I0662657

MARTIANS, MONSTERS, AND PEPPERONI PIZZA

100 SPECULATIVE FICTION TALES

MICHAEL A. KECHULA

BooksForABuck.com
2012

BooksForABuck.com
December 2012

PUBLICATION HISTORY

A CHANGE OF PACE. Flashes in the Dark Magazine Feb 2009 as BOREDOM.

A GOOD EUCATION PAYS OFF. Post Card Shorts Magazine Apr 2009.

A HELLISH THING. Jake's Monthly Bizzaro Anthology May 2012.

AIN'T LOVE GRAND. Weirdyear Magazine Jun 2010.

A NOBLE CAUSE. Fiction at Work Magazine Aug 2008.

ATTACK FROM BEHIND. Concepts SciFi Magazine (England) Sep 2008.

BAD GENES. Concepts SciFi Magazine (England) Mar 2012.

BEAKS. Weirdyear Magazine May 2010.

CON ARTIST. Weirdyear Mag May 2010.

COPY CATS. Postcard Shorts Magazine Nov 2010.

CRAZY JOEY. Short Humour Magazine (England) Jan 2009.

ELIXIR 140. Tomfoolery Review May 2010.

FLASH FROZEN. New Flesh Magazine Sep 2010 as WONDERFUL SNACKS.

FLUIDS. Flashes in The Dark Magazine Apr 2009.

FREEBIES. Alien Skin Magazine Jun 2010.

GENOCIDAL BASTARDS. Yesteryear Magazine May 2010.

GROSS MISINTERPRETATION. New Flesh Magazine Aug 2010.

HIT AND RUN. Short Humour Magazine (England) Jan 2010.

IF ONLY THE PORTUGUESE HADN'T DIED. Flashes in the Dark Magazine Mar 2009.

INCREDIBLE INVENTION.Yesteryear Mag Jun 2010 as INCREDIBLE DISCOVERY.

INVISIBLE MAN. State of Imagination Magazine Nov 2010.

JACOB IS MISSING. Full Armour Mar 2010.

LESSONS FROM GRANDMA. Flashes in the Dark Magazine Mar 2011.

LET'S TRADE. Micro-Story A Week Magazine Oct 2011.

REVELATION. Weirdyear Magazine Jul 2010.

ROB-A-STORE DAY. Weirdyear Magazine Jul 2010.

SNEAK ATTACK. An Electric Tragedy Jun 2011.

SNEERS. Flashes in the Dark Magazine Aug 2011.

THE BASTARDS OF HOLLYBIRD. Eclectic Flash Magazine Jan 2010.

THE BATTLE. Flashes in the Dark Mag May 2011 as A STRANGE WORD.

THE BIG SWAP. Weirdyear Magazine Jul 2010.

THE BONUS. Yesteryear Magazine Jun 2010.

THE BREAK UP. New Flesh Magazine Sep 2010.

THE RUBY IDOL. New Flesh Magazine 2010.

THE WHITE DRAGON. Firepower Magazine Sep 2010.

THIRD PRIZE. New Flesh Magazine Oct 2010.

TOAST AND COFFEE. Dark and Dreary Magazine Sep 2009.

TOYS. Dark and Dreary Magazine Sep 2009.

WALLS. A Cup of Joe Coffee House Flash Dec 2011.

WEAPONS OF MASS DESTRUCTION. Weirdyear May 2010.

WEEDS. An Electric Tragedy Jun 2011.

Contents

THE BIG SWAP

In January, 2011, ten thousand UFO sightings were reported in the U.S. The same month, over twenty thousand Americans reported they'd been abducted by Martians. After several days of captivity, all were returned to Earth. When questioned by the FBI, they claimed they were examined by strange-looking creatures, then shown to the Emperor of Mars. They said the Emperor spoke to them through translating machines. The Emperor boasted he would soon conquer Earth.

Considering the seriousness of the abductees' statements, the government insisted they take lie detector tests. Results showed all had spoken the truth. Consequently, President Kirk was convinced that Martians would soon invade Earth.

During an emergency cabinet meeting, Kirk said, "I'm preparing a message for transmission to Mars to arrange a meeting with the Emperor. We must find a way to prevent interplanetary war."

Kirk conferred with leaders of the Amalgamated Nations. All agreed with his conclusion and the content of the message he wanted to transmit to the Emperor. They selected Kirk to represent the interests of every nation on Earth.

Two hours after Kirk's message was transmitted to Mars, he received a reply. The Emperor agreed to meet him in Roswell, New Mexico, site of the first Martian landing in America.

They met on the field where a Martian flying saucer crashed in 1947, killing its occupants. After an Army band played the national anthems of both planets, the Emperor laid a wreath to honor the aliens who died on that very spot.

"Let's get down to business," Kirk said. "I understand you intend to invade our planet. Why would you do such a thing?"

"I have no choice," said the Emperor. "My astronomers discovered a comet twice the size of the Sun heading toward my planet. It will strike us and destroy everything. I must relocate all my subjects. Our surveys indicate that your planet would be best for us. I suggest you surrender now."

"And if we do, what will happen to the billions that inhabit this planet?"

The Emperor didn't answer.

A shaken but poker-faced President said, "Surrender is not an option. When will the collision occur?"

"In one hundred years, three months, two weeks, and five days. You can understand the need for us to occupy your planet very soon when you consider the logistical nightmare I'm faced with."

"Instead of invading us, which would cause extensive bloodshed on both sides, let's compromise."

"What do you have in mind?"

"Suppose we trade planets? Relocate all your subjects to Earth, and we'll move our entire population to your planet."

"You'd do that, knowing that my planet will be destroyed?"

"Yes. We'd have to borrow lots of your flying saucers to transport our people to your planet. To sweeten the deal, I'll ensure that every building on Earth is left intact when we leave. That way, your subjects could move right in when they arrive. Think of the savings you'll realize by avoiding construction costs. What do you have to lose? You'll gain Earth, a planet that has a bright future, while we'll face a dismal future and certain annihilation."

"It's a deal," said the Emperor.

The Emperor became a hero to his subjects for obtaining such a fabulous concession from Earth. They snickered, calling Earthlings weak and stupid for giving up their beautiful planet without a fight.

In contrast, Kirk's popularity plummeted 90%. Many around the globe said he'd made a lousy deal. Several attempts were made on his life.

Kirk appeared on TV to assure the world's masses. "It's not all that bad. True, we'll have to live in caves formerly occupied by Martians. That will take a bit of adjustment, considering their stench. And we'll have a hundred years to find a way to save our new home planet from destruction. With our intelligence and ingenuity, I'm sure we'll find a way and live happily ever after."

During the rest of 2011 and most of 2012, both planets undertook the massive project of swapping their entire populations.

On December 20, 2012, ceremonies were held on Mars and Earth to celebrate the successful end of the project.

The next day, President Kirk spoke on TV to all Earthlings now living on Mars.

"I'd like to thank all of you for your cooperation. The tremendously complex relocation project has been completed on schedule, on budget, and without casualties. On behalf of the Relocated Amalgamated Nations, I'd like to offer my profound thanks to the Emperor for his cooperation and for lending us thousands of flying saucers to transport our population to Mars. The leaders of the Relocated Amalgamated Nations and I wish to invite you to participate in a ceremony tonight, when we will salute our former planet for the last time. If you'll participate in this historical event, please leave your caves at 7:45 and face in the direction of Earth. At exactly 8:00 PM, we'll wave goodbye. Afterward, all government agencies will begin brainstorming sessions to figure out how we can save our new planet from destruction."

At 7:45, Earthlings all across Mars left their caves to assemble for the ceremony.

A few minutes before 8:00, Kirk transmitted a final message to the Emperor, who now occupied the most beautiful palace on Earth. Kirk thanked him for avoiding war and conducting a peaceful swap.

The last line of the message said, "Your Highness, on this the twenty-first day of December, in the year 2012, I wonder if you ever heard of the Mayans and their prophecy about this very day?"

"Who were the Mayans?" asked the Emperor's return message, as Earthlings were waving goodbye to Earth.

Suddenly, Earth exploded with a tremendous roar that was heard throughout the entire Solar System.

Raising his fist in defiance, Kirk said, "Well, as you just found out, the Mayans were a helluva lot smarter than you and your freakin' astronomers."

BEAKS

Harry woke with a start. "Where the hell am I?" he yelled when he looked up from the ground and saw a huge, black, iron snake coiled on a concrete pedestal, as if ready to strike. "Why are my wrists and ankles tied to stakes? Help! Police!"

"Save your breath," somebody said. "Nobody can hear you."

"What am I doing here?" Seeing lots of trees, he figured he was in a large park.

"You tell *us* what you're doing here, and why you egged the sacred statue of Jaxil, our most beloved and holy God." The voice came from a man wearing a mask that made him look like a weird bird. A long, jagged beak protruded from the mask.

"I don't know what the hell you're talking about."

"See this egg carton? It held eighteen eggs. You brought it here and threw every one of them at God, striking him eighteen times. You've committed horrible, multiple sacrileges!"

"Look. I don't know anything about eggs, or your god. Last thing I knew I was driving home from a bachelor party in Mill Town. Am I still in Mill Town?"

"It doesn't matter where you are. You were drunk and raged at our God. You called Him an ugly monstrous bastard. How dare you! That's not only blasphemy but also a dastardly hate crime. Now you must pay."

"I'm positive I didn't do anything to your god. You got the wrong guy. I wouldn't do anything to offend anybody's religious beliefs or insult their god."

Harry heard screeching birdcalls. When he strained to see where the sound came from, he saw six others wearing bird masks heading his way. All carried supermarket shopping bags.

The masked men surrounded Harry. The one with the largest beak said, "Time to pay for your heinous crime."

They tore off Harry's clothes. Standing a few feet away, they made shrill bird noises, as they removed egg cartons from their shopping bags, and pelted him with eggs.

"Ow! That hurts! Please stop!" he hollered, as eggs crashed against his body. "I'm sorry. I'll never do it again. I swear!"

They threw the eggs with more force. Soon Harry's entire body was covered with slimy yolk, egg whites, and shell fragments. His face was so saturated, egg goo flooded his nose each time he inhaled.

Before long, streams of muck ran down his throat and into his lungs. Straining to breathe, Harry turned blue and convulsed. Still the eggs came.

When they ran out of eggs, someone felt Harry's pulse.

"He's dead."

Cutting the ropes that bound Harry, they dragged his slimy corpse closer to the statue. Removing twelve bags of grated cheddar cheese from their shopping bags, they offered it to their Snake God with high-pitched bird squawks. Then they sprinkled the cheese all over Harry's corpse.

With outstretched arms they cried, "Accept this human food offering, Great and Mighty Jaxil."

Hopping like birds and chanting, "May this sacrifice ascend as an odor of sweetness to propitiate for this man's most horrendous and grievous evils," they circled the statue three times. Then their leader poured charcoal fluid over Harry and struck a match. When his cheese and egg covered corpse caught fire, their hops and squawks became more frantic.

Suddenly, they fell on their knees.

"Almighty Jaxil has spoken to me," their leader said. "He has graciously accepted our sacrifice and is appeased. Now he invites us to commune with him by partaking of this sacred omelet."

Frenzied beaks tore into the mass of toasted eggs, cheese, and human tissue.

ROB-A-STORE DAY

Fred expected to have the time of his life stealing things at Santa Buffoona Mall during its annual Rob-A-Store Day.

That was the day the mall sanctioned robbery, giving customers an opportunity to act out shoplifting fantasies without being arrested. Kids were especially welcome. To encourage kiddy thievery, stores placed a wonderful array of highly desirable toys on tables low enough for tots to snatch.

The mall provided every participant a long black coat that was specially designed by the Mafia for shoplifting. They also distributed free masks to protect participants' identities. Prominent citizens who joined the robbery festivities greatly appreciated this.

When thieves filled their coat pockets, they were to leave the mall and unload their loot onto tables for immediate recycling. Then they could go back inside for another round of theft. This cycle could be repeated until closing time.

When Fred asked why Santa Buffoona Mall sponsored such a bizarre event, they told him the mall had the worst record for shoplifting losses in the world. Consultants were hired to find ways to eliminate the losses. They suggested that the mall sponsor a Rob-A-Store Day to let customers act out shoplifting fantasies without penalties. Thus, potential thieves of all ages would have an opportunity to experience how unglamorous and destructive shoplifting really was. Hopefully, once they gave it a try on Rob-A-Store Day, they'd never want to do it again any other time.

The experiment worked. None of the mall's 100 stores reported a single loss from theft for two years. Mall management decided to repeat the special event every year.

Fred hurried to the mall on Rob-A-Store Day, hoping to snag some expensive items for which he'd lusted, but couldn't afford. He figured if he couldn't own them for real, at least he'd have the pleasure of having them in his possession for a little while.

After registering at a booth in the mall's parking lot, he donned the mask and coat they gave him, and entered the mall. Inside, he saw shoplifters racing from store to store, grabbing whatever they could. People were elbowing each other, shoving each other, pulling things away from each other. A teenager got punched and fell to the floor with a bloody face.

An eighty-year old woman tripped as she raced toward a table filled with expensive handbags. "Ow! I think I broke my hip! Please help me."

Nobody responded. They were too busy scrambling in all directions, manically grabbing everything in sight and jamming it into their shoplifting coats.

Although Fred felt a tinge of compassion when he passed the crying woman, he ignored her. "I didn't come here to waste time helping injured people," he mumbled.

The mall was so crowded, Fred was unable to snag any of the fancy items he'd hoped to steal. They were either gone, or he couldn't get near them because of the crowds. So, in keeping with the spirit of the day, he grabbed whatever he could just for the sake of shoplifting.

Before long, his coat pockets were full of paint brushes, knick-knacks, scented candles, and women's panties. He raced to the exit, unloaded everything on a collection table, and hurried back inside for another round.

After four trips to unload things that were of no interest to him, he realized he wasn't having much fun. Especially since he'd been kicked, shoved, pushed, and almost knocked down.

During his fifth run, he was so caught up in the orgy of larcenous lunacy, he yanked a Beanie Baby from a seven-year old girl's hand before she could stuff it inside her black coat.

Following his sixth trip, Fred decided to grab a snack at the food court. He found dozens of people showing each other what they'd shoplifted.

"Look at this neat Swarovski crystal chicken, I stole," a kid told his mom. "The price tag says it's worth $250."

"I'm so proud of you," said his mom. "Let's eat fast so we can steal some more."

A six year old girl said, "Mommy, look at all the Barbie dolls I stole."

"What's so great about that? They're a dime a dozen. I told you to practice snitching porcelain collector's dolls. I ought to ground you for not listening!"

Returning to the fray, Fred found the situation even more frantic than before. Somebody was pushed through a store window. Store decorations were in tatters. Somebody's blood was on the floor.

Unable to stand the pandemonium any longer, Fred hurried to an exit. After dropping his mask and thief's coat on a table, he headed for his car. On the way, he was approached by a mall security guard.

"I got a complaint about you," the guard said.

"Whadda ya mean?" asked Fred."

"You stole a Beanie Baby from my daughter right after she shoplifted it. It's against the rules to steal from shoplifters on Rob-A-Store Day. Poor kid has been practicing for months to swipe that particular Beanie Baby. And then you come along and botch things up."

"I didn't steal anything from a kid. You got the wrong guy."

"She said the crook had red hair and blue tennis shoes. That describes you perfectly. Nobody robs my daughter and gets away with it."

The guard punched Fred, knocking him unconscious. Calling his daughter with his cell phone, he said, "I found the crook who stole the Beanie Baby you swiped. Whadda ya think I should do with him?"

The following week, Santa Buffoona Mall announced its 1st Annual Piñata Day. The brightly decorated piñata kids saw in the middle of the mall was filled with candy, gum, and cookies.

Kids were blindfolded and given broom sticks. They were told to whack the piñata until it broke open and all the goodies fell out.

Instead of the traditional animal-shaped piñata, this one was formed like a man with a bloated belly. Festooned with brightly colored tissue paper, it had the cutest red hair and blue sneakers.

FREEBIES

The Emperor of Mars sent 7-billion pepperoni pizzas to Earth as a peace gesture. Earth's Illustrious Pooh-bah was so grateful he declared a global holiday to honor the Emperor. Everyone on Earth received a pizza, and gobbled it up.

That night, Illustrious Pooh-bah yelled over TV, "This is an emergency. The FBI discovered the pizzas contain tiny nuclear bombs. Martians might detonate them any minute. Induce vomiting. Rush to hospitals!"

Vomit flooded the streets. Hospitals were overwhelmed.

The Emperor pressed a button. Billions of Earthlings exploded.

"I told you they'd eat free pizzas," General Ggg told Mars' Emperor, as they viewed billions of nuclear mushroom clouds through telescopes.

"True. But some vomited enough to eject the bombs."

"No problem. Let's send Earthlings chocolate chip cookies with bombs inside."

"Can we fool them twice?"

"Sure. They have notoriously short memories and can't resist chocolate chip cookies."

Mars conquered Earth without firing a shot.

WEAPONS OF MASS DESTRUCTION

When Charlie left the bakery with a bag full of donuts, he was abducted by aliens. The next thing he knew, he was sitting in a chair in their spacecraft with the donuts in his lap. Facing him were a dozen green Martians. All were holding clipboards and taking notes.

"Welcome aboard," said the tallest one. "My name is Glurp. We won't keep you long. We just want to remove one of your eyes for analysis. Don't worry, you won't feel a thing. What's that in your lap?"

"A bag of donuts."

"What's a donut?"

"Something good to eat."

Glurp nudged the greenie next to him. "Take one and taste it. If it's really good, we'll reverse engineer it, duplicate it, and open donut shops back home."

As the Martian approached, Charlie extended a glazed cinnamon twist. When the alien took a bite, he screamed, and fell to the floor convulsing. In seconds, he disintegrated into a pile of dust.

Charlie grabbed another cinnamon twist from the bag and pointed it at the Martians. "Okay, you bums. Put your hands up. This bag's full of weapons of mass destruction. The one I'm holding is powerful enough to blow this spaceship to smithereens. If you don't return me to Earth immediately, I'll set it off."

Trembling, the Martians did as Charlie commanded.

"Where the hell have you been for the last three hours?" asked his wife. "I've been dying for a donut."

When he tried to explain, she called him an idiot.

"You don't understand," he said. "I've made a remarkable discovery. Donuts are more than what they seem. In fact, they can be used as very effective weapons against Martians. Do you realize with a cinnamon twist, we may be able to end alien abductions forever? I'm gonna call Homeland Security right now and tell them."

The agent who answered the phone called Charlie an idiot and hung up.

Charlie wrote to the President, Congress, and heads of the armed forces. Nobody bothered to respond.

When he called radio talk shows, the hosts derided him and terminated his call before he could explain how donuts could be used to kill Martians and defend the country against invasion.

The only way I'll be able to convince anybody is if I run for Congress, he mumbled. *When I'm elected, I'll have some clout. And when they interview me on CNN and Fox News, I'll be able to tell everybody about the fantastic power of donuts.*

Charlie got elected to Congress and managed to wrangle an appointment to the Armed Forces Committee. During a secret hearing about UFOs and what the Air Force was doing to defend the country against alien intrusions, he finally got a chance to tell a general how cinnamon twists affected Martians.

During a break in the hearings, he approached the general in charge of US Air Defense Forces and explained his ideas on defending the nation against Martians.

"You want me to remove one of our four air-to-air missiles on our UFO chase planes and replace it with a donut?" asked the incredulous general.

"Right. I have reason to believe that all UFOs come from Mars. I have reliable information about a situation where an abductee killed a Martian with a glazed cinnamon twist. Not only that, the guy got away by threatening to blow up their spacecraft with a cinnamon twist. I figure by now the word got around Mars, and every UFO pilot and crew know about this. So, I figure if we shoot cinnamon twists at UFOs, instead of missiles, we'll scare them off for good. I suggest we run a test."

The general agreed. A month later, two Air Defense fighter planes were scrambled to intercept a UFO over Detroit. Instead of shooting missiles to scare it away, each pilot fired an oversized cinnamon twist. The pilots were amazed when the UFO suddenly changed direction and hightailed it into outer space at warp speed. After that incident, no UFOs were ever again seen over Detroit.

The same thing happened when UFOs were spotted over Chicago and New York. Consequently, the President issued an executive order stating that all Air Force attack planes guarding against UFO intrusions were to be armed with four oversized, glazed, cinnamon twists.

Some UFO's managed to get through the global radar shield and abducted dozens of Earthlings. When Congressman Charlie learned this, he spoke of his abduction experience during a congressional hearing. Afterward, he sponsored a bill to provide every citizen in the United States with a fresh cinnamon twist, every day for life.

Before long, all citizens wore cinnamon twists around their necks, 24/7. As a result, alien abductions ceased completely.

Now, Earthlings can once again enjoy munching cinnamon twists, instead of wearing them in self-defense.

CON ARTIST

Frank was whale watching off the coast of Santa Buffoona when he heard a whale call, "Hey, Mister, what's your name."

"Frank," he said, wondering if he were hallucinating.

"Well, Frank, could you do me a big favor?"

"Depends on what it is," he said, wondering if the whale was gonna hit him up for a few bucks.

"It's not complicated. I'm the King of the Whales. I'm facing open rebellion. Some of my subjects are fed up with their diets. Not so long ago a tour boat was in this area, and it was full of kids eating something they called *pepperoni pizza*. A few pieces of it fell overboard. Some of my subjects were in the area and tasted the stuff floating on the water. Now they're hooked. Seems they particularly liked the yellow stuff on top. It was kind of stringy. Do you know what that stuff's called?"

"Mozzarella cheese," Frank said.

"They also liked the little round red thingees on top of the mozzarella. What's that called?"

"Pepperoni."

"I'd be eternally grateful to you, Frank, if you could get a few pepperoni pizzas and put them in the water. I'll add some poison. That would get rid of my rebellious subjects before they spread the word about pizza and infect more in my empire with their weird dietary ideas."

"How many pizzas do you think you'll need?"

"I figure seven-hundred extra-large ones would do the trick. The guys who'll eat this have gigantic appetites."

"Do you have any money?" Frank asked. "Extra-large pizzas are pretty expensive, especially when they're covered with pepperoni."

"Where the hell would whales get money?" asked the King.

"I thought maybe if pizza fell overboard from passing boats, maybe a purse or two, or a few wallets might have also have dropped into the drink at one time or another."

"No such luck. Look, my credit's good. I am, after all, the King of the Whales. I got connections. I could, in exchange for your generosity, fix it with great white sharks so that they'll never attack you in case you ever fall overboard into shark infested waters. Or I could make an arrangement with all the alligators so you never get your hands bitten off, in case you ever want to pet one when you're in Florida."

"I appreciate your offer," said Frank. "But you're talking about an expenditure on my part of about $14,000, unless you got some Pizza Hut discount coupons on hand."

"What are coupons?"

Frank explained.

"Nope, we don't have any of those. Tell you what I'll do. I have a beautiful daughter. I've put together quite a dowry for her. Perhaps you'd be interested in marrying her."

"What's her dowry worth?"

"Oh, it's quite rich. Two thousand tons of briny kelp. Five thousand tons of delicious seaweed."

Frank did some quick calculations, figuring he could sell the kelp and seaweed to sushi restaurants for mega-bucks. That'd cover the cost of using his credit card to buy 700 pepperoni pizzas, ten-thousand times over.

"It's a deal," Frank said. "I'll run and get the pizzas. Give me a few hours. It's gonna take a while for them to make 700 extra-large pepperoni pizzas."

"Okay," said the King. "Meanwhile, I'll get my daughter and her dowry ready for you. We can conduct the ceremony when you return. Sound good?"

"Sounds great," Frank said, trying to calculate how much he'd profit from selling a female whale to Japanese fishermen. "When I come back with the pizzas in a boat, how will I find you so I know where to drop them?"

"I'll set off flares," said the whale King.

Ten hours later, Frank arrived with 700 pepperoni pizzas. The King heard the boat's engines, came to the surface, and set off several flares.

After Frank dropped all the pizzas overboard, his future bride came to the surface along with her dad, the King.

"Oh, he's cute, Daddy," she said. "He looks good enough to eat."

"Indulge yourself, my sweetie-pie," said the King.

Frank was gone in one gulp.

The King dried the 700 pizzas, and sold them to hungry tourists who came in boats to watch whales frolic in the Pacific. He made so much money, he bought the island of Tahiti, where he lived happily ever after with his subjects—none of which had ever heard of pepperoni pizza, or ever tasted it.

WALLS

"The strangest thing happened to me in my *Witchcraft and Religion* class," said Lisa, as we lunched in a coffee shop. "On Tuesday, the prof said we had a guest speaker. A practicing witch."

"I heard they do that in that class," I said. "Was she good looking?"

"She was stunning. All the guys were going crazy over her. Anyway, she started talking about black magic, which she said she didn't practice. And while she was lecturing, I don't know why it happened, but I suddenly saw her tied up and burning at the stake. I even heard the flames crackling. All of a sudden she stopped talking in mid-sentence and looked right at me. Her face looked so twisted and distorted. And in the creepiest voice, she said, 'I know what you're thinking.' That scared the hell outta me."

"Geez, that's weird," I said, as chills raced down my arms.

"As if that wasn't bad enough, she pointed right at me, and suddenly I saw a brick wall rushing toward me. It was as real as the chair I'm sitting on. Just as it was about to smash into my face, I screamed and ran out of the room. I heard her calling to me, 'Don't ever try that again!'"

"Wow!"

"I dropped the class, immediately. I've been scared ever since. What if she's pissed, because I sensed that she really does practice black magic? What if she checked the seating chart, or asked the professor my name? What if she finds out I have a baby? Will she hex me and my daughter?"

"I think you better start praying."

"I haven't stopped since it happened. I'm telling everybody I know never to take that class."

Suddenly, Lisa grabbed my arm. "Oh my God! She's here! She's standing by the door. She's staring at me."

"Don't worry," I said. "I'll protect you."

"Well, well, well," said the gorgeous woman, as she approached our table, "if it isn't the little lady who wants to see me burned at the stake."

Lisa blanched, then screamed.

During the pandemonium that followed, I remember the woman pointing at me and saying, "What do *you* see when you look at me?"

"I see you naked on a bed."

"Good. Look me up. I think you're hot."

Then I swear she disappeared.

When the cops arrived, I told them, "When Lisa saw the woman, she screamed. Suddenly her body flew backward about ten feet, as if something had slammed into her. Her face was smashed to a pulp."

I didn't tell them what happened in Lisa's class. Nor did I tell them that the woman pointed at me, asked what I saw, then disappeared into thin air. I didn't want to spend time on the Funny Farm in a straightjacket.

Lisa was buried a few days later.

Since then, every night I've dreamed about her death. I see a brick wall rushing toward her and smashing her face. But the next dream is about the stunning woman I saw in the coffee shop. I see her in bed in every dream. And I'm right there with her.

The dream about the witch always arouses me tremendously. So much so, I've thought about finding out where she lives. But, if we end up in bed together—like in my recurring dream—what'll happen to me if I look at her lovely face...and see her burning at the stake?

THE BASTARDS OF HOLLYBIRD

It's very easy to kidnap somebody. I know. I did it, and got away with it.

It wasn't done for ransom, political reasons, or rape. I'm extremely wealthy, apolitical, and get serviced regularly by a bevy of acrobatic call girls.

I did it to get satisfaction for receiving eight, preprinted, nondescript, 3 x 4 inch, generic, rejection slips from those bastards at Hollybird Publishing.

I'd sent them magnificent novella manuscripts. Eight in four years. And they didn't have the damn decency to type or write a single word on their rejections. The preprinted rejection slips they stuffed into my self-addressed stamped envelope were barely legible. And they all said the same thing about my novellas not meeting their current needs. Damn jerks!

Before I even dreamed of kidnapping, I was pretty happy-go-lucky. Money does that. At thirty-six, I'd seen it all, been everywhere, and done it all, with one exception: I'd never written a best seller. It shouldn't have mattered. But one day, walking into a huge library, I noticed the mountain of books. Not a single book bore my name. The thought bugged me.

As new books were added to library shelves, my frustration increased. To relieve my distress, I wrote eight, sci-fi western novellas. Masterpieces. Followed every rule of fiction. My opening sentences had gripping hooks, the kind that knock your drawers off. My descriptions were divinely inspired. The dialog was crisp, dynamic, incredibly moving.

Self-publish or use the vanity press? Nope. Anybody can do that. I wanted my creations to bubble to the top by their sheer magnificence. I wanted to inspire readers and change their lives.

But all I got were crummy reject slips.

Enough! I'd make them pay. Principle was involved. I made a plan.

First, I added a 40 x 50 foot, luxury bedroom and bath to my estate. Installed every convenience.

Then, a few calls to Hollybird identified Victoria Chubbs as Editor-in-Chief. I paid triple the going rate for a private investigator who'd keep secrets. I learned where Chubbs lived, dined, and shopped. White Plains. Tavern on the Green. Macy's. But, she'd bought groceries at Wal-Mart, ten Sundays in a row.

That's where I snatched her.

I locked her in the new bedroom.

When the chloroform wore off, she panicked. "Where am I? What's going on? I wanna go home."

"There's nothing to worry about," I said gently over the intercom. "The bar's full. Snacks are behind the bar. You'll get gourmet meals. All your needs will be met scrupulously and respectfully. I'm not a rapist, or insane."

"Please let me go."

"After you complete certain tasks, I promise to release you unharmed, with twenty thousand dollars in your handbag. Make yourself at home. Look around. You'll never rest your head in a more sumptuous room, and enjoy better food. Wait until you see the bathroom. Think of this as a vacation. A working vacation."

"What do you want me to do?"

"In the desk are eight manuscripts. Each bears a rejection slip from Hollybird. Read all manuscripts and write in longhand why they were rejected. Make suggestions for improvement. That's all. Just that."

"You gotta be kidding."

"Nope. Dinner is at 7:00. Coq Au Vin. I'll serve it through the dumbwaiter by the bar. Meanwhile, have a drink to settle your nerves."

She looked around warily. Hopefully the fabulous surroundings and the vodka she poured would help calm her.

The surveillance camera showed her heading for the bathroom.

"I guess you're gonna watch," she said.

"The bathroom's surveillance-free. I'm not a voyeur."

Later, she ran her hand down the beautiful marble columns and exquisite tapestries. She examined paintings, and toyed with the satellite radio. She watched *CNN* on wide-screen, high-definition TV.

After dinner, she opened the first manuscript.

"Are you there?" she called.

"Yep."

"I guess I have to say everything is just peachy, or else you'll—"

"I won't harm you. I'll accept your honest opinion. Let the chips fall."

"This opening line is… well… unsatisfactory, 'It was a dark and stormy night when Brace Brute, the ambidextrous, bi-sexual, Martian sheriff half-galloped toward the groveling town of Destiny, heading for the Bucket of Blood saloon, knowing that buried beneath was the Ark of the Covenant.'"

"Write down why you think it's bad."

She scribbled.

"This description doesn't work. 'His nose dribbled like the anus of a horse with diarrhea.' It'll turn your readers off. Makes me wanna vomit."

"Don't tell me everything. Write it all down."

Four days later, all eight manuscripts had been critiqued.

After feasting on Boef de l'Orange de Mandarin, she complained of dizziness.

"A sedative was in your espresso. When you awake, you'll be near a pay phone. Hang on to your purse. I've put twenty thousand dollars inside. When you return to Hollybird, burn those miserable preprinted rejection slips. Henceforth, make your readers and editors handwrite comments on all rejections. Show some respect for writers."

"But, we get hundreds of unsolicited manuscripts every day."

"Find a way to do it. And sign them yourself. Oh, and I wanna see faster turnaround, too. Unless you'd like to return here for an extended vacation."

She shook her head and passed out.

At midnight, I took her to a park, then called 911.

I read her critiques. What a bitch! She wouldn't know talent if it bit her in the ass.

Four months later, I sent a fabulous 500-page pirate story to Hollybird Publishing.

After three weeks, a two-page rejection letter arrived signed by Victoria Chubbs. Her highfalutin words said my story stank.

Originally against the idea, I decided to self-published the pirate story. It was too good to leave unpublished. I donated copies to all the libraries in town. It looks good on the shelves.

I'm bored with writing.

I think I'll compose a symphony.

A MONEY MAKER

I walked in as the bartender was telling the punch line of a farmer's daughter joke. The three mangy-looking guys at the bar howled.

"My turn," said the guy in a checkered shirt. Ever hear about the dog who knew karate?"

"You told us last week," said the bald guy.

"How about the priest who ran into a rabbi at a Honey Roasted Ham Store?"

"You told that one, too," said the toothless guy.

The bald guy turned to me. Swaying on the barstool he asked, "Hey, buddy, how about you? Got a good joke for us? Don't make it too dirty, 'cause me and the boys have virgin ears."

They guffawed.

"I haven't heard any lately," I said. "But I know an interesting story. It really happened. I ain't sure if you'd consider it funny."

"Hey, what the hell," Baldy said. "It's getting dull around here looking at these ugly faces night after night, and listening to their booze talk. I'm up to a good story. Even if it ain't funny."

I took a big swig of beer. "I once had a red coconut. Red as a fire engine. Found it in Hawaii. It fell from a tree. Just missed my head by inches."

"So what's so interesting about a damn coconut?" Toothless asked.

"This one could talk."

"Oh sure. What did it say?"

"Lots of things. When it fell and almost hit me, it said, 'Beware the Ides of March.'"

"What the hell does that mean?" asked Checkered.

"It's from Shakespeare," said Bartender.

"When I picked it up, it said, 'To be or not to be, that is the question.'"

"Sounds weird," said Baldy. "Then what?"

"I tried to figure out how to turn the coconut into a money maker. I put up a sign on my house. 'See the Red Talking Coconut. 25 cents.'"

"How'd that work out?"

"Only made three bucks. I guess people just ain't interested in talking coconuts. So, I thought maybe I could teach it to sing. I bought some Frank Sinatra albums for the coconut to listen to."

"Great idea. Did the coconut like Sinatra?"

"Probably not. After a few weeks, all it would sing was, 'Do-be-do-be-do.' Just as I was about to give up, Pavarotti comes on TV singing opera. The coconut heard him and started warbling like a canary. I mean, it sang its heart out. Imitated Pavarotti perfectly. What a terrific voice that coconut had."

"Any coconut that can sing that good oughta be worth big bucks," said Bartender.

"That's what I figured. So, I took the coconut to a big-time booking agent in New York. He loved what he heard. 'But this is a coconut,' he said. 'I can't book an opera-singing coconut.' Just as I was ready to leave, he said, 'Hey, maybe you could make like you're a ventriloquist. Put the coconut on your lap. Paint a funny face on it. It already looks hilarious with that scrubby red color.'"

"Smart idea," Checkered said.

"So, I had a heart-to-heart with the coconut. Got it to agree. But, it didn't like the idea of acting like a ventriloquist's dummy. Especially when I came up with the stage name of Coo-coo the Singing Coconut."

"Hey, I don't blame the coconut. You musta hurt its feelings," Toothless said.

"Anyway, the agent placed us in the Catskills. During high season. We were a big hit. Got rave reviews."

"Sounds fantastic," Baldy said.

"It was. Until Coo-coo got laryngitis. With its resistance lowered, it caught a rare coconut disease—coconut-itis. Where all the milk dries up inside. Even the Mayo Clinic couldn't help. Buried Coo-coo a month ago. A few miles from here. Things ain't been the same since."

Checkered took out a grimy handkerchief and dabbed his eyes. Bartender's mouth was wide open in shock.

"Give the man a drink on me," Baldy said. "That's the saddest damn story I ever heard."

"Cognac," I said. "Best you have."

The bartender poured. "So I guess it's rough not having your coconut around."

"Yeah. We were real close."

"So whadda ya doing these days?" Baldy asked.

"I wander here and there. I'm still in mourning."

Next thing I knew, the boozers pushed money my way. Toothless, looking downcast said, "Buy flowers for the coconut's grave. Just say it's from the boys at Louie's Lounge."

"Thank you gents. Coo-coo would've appreciated it and would've sung something nice for you."

"Have another drink on me," Checkered said. "It'll help ease the pain."

When I left with twenty bucks more than I came in with, they were fist fighting over whether or not a coconut has a soul.

Damn, it was so easy to con booze and bucks from half-wits like that bunch. This week it was the coconut story. Next week, I'll hit more taverns and tell the story about the orphan elephant I adopted. The one that read palms. Until he lost his sight because of global warming.

TOAST AND COFFEE

Joe was munching toast in a diner when the clock struck midnight. This was the third diner he'd visited since arriving in Jersey City. If this were the right one, a woman with terrible body odor would soon show up and take the stool next to his.

As he raised a cup of coffee to his lips, a reeking woman flopped onto the seat next to him. Her stench was so terrible, he thought he'd vomit.

The woman elbowed him so hard in the ribs, his cup went flying. Exactly as predicted in the manual he received when attending a special, secret workshop.

"What's your problem lady?" Joe said, using the words he'd memorized from the manual.

"My problem?" she hollered. "What's yours, you freakin' jerk!"

Her words were predicted verbatim by the manual. So were those of the owner when he said, "Hey! I don't want no hassles here. If you can't settle down, get the hell outta my diner."

"Tell him, not me," the washed out, baggy-eyed woman said. "He was supposed to meet me at Louie's Lounge last night. The bastard never showed up for our date."

"I don't know this woman," Joe said. "I don't date anybody. I'm a priest."

"He's a damn liar," the woman shouted. "I'm his girlfriend. And he sure as hell ain't no priest."

"You don't look like no priest," the owner said on cue. "Are you perfectly sure you are one? Or are you imagining things?"

Joe removed a small bottle of holy water, crucifix, and book of psalms from his jacket and put them on the counter. "Who else but a priest would have stuff like this in his pocket?" he asked.

Everyone in the diner sneered, then removed the same things from pockets and handbags and laid them on tables. All stared menacingly at Joe, waiting for his next move.

Reaching inside his jacket, Joe removed a purple stole that Roman Catholic priests wore when conducting religious rituals.

Everyone else in the diner took out a purple stole that looked exactly like Joe's.

"Okay," Joe said. "I see you wanna play games. That's fine with me."

"Do you really have the guts to put that thing on?" asked a customer. "Did your bosses in Rome ever tell you what happens to those who don't truly believe? You look very nervous to me. Are you sure you're up to the task? If you put that thing back in your pocket and leave right now, we'll all make believe you never came through that door. That is, if you never go to another diner again. You're awfully young to be hanging around diners. Too young to be wasting your time here. Tell you what I'm gonna do. I'll toss in a bonus. Besides sparing your life, if you leave right now, the most exquisite woman in the universe will be out front within sixty seconds. She'll give you the time of your life, a hundred times over. You'll bless the day you reached out to stroke the gorgeous flesh under her skirt. So, what do you say?"

Placing the stole around his neck Joe said aloud in Latin, "Out of the depths have I cried to Thee, oh Lord."

Instantly, everyone except Joe was frozen in place.

Starting with the owner, Joe went to every entity and splashed it with holy water. Each time a drop struck one, it disappeared with a loud pop. He saved the woman who'd elbowed him for last. Checking her scalp as if searching for lice, he found two hard nubs that would soon become six-inch horns.

"Demon in training," he muttered in Latin. "And this one's close to getting her diploma."

When he threw holy water in her face, she too disappeared with a pop.

Outside the diner, he swigged the blessed water to decontaminate the toast and coffee he'd ingested in the unholy place. Forgetting to do so would have resulted in a fatal stomach disorder.

Removing a portable flame thrower from his car, Joe muttered prayers of exorcism, and torched the diner.

"One down," he muttered, as he drove away.

After a good night's rest, he drove to Hoboken to check out the town's four diners.

Ten minutes before midnight, Joe took a counter seat in a diner. Ordering plain toast and coffee, he waited for the next horrible-smelling demon to take a stool and elbow him in the ribs.

Nobody showed up.

When he paid the cashier, Joe wondered how long it would take to exorcise the remaining sixty-one diners declared by the Vatican as the most demonically possessed eateries in the United States.

BANANAS

"I'm the President of the United States," said the gorilla to the zookeeper. "I was kidnapped, injected with something, and now here I am in the zoo."

"So if you ain't Bonzo the Dancing Gorilla, where's he?"

"I don't know. They must have taken him away when they put me here. Please call the CIA. Tell them I'm here. They'll know what to do."

"That's crazy. They'll think I'm nuts."

"Not if you give say this word: goober-nobers."

"What's that mean?"

"It doesn't mean anything. It's a top-secret doomsday word, if a worst-case scenario occurs involving the President. It'll activate thousands of agents. Just say that word. You'll get a big cash reward. The American people will be eternally grateful, and I'll give you a big-paying job in my administration. I'll create a special position in my Cabinet. How does Chief of Gorilla Affairs sound?"

"Great. Okay. I'll call them. What's their number?"

"It's a special one. Twenty-seven digits long. It begins with 757. No wait. It's 575 followed by... no, that's not it. Hmm. I knew I should have tattooed it on my arm, but the missus wouldn't let me. It's on a slip of paper in my wallet. Did you happen to find a wallet around here anywhere?"

"Nope."

"It figures. Well, give me a few minutes. I'll think of it."

"Does anybody else know the number?"

"Nobody, except the Director of the CIA. And he's on a secret mission somewhere in the mountains of Afghanistan. Let's see. It's 838..."

"Mr. President. While you're trying to remember the number, what about some breakfast?"

"Yeah. I'd like eggs over easy, hash browns, and rye toast. And a piece of apple pie. Heat the pie."

"I'm sorry, Sir. All I have is bananas."

"Bananas give me indigestion. Do you have a cell phone? I can call the White House and have the chefs bring me breakfast."

"I'll dial it for you, Sir. What's the number?"

"Damn. I don't know. I never called the White House."

"You don't seem to know anything," said the keeper. I think you're kidding me. You're about as much the President of the United States as I'm Napoleon."

"Damn!" said the gorilla. "Thought I'd fooled you this time. What game shall we play tomorrow? Hmm. What about Monopoly? Then you can pretend to be Donald Trump."

"We did that last week," the keeper said.

"Oh yeah. What about this game—when you come to feed me breakfast tomorrow, suppose I play King Kong and you play the woman. Can you scream loud?"

"I don't know. But it's not a bad idea. Meanwhile, here's some bananas. See you tomorrow morning."

ATTACK FROM BEHIND

"I'm sorry, Sir, but you can't go in there," said the Marine Guard. "The President's in an important conference."

"Hold on, Sergeant. Don't you recognize me?"

"Yes, Sir. You're General Sims, Chairman of the Joint Chiefs of Staff. I'm sorry, Sir, but I have explicit instructions from the President himself that he's not to be disturbed."

"This is a vital matter of national security!" The general pushed the Marine aside and opened the conference room door.

"What the hell—" yelled the President, who was on the floor playing Tiddlywinks with his six year old son.

"Sorry, Mr. President. We've intercepted a signal from somebody claiming to be the Emperor of Mars."

"What? Are you sure?"

"Yes, Sir. Might have something to do with all those UFO sightings over the White House last night."

"What does the message say?"

"Stop sending space probes," the general read. "They're affecting our weather and scaring our children."

"How many probes have we sent to Mars so far?"

"Two."

"Somebody's bitching about two lousy probes? Nonsense! Our probes showed there's no life on Mars. I'll bet this is the raving of a save-our-solar-system crackpot who's found a way to bounce signals off Mars to our receivers. Can you send a message over the same frequency?"

"Yes, Sir."

"Send this one: 'We got your message. Next time you're in town, we'll have a barbeque in your honor. Bring the wife and kids. Oh, and add this: 'Do you like your chili mild or hot?'"

That night, General Sims was ushered into the Presidential Bedroom.

"I'm sorry to wake you, Mr. President. "We intercepted another message from the guy who says he's the Emperor of Mars."

"What's it say?"

"Be reasonable. Our weather is getting worse. Our children are afraid to go outside. Many are getting sick. Their pet wurpsuls are dying at an alarming rate. Millions of our children are weeping. Stop this wurpsul genocide immediately. Don't force us to take hostile action."

"Damn!" said the President. "This is probably a terrorist diversion. Tell Homeland Security to raise the terrorist alert level. Double air cover over our cities. Send a new message."

"What do you want to say, Mr. President?"

"Just three words: 'Up your kazoo!' Dammit, I'm losing sleep over a crackpot!"

After reading the President's message, the enraged Emperor of Mars dispatched 100,000 troop carrier squadrons to penetrate Earth's atmosphere. By morning, the sky was filled with so many crisscrossing chemtrails a heavy fog fell covered the entire globe.

By the time the fog cleared, 1,000-bazillion Martian, microscopic, nano-robot bugs covered every square inch of Earth's surface. Vicious and razor-clawed, they were indestructible. Even worse, they were so tiny their presence went undetected.

After removing and burying their minuscule parachutes, the nano-robot bugs penetrated every sewer system, garbage dump, trash pile, latrine, dung heap, privy, port-o-potty, and outhouse on Earth. Within hours, they obliterated Earth's entire rat population.

The Emperor signaled Earth. "Because of your stubbornness, we've massacred all your children's favorite pets. Now YOUR children will weep."

The President released the Emperor's message to *CNN*. Upon hearing it, billions of Earthlings roared with laughter.

"Rats our kids' pets? Martians are raving idiots," many citizens said, while celebrating Global Rat Genocide Day, a holiday hastily declared by the Amalgamated Nations.

While Earth celebrated, the President ordered the Space Agency to send another probe to Mars.

Martian weather worsened. Children's fright increased. Many sickened to the point where their greenish skin turned blotchy blue-gray. Millions more wurpsuls died.

In retaliation, the Emperor ordered his microscopic robots to infiltrate one of Earth's most cherished commodities. Within hours, 100-million Earthlings died from vicious robot attacks while using toilet tissue.

"This is a national emergency!" yelled the President over TV. "We're under massive attack from behind! Don't use any wipes until Homeland Security declares it's safe to do so!"

Unfortunately, thousands of space scientists and personal hygiene product developers had wiped vigorously that morning upon arising.

Their demise at the hands of nano-robots caused the total collapse of Earth's space programs and personal hygiene research programs.

Earthlings everywhere mourned the loss of toilet tissue. Wailing and gnashing of teeth could be heard from Pole to Pole. Every attempt to devise suitable replacements, such as aluminum foil, plastic wrap, wax paper, newspaper, sandpaper, and foliage was sabotaged by Mars' nasty, microscopic robots.

News of Earth's scatological catastrophe and permanent inability to launch additional probes reached Mars. The Emperor rejoiced.

All of Earth's probes on Mars were located and destroyed.

Soon afterward, Martian weather returned to normal, wurpsuls stopped dying, and Martian children played outside again.

WEEDS

"What are my orders?" asked Kemper.

"When the band plays real loud, I want you to put an exploding bullet in the center of the bastard's forehead," said Atkins.

"I'll put it anywhere you want," Kemper said, "considering the kind of dough you guys paid."

"We pay a premium for genius, and that's what you are with a sniper's rifle."

"I had plenty of practice. Tell you what—I'll throw in her partner for free."

"No. One assassination's enough. Once you zap that freak, their political party will be in shambles."

"I heard rumors they started infiltrating back in 1947 at Roswell, New Mexico," Kemper said. "Is it true?"

"Yeah. But I'll bet you didn't hear about this: after the Army caught a dozen of the smelly bastards, those freaks got wise. They transformed themselves into the shapes and biological compositions of trees, and fled to California. We didn't know about it then. Meanwhile every year, more came from outer space surreptitiously, and changed themselves into trees, causing several new forests to show up in California's Redwood Country. The government estimated that 20 million of them were here illegally, posing as trees."

"Maybe they oughta burn down the forests," Kemper said.

"What do you think the recent California forest fires were about?" Atkins said. "But nobody's sure if we got them all. Meanwhile, about ten years ago, so many were here, a few thousand decided to rearrange their biological structures. They reshaped themselves from trees into entities that looked like beautiful, blonde Earth women. Stupid bastards all looked exactly alike, except for marks on their earlobes. They were tolerated because they took stripper and hooker jobs. But then they formed their own political party. Well, they're in for a big surprise tonight at their first convention, when they nominate that stupid one they call Glixa to run for President of the Amalgamated States of America, and you blow her brains out."

* * * *

When delegates stopped cheering, Glixa said, "Fellow Martians. We've come a long way. When we first arrived on Earth, we had to pose as trees for our own safety after some of our comrades ended up on autopsy tables at Roswell. Well, I say to you and to the humans of this nation: NEVER AGAIN!"

As the crowd roared approval, Kemper fired his rifle. Glixa's head exploded.

The audience was so shocked, nobody uttered a sound. Then, one by one, they began to turn back into trees. Just what Atkins was waiting for. Sealing all exits, his goons bored holes into the auditorium and pumped in gas to put delegates into a stupor.

One by one the intoxicated trees were removed from the convention center, taken to Army bases, and incinerated.

With the Martians out of the way, the Republicrats won the election. Atkins was appointed Secretary of Defense in appreciation for his efforts to swing the election away from the Martians. To make sure all Martians were eliminated, he ordered all trees in the nation burned.

What he didn't know was that millions of Martians, who arrived immediately after Glixa's assassination, transformed themselves into weeds.

MIRROR, MIRROR ON THE WALL

"Can I have the key to the men's room?" Harry asked the old timer at the dilapidated gas station in the middle of the Mojave Desert.

"Yep," said the guy wearing the JASPER name tag. "But use it at your own risk."

"Well, if it's that filthy, forget it."

"It's clean. Just stay as far away from the mirror as you can."

"What's wrong with it?"

"It's hexed. The last five guys who looked at it had heart attacks and died right on the spot."

"You gotta be kidding."

"Nope. You gotta trust what I'm telling you. Use the toilet, but don't look in the mirror."

"This is the craziest thing I ever heard. If such a thing happened wouldn't a guy's family sue the hell outta you?"

"Some tried. But, I make everybody sign this here release form. It says I can't be responsible for people who look in the mirror, then fall over dead."

"So why don't you remove it?"

"I was told it's imbedded in such a way, half the building would collapse if it was removed. I ain't got money to rebuild. Look, Mister, do you wanna use the men's room or not? I can't stand around here all day talking about mirrors."

"Sorry. Didn't mean to make you mad."

"Well, either you believe me or you don't. Why don't you just go outside and do your business in the damn desert. On the other hand, if you give me twenty bucks, I'll remove the hex and you can look in the mirror all you want without a problem."

"Why in the hell would I do that?" Harry asked.

"To see the show. They say it's incredible."

"What kinda show?"

"Never saw it myself. I can't remove the hex for myself. But everybody who saw the show leaves here laughing their asses off. So, if you want a good laugh, pay me twenty bucks and see the show."

"Twenty bucks seems like an awful lot for a few laughs."

"I'll throw in a free bag of popcorn. Meanwhile, how much gas do you want?

"Fill it. Free popcorn, eh?"

"Yep. And I put *real* melted butter on it, not that lousy chemical gunk they use everywhere else. Here's a sample. Tell me what you think."

"Hey, this is fantastic. Okay, here's twenty bucks."

"While you're watching the show, I'll vacuum your car."

"That's great."

When Harry entered the men's room, he didn't see any mirrors. "Well, I'll be damned! Whatta crooked bastard!" he muttered, as he relived himself. "I'm gonna kick his stupid ass!"

Harry ran back and hollered, "Hey, gimme my money back!"

"Why?"

"There's no mirror in that room."

"Well that don't make no sense."

"I said give me my twenty bucks back, you damn crook!" Harry raised his fists.

"Okay…here. But now that I have, the hex automatically goes back on the mirror. Would you go back there with me so we can both look to see if the mirror's there?"

"You're nuts. I'm getting the hell outta here. How much for the gas."

"Fifty bucks. But for you, it's free."

"Why would you give me free gas?"

"For your inconvenience. You sound mad. I don't want you telling everybody I'm a crook. It's bad for business."

"Well, you don't have to go that far," Harry said, putting a fifty on the grimy counter. "I don't want something for nothing."

"Before you go," said Jasper, "I'll bet you a hundred bucks you can't prove there ain't no mirror in the men's room."

Just about at his wits end, Harry figured to hell with it. Let the old fool pay for jerking him around so much.

"Okay. You're on. Let's go."

"Put up the hundred first," Jasper said. "And sign this here release form."

Harry put five twenties on the counter and signed the form.

When they walked inside the men's room, Harry said, "See there ain't no damn mirror anywhere on the wall. You lose."

"I never said it was on the wall."

"Then where the hell is it?

"In the toilet."

Harry leaned over and looked into the bowl. "What the hell you talking about, I don't see no damn mirror down here."

"That's because you didn't flush after you used the toilet. Flush it, then take a look."

"I didn't flush it because I couldn't find a lever."

"This one uses a pressure plate. See that little button on the floor? Press it with your foot."

The toilet flushed, and Harry looked inside.

Jasper left, took Harry's hundred dollars off the counter, and went back to the men's room with a body bag.

HIT AND RUN

A van skidded off the mountain road and crashed into a tree. A passenger got out and staggered toward the road.

"Martha, look at that thing coming out of the van," exclaimed an old timer, as their recreation vehicle approached the crash site. "What the hell is it?"

"Don't know. Maybe it's one of them aliens from outer space. Oh dear! A car's coming. Oh no! The driver squashed it and didn't stop."

"Watch for more cars," Frank said, as he raced toward the victim. "Try to stop them. I'm gonna check to see if it's still alive."

Frank approached the mess. "Hey, it looks like a giant, powdered, jelly donut. Look at all the purple goo that came out of it."

Running a finger through the goo, he sniffed it. "This stuff smells like grape jelly. Yum. It *is* grape jelly. Best I ever tasted. Try some."

"You know I only like blueberry," she said. "Maybe you should check the van to see if more jelly donuts are inside. One of them might be filled with blueberry."

Peering inside the van, Frank said, "There's three more. One's powdered. The others are glazed. I'm gonna cut them open to see if any are filled with blueberry jelly."

"You better check to see if they're still alive before you start slicing and dicing."

Frank pinched the things. None responded. Pressing his ear against each, he didn't hear heartbeats. "They're all dead. Damn! These critters are so tough I can't cut them. Come here and help me get them out of the van."

When they removed all the passengers, Frank sniffed the glazed one. "This smells like it's loaded with blueberry jelly. But if I can't cut it open, how am I gonna get the jelly out so you can have some?"

"Let's just put it on the road and wait for the next car to squish it," Martha said.

They hid in the bushes and waited. Within minutes, an 18-wheeler loaded with logs came roaring down the road. It squashed the glazed thing so hard, blueberry jelly flew everywhere. Some splattered Martha's face.

"Wow," she said. "This is absolutely delicious."

They did the same with the remaining two passengers. Soon, the road was covered with grape, blueberry, cherry, and strawberry jelly.

"We shouldn't let all this good stuff go to waste," Frank said.

Martha helped him shovel all the tasty goo into their RV.

When they arrived at the next town, they found a bakery. The owner tasted a sample of the jelly and found it so delightful, he bought it all for his pastries.

Realizing they'd discovered a potentially lucrative source of income, Frank and Martha decided to cause more accidents along mountain roads and to check each of their victims for jelly content.

Today, these two entrepreneurs have several patents for rapid jelly removal, and highly profitable franchise operations in 150 countries.

THIRD PRIZE

"Congratulations," said the voice on Harry's phone. "You won third prize in our Birthday Boy contest."

"But I didn't enter any contests."

"You didn't have to. Our company's computer selected your name from thousands of American men whose birthday is today."

"What's the name of your company?"

"Zombies-R-Us."

"Never heard of you."

"I'm surprised, considering we're a multi-billion dollar company with stores throughout America."

"So what did I win?" Harry asked.

"One of our delightful pet zombies. It does everything dogs, cats, and birds can do. It comes with a rotary switch and keyboard embedded in its back. If you want it to be a canary, just turn the switch to the bird setting. When a light blinks on the keyboard, type the word canary. Your pet zombie will hop around and warble like a canary. If you get tired of having a canary around, you can turn the switch to one of dozens of dog and cat breeds. On the other hand, if you just want it to be a zombie, don't touch any of the switches."

"I have a dog. What do you suggest I do with it when my pet zombie arrives?"

"Throw it in the trash, feed it to your new pet, or trade it in for a discount on a bag of our wonderful zombie food pellets which are chock full of vitamins, minerals, antioxidants, and putrefaction retardants."

"What's putrefaction?"

"Rotting of skin and body organs. Our pet zombies are inoculated and coated with shellac to keep their rot rate to a minimum. However, to keep your pet zombie fresh and supple, just feed it one food pellet a day. By the way, if you let the zombie eat your dog, you won't have to feed it for a whole week."

Ignoring the comment about his dog, Harry asked, "How much is a bag of food pellets?"

"A dollar for three months' worth. So, where would you like us to deliver your prize?"

Harry gave his address.

"Congratulations once again. I'm sure you'll just love your new pet."

"Wait a minute," Harry said. "Don't zombies eat human brains?"

"Not the ones we sell. On the other hand, in the extremely rare situation where there's a slight malfunction, and one bites your skull open while you're sleeping, we stock blood-and-brains stain remover for your pillow case. Comes in a spray can. So, have you decided what you'll do with your dog now that it's obsolete?"

"Yeah. I'll feed it to the zombie."

"Ah, a most humane decision. We'll bring a container shaped like a zombie food pellet when we deliver your prize. But we need to know the size of your dog."

"It's a tiny, teacup poodle."

When Harry hung up, he picked up his doggie, Honeybun, looked into her loving, sparkling eyes, and said, "You've been a pretty good pet. But it costs two dollars a week to feed you. You just ain't cost effective anymore, considering these terrible economic times."

Thinking she was being praised, Honey Bun wagged her tail and licked her beloved master's hand.

* * * *

Honeybun thought she was playing a new, exciting game when Harry pushed her into a container shaped like a zombie food pellet, and handed it to his new, salivating pet.

GENOCIDAL BASTARDS

World War Seven broke out while I was inspecting the Doomsday Shelter twenty miles below Area 51. I was incommunicado the whole time, so I had no way of knowing.

I was in the Shelter only three days. But during that time, Martians staged a sneak attack, waged nuclear war, won, and departed Earth with the spoils.

When I came to the surface, I checked nearby Las Vegas. No survivors. I checked Los Angeles, San Francisco, and Phoenix. Same thing. Horrors! Beside me, the only other survivors were cockroaches.

Fortunately, the Doomsday Shelter had lots of supplies. Except for human companionship, life was as normal as possible.

I spent my mornings working out in the massive gym that was built for 500,000 people. Afternoons, I whiled away the time reading in the Shelter's vast library of a billion volumes. The days passed quickly. But after six months, I found myself dying of loneliness.

Then I discovered a most unusual series of books that contained photographs of all female cockroaches in the United States. The covers said they had been published by the Royal Cockroach Press, commissioned by His Royal Highness, The King of North American Cockroaches. The address of the publishing house was in Las Vegas, just a few blocks from Caesar's Palace Casino.

Waving a white flag, I approached the place.

In seconds, I was surrounded by some very nasty looking, heavily armed cockroaches. I told them I came in peace, and I wanted to see their King.

Recognizing that I was human, they put away their weapons, and shook my hand. Then they told me to lie on my back. When I did, untold numbers crawled under me, lifted me, and carried me to the royal chamber.

"Your Highness," I said, as they put me down at the foot of the King's throne. "I'm so glad to see you. And I'm pleased that you and so many of your people survived."

"We all survived. Your scientists were right."

"In what way, Your Highness?"

"They predicted that after nuclear war, the only survivors would be cockroaches. So, how did you manage to stay alive, seeing that you aren't one of us?"

"I was inspecting the Doomsday Shelter. The one I designed and built for this nation at a cost of 75 trillion dollars. I was twenty miles below the surface inspecting the wiring. When I came to the surface, I saw bodies laying everywhere, and all the destroyed buildings. I saw some of your kind scurrying here and there, so I knew that there were other survivors beside myself."

"So what brings you here?" he asked.

"I saw your books in the Shelter's library."

"Ah yes. I had those published to show how beautiful my female subjects truly were. I sent copies to all the casinos in town, hoping to convince them to hire my subjects as show girls."

"I see. Considering how beautiful they are, I can't imagine why I never saw any of them on stage at any of the casinos. Actually, that's why I'm here. I have an idea."

"Let's hear it," he said.

We spoke for hours. When I finished he heartily agreed. He immediately ordered a beauty contest in which only the most stunning of his subjects would participate.

The contest was held on the stage in what was left of Caesar's Palace. It rivaled in grandeur any Miss America Contest I'd ever seen on TV. Not only were those cockroaches talented, but they were also incredibly beautiful. Seeing them posing in swim suits was something to behold.

With the king's approval, I married the winner.

Since then, we've mated hourly to repopulate Earth. The cross-species pollination is working. When we have sufficient mutated offspring, I'll build a humongous army, nuclear weapons, and rocket ships.

Beware, you genocidal Martian bastards! The cocka-humans are coming to get you!

THE MONUMENT

"**G**reetings from the Zayans," said the parchment Frank found inside an old bottle that washed ashore. "We are an ancient, honorable, and enlightened tribe that had the terrible misfortune of living too close to the jerky Mayans who practiced human sacrifice. Don't believe anything those bozos said. They got it all wrong. Their schools were dumbed-down long ago. Earth will NOT be destroyed on December 21, 2012 like they say. The only reason why their calendar doesn't go beyond 2012 is because they never learned to count any higher than that. The real date for Earth's destruction which we enlightened Zayan soothsayers have discovered through extremely accurate crystal ball gazing is: July 15, 2012 at the seventh hour past noon. (Turn this parchment to the other side, if you want to find out how to save Earth from total destruction.)"

"Geez," Frank mumbled. "That's today. Only ten hours from now. Am I ever glad I found this old bottle. I better call 911 as soon as I read how to save the planet."

Frank turned the parchment over and continued reading. "There is only one way to avoid this catastrophe. The planet's entire population must go outdoors one hour before Earth's scheduled destruction. Everyone must stand on one leg in piles of dirt, and hop continuously while chanting the lyrics from our beloved Zayan National Anthem: 'Gimme a one. Gimme a two. Gimme a one-two-three.' Chant these sacred words while hopping until the seventh hour past noon. If, at the seventh hour brilliant lights appear in the sky, you will know you have succeeded, and the gods have granted a reprieve for another million years."

The parchment was signed by the Illustrious Poo-bah of the Zayan Soothsayer's Guild and dated, "Year 1025 After The Great Solar Eclipse."

Frank keyed 911 on his cell phone.

After hearing the contents of the parchment, the operator alerted Homeland Security. Within an hour, the entire world was notified.

As the Zayan parchment directed, everybody on Earth went outside and stood in piles of dirt. At exactly the sixth hour past noon, they stood on one leg, hopped, and chanted the ancient Zayan National Anthem.

Seven billion legs hopping in dirt created a massive dust cloud. In fifteen minutes, it moved skyward. After thirty minutes, the dust cloud entered the atmosphere, forming a belt of thick smog that circled the entire globe. Meanwhile, the sounds generated by seven billion chanting voices created tremendous vibrations that also moved outward and circled the globe.

Unknown to Earthlings, earlier that day Martians launched a massive invasion force to conquer Earth. This included 100,000 troop transports and 10-million assault troops.

When the Martian armada approached Earth's atmosphere, they ran into the dust cloud kicked up by the chanters. They panicked when realizing they could no longer see the landing sites they'd selected years in advance. Even worse, their spacecraft began to shake violently, as they entered the sound waves generated by the Earthling chanters. One by one, the Martian craft exploded. The sight of 100,000 spacecraft exploding created a fabulous light show on Earth.

When normalcy resumed on Earth, every scrap of information known about Mayans was considered suspect. Since little was known about the ancient Zayans, an international, blue-panel, anthropological study group was formed to investigate why nobody ever heard of them or their culture.

Meanwhile, The Amalgamated Nations (AN) declared an international holiday to honor the Zayans and their crystal gazing soothsayers.

Since Frank discovered the bottle and parchment, he was appointed AN Secretary General for life for his contributions in saving the planet.

As to the parchment and bottle, a colossal monument to house them was proposed for Washington D. C. However, a problem arose. Since every Congressman and Senator had already built colossal marble moments to honor themselves, no room was left anywhere in Washington for another moment. A monument already standing would have to be destroyed before construction for the new one could begin.

Alarmed, at the prospect of losing one of their members' monuments, Congress quickly passed a law prohibiting the destruction of any member's monument. Attached to the bill were 7,321 earmarks.

The President addressed the nation on TV. "We need to make room in Washington so we can build a monument to honor the Zayans for saving our planet. To do this, we must eliminate one of our present monuments. After reviewing the value of each monument has to our history, I'm compelled to ask you which is more important: the monument for Abraham Lincoln who lived a long time ago? Or a monument that will contain the recipe that saved Earth for another million years? I'm asking all our citizens to call or email the White House to give their opinions."

Two days later, the Lincoln Memorial was destroyed.

STICKS AND STONES

Harry screamed so loud he woke the neighbors.

"Easy, Honey," his wife said softly.

She knew better than speak above a whisper at times like this. Until he snapped out of it, he might think she was a Chinese soldier and attack her in self-defense.

She knew he was dreaming again about that horrible night in Korea that devastated his psyche. The night an enemy sapper wearing sneakers slipped through the barbed wire and knifed the other Marine in his foxhole. Left Harry alive on purpose. To destabilize him. It'd worked. The event left a psychic scar so deep nothing could excise it.

"Sonovabitches! I'll get those bastards!"

"Easy does it, Honey."

"Huh! What? Oh, God. How horrible."

Liz led him to the bathroom. She lovingly wiped perspiration from his face with a cool cloth.

"I'm okay now," he said kissing the angelic hand that tended him.

"That's three times this month. Better call Dr. Katz in the morning. You've reached that threshold where you should see him again."

"I don't need Katz. It wasn't about the Chinese sapper. I dreamed Los Angeles was nuked. I saw the bright light coming through the bedroom blinds. Then, a minute later, the whole house shook. Geez. Four hundred miles away from LA, and I could see the light from the blast, and feel the shock wave."

"At least it wasn't about Korea," Liz said.

"This was far worse. In my dream, I had the radio tuned to classical music, when suddenly that god-awful noise filled the room. That sound you hate so much when they do the monthly test of the Radio Emergency Alert System. I figured another Amber Alert. But it wasn't. Somebody very shaken said, 'This is not a drill. Los Angeles is gone.'"

"Well, Los Angeles is still there. It was just a horrible, vivid nightmare."

"But the details seemed so real. Nothing was distorted. The announcer said, 'It is believed that the city was struck by a ten megaton nuclear explosion. This is a preliminary report. All commercial broadcasting is hereby suspended. Martial law has been declared throughout the United States. If you are in the Western States, stay indoors to lessen the effects of radioactive fallout. Stay tuned to this station for further announcements. The President will speak in four minutes.'"

"No wonder you were perspiring so badly. Worse than I've ever seen. Well, look. It's over. It was only a dream. You know how real they can be at times. Let's go and raid the fridge. I could go for some potato salad. Can I make you a nice salami sandwich?"

"At 2:30 in the morning? I'll get bad indigestion. Gimme some potato salad."

Suddenly, the house was filled with an eerie, intense light lasting a few seconds. A minute later, the entire house shook.

Liz screamed along with everyone else in Phoenix.

Harry ran for the TV. Only lines appeared across the screen.

A moment later, a face came on.

"Los Angeles is...."

Static.

"Oh my God!" Harry yelled.

"Martial law has..."

Picture and sound disappeared for several seconds.

"Houston, Miami, and Seattle have been invaded by...."

The signal was lost again.

"Arm yourselves!" a voice screamed over the TV.

"Arm myself with what? A pipe wrench? A broomstick? They confiscated all our weapons last year. Said that we had to conform with the wishes of rest of the world. Bastards!"

The electricity went out.

Trembling, they held each other tightly. "Is this the end?" she asked, sobbing.

He didn't know how to answer. All he could think of was his buddy getting knifed by a sapper in their foxhole. And how traumatized he was when waking up. Bombing Los Angeles was the same idea. Kill one city. Then every other city will be traumatized, destabilized.

"That Chinese general threatened ten years ago they'd take out Los Angeles if we reacted to their moves against Taiwan. The sonovabitch said, 'What would you rather have? Taiwan, or Los Angeles?' Instead of nationwide outrage, there was silence. That's because the freakin' newspapers wouldn't carry the story. Didn't mesh with their agenda. Didn't wanna make our trading partners look bad. Only the *Dallas Daily Bugle* carried the story, and got shut down because of it. So, hardly anybody knew of the threat against LA."

"What'll we do?" Liz asked weakly.

"I don't know," he said, slumping into a chair, wondering where he could get some sticks to sharpen and heavy rocks to throw.

REVELATION

"There's something I've wanted to tell you for quite some time," Shakira said, as she sat across from Harry, sipping coffee.

"What's that?" he asked.

"Well, promise you won't laugh."

"I promise. Unless it's something really funny, then my promise is nullified."

"It's not funny in the slightest," she said.

"Well, are you gonna tell me or what?"

"Yeah. Do you remember me telling you that I was born on a Pacific Island?"

"Right. You've mentioned that from time to time. And you've told me several times your mom and dad were sole survivors of a shipwreck—while your mom was preggers with you. And the stress of the incident caused her to go into labor weeks before she should have."

"Well, Harry, that was all a lie. I came from the Pacific, but not from an island. The truth is... I'm a mermaid."

"Yeah, and I'm Superman," he said chuckling. "You're one of the funniest women I've ever met, Shakira. Always joking. That's what I like most about you."

"I'm not joking. It's true. I wanted you to be the first to know."

"It's true, eh? So, where's your tail? Don't all mermaids have tails?"

"Yes, they do. Mine is just starting to develop. It takes about three hundred years for a mermaid's tale to develop properly. I'm only a hundred and five. So, all I have is a stub. In a hundred and ninety-five years, my tail will be fully developed. Too bad you won't be around to see it."

"What an imagination! Mermaid. Heh-heh."

"Cross my heart and swear to God, it's true," she said.

"Yeah, sure." Suddenly, Harry shouted to all the customers, "Hey, everybody, see this woman sitting across from me? She's a mermaid. Ain't that a scream?"

"Where's your tail, Honey," an old guy called out, then guffawed.

A pony-tailed guy yelled, "Hey, Ariel. Can I have your autograph?"

Shakira turned red. "Harry, what the hell are you doing? Why did you betray me like this and tell everybody my secret?"

"C'mon, Shakira. Enough is enough. Want another donut?"

"No. In fact, I'm leaving. I never want to see you again, you bastard!"

"Geez," Harry said. "Take it easy. What's your problem? PMS?"

"Dammit, Harry! I don't get periods. I'm a mermaid, for crying out loud. Why the hell didn't you believe me when I told you? Why did you have to yell it out to everybody? I wanted to keep it a secret, especially since I got that slot as a TV Weather Woman on station KZIX. What if they find out? They'll fire me before my first broadcast."

That said, she stormed out.

Several customers yelled, "Bye, Mermaid."

Harry was stunned. He'd never seen her act like this before. While he pondered the incident, a woman slid into the chair Shakira had vacated.

"Do you mind if I sit?" she asked.

Harry couldn't believe his eyes. The most stunning blonde he'd ever seen was sitting across from him.

"Not at all," he replied.

"I heard what she said. Perhaps it's true. Several women have come out of the closet and told the truth about what they really are."

"I suppose they said they were mermaids."

"Right. Lots of people scoffed. It's a perfectly normal reaction. But the women were examined at the university hospital. Turns out they really were mermaids."

"Aw, c'mon. I never heard anything about that. If such a thing happened, *CNN* and *Fox News* would have blasted us with that around the clock."

"But it's true," the blonde said. "The world's not ready for the announcement yet. But it will come."

"So, how do you know all this?" Harry asked.

"Because I'm a mermaid too."

Harry had enough. He left without saying another word.

On the way to his car, he noticed a meter maid writing him a ticket. "Hey, Officer. Gimme a break. I was on my way to put another quarter in the meter."

"Yeah, that's what they all say," she said, handing him a ticket.

Harry crumpled the ticket, threw it on the ground, and stepped on it.

Before he knew what happened, he was flat on the ground.

"Wise, guy, eh?" the maid yelled. "Now you're going to jail."

Harry couldn't believe when she cuffed him, picked him up and threw him over her shoulder.

As she carried him toward the nearest police station, he said, "Officer, I'm 260 pounds. How the hell did you pick me up with one arm and throw me over your shoulder?"

"For me to know and for you to find out," she said.

"Do you by any chance come from a Pacific Island?" Harry asked.

"Yeah, how did you know?"

"And do you tell everybody your mom and dad were the only survivors of a shipwreck while your mom was pregnant with you?"

"You're a mind reader," she said.

INCREDIBLE INVENTION

"Ladies and gentlemen," said Dr. Dumont to the thirty military observers in the research pavilion, "thank you for coming today. What you are about to see will radically transform life as we know it. This includes how we wage war. Let's begin the demonstration."

Spotlights focused on a human form covered by a sheet.

"What we have here is a zombie unlike any we've ever seen before. This one is so different it boggles the mind. Though it is a horrendous threat to human life, it has peculiar properties that can benefit mankind in ways that exceed our wildest dreams."

While the observers digested Dumont's profound paradoxical statement, he lowered the sheet to expose the zombie's shoulders and upper arms.

"What's that silver-colored material wrapped around its upper arms and shoulder?" a general asked.

"Duct tape."

Some observers snickered.

"Notice what happens when I remove the tape." Dumont grabbed one end and yanked it loose.

Loud murmurs rose when the zombie's arms fell off.

"Believe me, I was just as surprised when I discovered this unusual invention. This monster grabbed its victims, tore their heads off, and pounded skulls with its fists to get at their brains. And yet, there isn't a single muscle, bone, or nerve connection between its shoulders and arms."

"Dr. Dumont, would you pass the tape around so we can examine it?" asked an admiral.

"Please bear with me a bit longer, and then my assistants will provide you with samples."

Dumont lowered the sheet further to expose the zombie's legs. More duct tape was wrapped around the area where legs were joined to the trunk. Once again, he pulled on the tape.

The observers were amazed when the zombie's legs fell off.

"This thing prowled the jungles with nothing more than duct tape connecting its legs to its torso. What we have before us is the strongest duct tape in the universe. With this incredible tape, we'll be able to change the world. Bridge structures could be a thousand times lighter and stronger if held together with nothing more than this tape. Steel girders in skyscrapers would no longer have to be bolted together with steel rivets if we bind them with this tape."

"Our tanks could be made more cheaply," said a colonel wearing insignia of an Army Armored Division.

"And our planes could be produced faster at far less cost," said an Air Force general.

"This tape has uncountable uses," Dumont said. "It can be used to cover wounds to stop bleeding. Thus, soldiers will no longer be incapacitated when wounded. This will allow them to fight on until they are killed. Imagine the tactical implications."

"It's a shame we can't make this edible," an observer said. "We could save billions. No more spoilage. No more refrigerated warehouses. No more food distribution logistical nightmares. No more need to provide vegetables, meat, and poultry."

"Exactly," Dr. Dumont said. "I'm pleased to tell you we've synthesized this tape and produced an edible version. My assistants will now pass out samples. Each of you will receive a single, one-inch square of edible duct tape."

"Why's mine green, when I see others with red, orange, and blue samples?" a colonel asked.

"We added colors to create a sense of variety. We all know how the stomach reacts when we eat the same thing, meal after meal, day after day. Actually, these duct tape morsels come in 120 distinct colors and 1,200 different flavors. We made arrangements with the Crayola Crayon Corporation to imitate colors selected as their favorites by the nation's children. Now, please eat your samples. You'll find some quite chewy, while others are so tender, they'll melt in your mouth."

Appreciative sounds came from the observers the moment they placed the duct tape into their mouths. One female officer accidentally burped loudly, when she proclaimed how delicious her purple morsel was.

"Mine tastes like pumpkin pie," somebody said.

"Mine tastes like a bagel with cream cheese."

"The blue one I have tastes like mashed potatoes and gravy."

A startled general said, "Mine tastes like a hot dog with mustard, onions, and sauerkraut."

The observers applauded enthusiastically. Some shouted, "Bravo."

"Notice how full you feel," said Dumont. "This feeling will last for 24 hours. Thus, your troops will only have to eat once a day. What's more, storage problems will be totally eliminated, because these duct tape morsels can adhere to helmets, shoes, rifle stocks, ammunition—to name a few. And to top it off, we've been able to produce these samples at a cost of 1 cent per thousand.

"Miraculous," somebody said.

"There's more. We're working on a version that will replace liquids. We hope to have this perfected within the next six months. We'll have duct tape morsels that taste like homemade lemonade, chocolate milk, coffee, Ovaltine, and so on. What's more, we'll be able to cut the size of the morsels in half."

The observers could barely contain themselves.

"I'll order a billion food units right now," said a four-star general. "Food this good will attract untold numbers of volunteers."

"If you can make a version to replace toilet tissue, I'd order ten million rolls immediately for my aircraft carriers," said an admiral.

Other officers expressed their desire to place orders for any version of the duct tape that Dumont's institute might devise.

One officer asked, "What is this tape made of?"

"One of our most plentiful resources," Dumont said. "Unfortunately, I'm not at liberty to give details. But I assure you, the raw materials are extremely plentiful."

As the observers shook Dumont's hand, tons of cemetery remains were being exhumed and loaded onto boxcars for shipment to his laboratory.

SWEET MAX

"**M**iss Jones, you're the first sitter we ever had for little Max. So, he may cry a bit if he wakes up and sees you instead of us. That's if he even wakes up. He usually sleeps through the night."

"Don't worry Mrs. Brown," said Jones. "I'll take good care of him."

"I'm sure you will. You were highly recommended by the agency. By the way, the agency said you had a Master's Degree in Babysitting from the Massachusetts Institute of Technology. I never knew there was such a thing, much less from MIT."

"Actually, they've been granting babysitting degrees for ten years. And several Ivy League Colleges have started undergraduate babysitting programs. Right now I'm working on my PhD."

"A PhD in Babysitting? That's remarkable. Just goes to show how the world is changing. Well, we're gonna leave now. See you in four hours. Bye."

"Enjoy yourselves," Jones said. "And don't worry about a thing."

The babysitter waited twenty minutes before removing a small, plastic case from her handbag. Popping the lid, she removed a syringe filled with purple fluid.

Approaching the sleeping baby, she asked "Okay...who'd like to volunteer to be part of a little experiment in brain stimulation?" After a few seconds of silence except for Max's deep breaths, she nudged him. When he groaned, she added, "Ah-hah! I see we have a volunteer. Very nice of you, Sir. Here's what we're gonna do..."

Twenty minutes later, Jones and Max were playing chess.

"Checkmate!" Max yelled through the bars of his crib.

While he laughed heartily, Jones scribbled some notes in her journal.

"So, whadda ya wanna do next, Bitch," he said, leering at her.

"I thought we might try a trivia game."

"What's that?"

"Oh, I ask you questions, and you answer."

"Go ahead," he said.

"Okay, what was the name of the Marx Brother who had his own popular radio and TV show?

"That's easy. Abraham Lincoln."

Jones scribbled in her journal again, injected more purple serum into Max, then asked the same question.

"Groucho Marx," he said.

"Good. And who played Superman in the serials of the same name in the 1940's?"

"Talking about Superman, I got something for you," he said. "Why don't you come into my crib, lay down, and relax a bit?"

Jones scribbled in her journal, then scrunched herself in the crib next to Max.

* * * *

When the Browns returned home, Jones told them how Max had slept the whole time. She reminded them that she was available to babysit Max any time.

After she left, Mr. Brown said, "Did you notice something peculiar about her?"

"What do you mean," his wife asked.

"She looked so dumpy when she arrived. But now she's, well, glowing might be the best word. Frankly, she looks like she just went through a helluva romp. Know what I mean? Kinda like what we're gonna do as soon as you undress."

"Come to think of it, you're right. Maybe she let her boyfriend in. I hope not. I don't want strangers in here. Well, she'll never get back in this house again."

Before she undressed, she checked Max. "Honey, come here. Look at Max. Look how he's smiling in his sleep. I never saw him smile like this before."

"Geez. You're right. Maybe he's having a Freudian dream."

"At his age?"

"More goes on with babies than we'll ever know," Brown said.

BILLY'S PILLS

"**W**anna buy some anti-stress pills?" asked the little kid at my door.

"Is this for a school project? Come back when you're selling candy."

"It's not for school. It's for me so I can raise money for college. I wanna be a chemical engineer when I grow up."

"You sure have big plans. What's your name?"

"Billy."

"Where do these pills come from, Billy?"

"I make them myself. With my chemistry set."

"Oh? What's in them?"

"Can't tell you."

"Why not?"

"It's my secret formula. I shouldn't even be telling you that."

"You can trust me. I won't tell anybody."

"Raise your hand and swear."

I did.

"I discovered this by accident," he said. "I was working on something to make airplanes invisible. But I slipped and spilled the yellow stuff into the blue stuff. I was so mad. But when I tasted the mixed up stuff, I felt better. So, I thought I invented something that takes away stress. Not for always. But for a couple hours."

Craziest thing I ever heard. Dumb kid thought he invented a tranquilizer out of spilled chemicals from a chintzy chemistry set. Now he was selling the result. His crappy pills would probably give somebody the runs for a week.

"I think you're gonna get in trouble," I said. "There's lotsa laws about who makes medicine and how they do it."

"The lady next door said that when she slammed the door."

"Have you sold any?"

"Nope. I hope you'll be my first customer."

"How many you got?" I figured I'd buy them all. Might be a way to get him off the streets and out of trouble. What the hell, the kid meant well. If nothing else, I'd be sponsoring a bit of his future education. And if his supply were gone, he'd be off the streets before somebody got mad and called the cops. Might scare the kid. Might make his parents take away his chemistry set.

"I got sixty."

"I'll take them all. I've had lots of stress lately. So how much do I owe you?"

"Twelve for a dime makes it fifty cents."

"Here's a dollar."

"I have to give you fifty pennies change."

"Tell you what. If you promise to stop selling your pills door to door, you can keep the change. In fact, here's another dollar. You can have it if you stop selling your pills forever. See, if certain people get their hands on your pills, some very smart chemists will analyze them. And they'll steal your secret. Then you'll have nothing. So, will you keep your formula secret and stop selling your pills if I give you this dollar?"

"I gotta think."

"It's now or never."

"Okay," he said. He gave me a small plastic pill bottle, and left.

* * * *

Seven years later, my company transferred me to New York. My wife refused to leave New Mexico. She filed for a no-fault divorce. Incredibly stressed, I thought I'd lose my mind.

Checking the medicine cabinet for something for my nerves, I noticed an unlabeled plastic bottle. Inside were yellow-blue pills. I wondered if they were the pills I'd bought years ago from the kid. Thought I'd trashed them long ago.

Maybe it was a suicidal impulse that made me open the bottle and take one of those dime-a-dozen, kid-made pills. Damn thing caught in the back of my throat. It was horribly bitter. Anything that bad should've killed me instantly.

Washing it down with whiskey, I waited for death. Instead, powerful euphoric feelings swept over me. I'd never experienced anything like it. In minutes, I was dancing around the room and singing every happy song I ever knew. I was King of the Universe... for twelve hours.

Even when the effects wore off, it happened gently. Even better, negative feelings didn't return. Talk about miracle drugs!

I flew to New Mexico to find the kid. When I asked around the old neighborhood, nobody knew who I was talking about.

My former neighbor, who'd shooed him, didn't remember.

School yearbooks helped me discover his name. William Van Kupnick. More checking revealed the Kupnicks had moved away years ago. Nobody knew where.

I thought about hiring a detective, but money was tight. Even if I found him, what would I do? Ask him for more pills? Maybe the kid had destroyed the formula. Hell, I'd done my part in discouraging him.

* * * *

Over the years, the remaining pills helped rescue my psyche from many gut-wrenching situations. I saved the last one for an unbearable tragedy yet to come

* * * *

I was downsized at fifty-seven. My gray hair kept the good jobs away.

I flipped burgers, barely making ends meet. I lived on rice, beans, cheap tuna, and day-old bread. Dogs had it better.

Then I got a letter from a law firm. They wanted to see me at their law offices.

When I went to their office, I left with a check for a million bucks and a letter from William Van Kupnick, PhD, CEO.

"Dear Mr. Downs," the letter said. "I finally found you...."

Billy'd kept the dollar I'd given him to stop peddling pills. Years later, with a PhD, a bio startup company hired him. He'd invested the dollar I'd given him in the company's penny stocks. They hit a biggie with his yellow-blue, anti-stress pills. Mergers, multiple stock splits, and international sales over thirty-two years had exploded the dollar's worth of penny stocks into millions. For Billy, it was payback time.

Taking the last pill from his original batch, I had it coated with gold and framed in platinum.

STRANGE OBJECT

"Good morning, Mr. President," a general said.

"Hello, General. So where's this thing you guys woke me about?"

"Right down the hall, Sir. If you'll please follow me."

Both men walked briskly until they reached an orange door guarded by four heavily-armed soldiers.

The general pressed his palm against the door. A split-second later, it unlocked with a loud snap and swung open.

Entering the laboratory, the President saw a dozen scientists surrounding a table on which rested a strange object brilliantly lit by flood lights. They parted when the President approached.

"What is it?" the President asked.

"We don't know, Sir."

"Where did you find it?"

"Seven meters outside the city gate."

"Where do you think it came from?"

"We have no idea. However, we've received a few reports of an unidentified flying object."

"What? Again? I thought our citizens all understood such things do not exist, have never existed, nor will they exist in the future."

"We continue our efforts to educate the public to eradicate any traces of superstition," a scientist said.

"Keep up your commendable work," said the President. "Meanwhile, we have this weird-looking thing sitting right here on this table. What about those red markings on the top. Any idea what they are?"

"No, Sir. However, our Linguistic Department has taken photographs and has already circulated them to the greatest minds on the planet. I suspect we should know something within the next few hours."

"Do you have an extra photograph that I can take?" asked the President.

"Yes, Sir. Would one be enough?"

"Yes. I want to show this curious thing to my wife. She's very intuitive. When I give her a gift, she can always guess what's in the box before opening it. She's quite remarkable that way. Maybe something will come to her mind about this. By the way, is this object hollow?"

"Yes, Sir. Our spectrographic analysis shows something round with a craggy surface. It's quite flat. The top is yellow and red. Several flat, reddish, round disk-like objects are also on the very top in a random pattern."

"Hmm. This gets stranger by the minute," said the President. "Well, it hasn't exploded, so I assume we're in no danger."

"We also have the same assumption," said the scientist.

"Well, thank you for waking me to see this thing. Carry on. I'd like a full report on my desk as soon as possible. Thank you."

Back in his bedroom, the President's wife woke as he slipped into bed.

"What's going on, Honey?"

"Something strange showed up outside the city's walls. They wanted me to see it."

"What does it look like?" she asked.

The President explained what he saw, and mentioned the picture he'd brought.

"Let me see it," she said.

Turning the lamp on, the President gave her the picture.

"What strange markings," she said. "What do you suppose they mean?"

"I was hoping your women's intuition could tell me. Got any strong feelings?"

"Yes. I'm starting to get the sense that it's a work of art from an ancient civilization. Could be from the 21st century. If so, it would be worth millions. I'm going to check it more closely with this magnifying glass," she added, as she stared intensely at the thing that had the inscription: *DOMINO'S PEPPERONI PIZZA.*

IF ONLY THE PORTUGUESE HADN'T DIED

In 1942, as the Second World War raged, a Portuguese coal miner in Pennsylvania collapsed and died. He was one of Grandma Winter's boarders from the Old Country. Since he had no relatives in America, Grandma arranged a proper Catholic burial.

His body was laid out in Grandma's parlor. On the evening of the wake, friends arrived, prayed, and pondered their own eventual return to dust. Women in black mourned in high-pitched, wailing voices.

"What's a wake, Mommy?" three-year old Billy asked, as they headed for Grandma's house.

"A party. But without cake and ice cream."

They passed a house where boy scouts were placing a coffin onto the front porch.

"What's that?" Billy asked.

"Hitler's coffin."

"What's a Hitler?"

"The name of a very bad man. He started the war."

"The war my daddy went to?"

"Yeah. The boys are collecting money for our soldiers. People give them a nickel so they can hammer a nail in Hitler's coffin."

"What's a coffin?"

"A box they put bad people into."

"If I'm bad will you put me in a coffin?"

"No I would never do that."

They ran into Billy's twelve-year-old cousin, Carl.

"Hi, Aunt Emma. Where you going?"

"To the boarder's wake. How about you?"

"I'm going to the movies."

Emma took Carl aside. "I couldn't get a sitter for Billy. And I don't want him to see a dead body in a coffin. It might give him nightmares. If I give you twelve cents for his ticket, will you take him? He'll be nice and quiet. He loves the movies. He sat through *Bambi* and *Fantasia* without making a sound. I'll even give you some pennies to buy candy."

Carl agreed.

Emma never thought to ask what was playing.

Wishing to spare Billy from the sights and sounds of a dead man's wake, Billy's mom inadvertently consigned him to something worse.

Showing that night were two of Universal International's most intense horror movies. Both featured Frankenstein, Dracula, and the Wolfman.

Billy was so shocked by the hideous images, he forgot to eat his candy. The sight of Dracula lying in a coffin petrified him. He screamed along with everybody else when the vampire drank people's blood.

The Wolfman looked like Billy's uncle—until the full moon rose. Billy cringed when he saw an ordinary man transforming into a hairy beast.

The Frankenstein Monster drew the most screams. His head was flat. Screws protruded from his neck. He roared ferociously, and strangled everybody who crossed his path.

After the show, Carl took a very frightened three-year old to Grandma's. Once inside, Emma covered her son's eyes when walking him through the parlor. She didn't want him to be shocked by the sight of a corpse in a coffin. But she didn't block his ears. To him, the women who wailed over the dead Portuguese sounded like the women who wailed over the victims of Frankenstein, Dracula, and the Wolfman.

Because his mom was staying over to help Grandma cook for funeral attendees, Billy was taken upstairs and put to bed. He kept looking around nervously, saying "Franken-stink...Franken-stink."

Emma didn't grasp what he was saying. She figured a bedtime story would settle him. So, she told him the story of the three little pigs that were gobbled up by a big bad wolf.

She left when Billy fell asleep.

Sometime later, he woke up and scampered down the dimly lit hall to the bathroom. While he was on the toilet, air raid sirens sounded signaling a blackout drill. To Billy, they sounded like screams he heard at the horror movies.

The town's entire electrical power was turned off from a central switchboard. When the bathroom turned pitch black, Billy cried out. That's when he saw Frankenstein, Dracula, and the Wolfman moving toward him. His screams pierced the entire house, shattering the frayed nerves of the mourners.

Stumbling through the darkness, Emma hurried upstairs. But it was too late. The imagined monsters had already ripped Billy's psyche apart.

A patrolling Air Raid Warden heard the commotion and ran into Grandma's house to investigate. A doctor was called. Questions were asked.

Carl ran away and hid for two days.

* * * *

In 1992, Billy, now known as Dr. William Winter, was about to give the keynote address at the International Robotics Association convention. He had a dynamite speech, fantastic visuals, terrific stage effects. At the point where he'd have the audience completely captivated, three of his company's most advanced robots would enter and dance a ballet.

Nobody except Billy's wife knew he was tottering on the edge of nervous collapse from overwork.

"And now, members of the Association," Billy said to the audience, "I present the most amazing robots in the entire world."

Lights dimmed. Spotlights focused on the stage. Three robots appeared and began to dance gracefully to tremendous applause.

Suddenly, a power failure darkened the room. Women's screams jolted Billy's raw nerves. Though the screaming stopped, it kept repeating in his head. Trembling, he found himself fighting an overwhelming urge to run for his life.

Somebody shined a flashlight onto the stage. The robots were no longer dancing. Now one had screws in its neck. Another was turning into a bat. The third howled as hair covered his face and arms.

When power was restored, Dr. William Winter was gone.

They found him in a fetal position in a closet, muttering, "Franken-stink...Franken-stink."

On the way to the hospital, he fell into a catatonic state.

Failing to revive him to normalcy, psychiatrists tried insulin shock. Though the effects would be temporary, he'd become lucid enough to communicate with them for a few minutes.

When they injected Billy, he sat straight up in bed.

"You're in a hospital," a doctor said. "Can you tell us what happened?"

Billy muttered something, then went unconscious.

"What did he say?" asked a doctor.

"Strangest thing I ever heard: 'If only the Portuguese hadn't died.'"

A NOBLE CAUSE

A man with a large black laundry bag slung over his shoulder flagged down a bus on a country road. As he paid his fare, he noticed four teens sitting in the back. Pointing at his bag, he hollered, "Hey, kids! Free jelly donuts. Come and get 'em."

"Can I have one?" asked the driver.

"Sure thing," the man said.

"What kind you got?"

"Any kind you want."

"I'll have cherry," the driver said.

The man rooted inside his bag. "Here's one with extra powdered sugar."

"Wow! I never saw a jelly donut the size of a grapefruit."

In seconds, the driver's face and fingers were smeared with cherry jelly. Every time he bit into the donut, some filling squirted out the other end and onto the floor.

"How about us?" yelled the kids.

"Don't worry," said the man. "I haven't forgotten you. I have plenty. Okay, Sonny, what kind do you want?"

"Blueberry."

Passing a huge donut from his pack, he asked the next kid.

"Raspberry."

"I'll have the same," said a girl whose top barely covered her ripeness.

The last kid said, "I don't like jelly donuts."

"You're really missing something, Lisa," somebody said. "This is the most fabulous donut I ever tasted. Stepping into a puddle of jelly that'd dropped to the floor, he added, "Well, if you ain't gonna have one, I'll eat yours."

"Young lady," the man said, "I hate to see you miss the treat of a lifetime. Sure you won't try at least one bite?"

"Nah."

"Would you try one if I gave you five dollars?"

"You'll pay me to eat a donut?"

"Yep."

"I don't believe you. Let me see the five bucks."

The man gave her a five-dollar bill. "What kind do you want?"

"Strawberry," she said, pleased that she'd just made five dollars for ingesting a stupid donut.

A moment later, her hands and face were full of jelly. A sizeable portion of the filling had dropped onto the floor.

"Do you like it?"

"It's terrific!" she said.

The man lit a match and stared at the flame. "If hadn't come aboard, you would've missed this wonderful, pleasurable experience. Have you ever noticed how everything has its opposite? Evil is the opposite of good. Cold is the opposite of hot. Pain is the opposite of pleasure. Now that you've felt pleasure, it's now time for you to experience pain to advance my holy cause."

He threw the match on the floor.

The jelly ignited instantly. Roaring flames surrounded the donut eaters. The residue on their fingers, faces, clothes also erupted.

They screamed horribly, as the man crashed through the front door. Watching the inferno, he muttered, "Let's see…five were on the bus. I paid a girl five bucks to try a donut. That works out to a buck each to field-test my new weapon."

When the flames died down, he took dozens of digital pictures of the charred remains from every angle. Removing a digital voice recorder from his pocket, he set it to the point where he boarded the bus. He chuckled when he heard the part where the donut eaters caught fire and were burning to death.

Then he muttered, "Bless all of you for giving your lives for a most noble and worthy cause. Now the Army will *have* to give me the attention I've demanded. Especially since I've just proven my new napalm formula is absolutely odorless… and wonderfully delicious."

A REALLY GREAT GAME

"Good evening," said the casino greeter. Welcome to our special roulette game for extremely honest players. Please take a seat."

Chairs scraped across the hardwood floor.

"Bibles have been placed at each player's position. Please put your left hand on the book, raise your right, and repeat after me… I promise not to cheat… I promise not to steal… If I do, may the Lord strike me dead."

Anna, Brad, and Chaz eagerly repeated the words.

Removing the Bibles, the greeter said, "Wonderful. Now, I'd like to present Fabio, our croupier."

A door opened. A tapping sound moved slowly toward them. A man appeared, wearing wrap-around dark glasses. Carrying a white cane, he tapped the floor ahead of him from left to right.

"He's blind," Brad whispered.

"Good evening, players," Fabio said brightly.

Two guards entered and placed stacks of playing chips on the table.

"They're all the same color," whispered Anna. "And they don't have any markings to identify their value."

The greeter wished everyone good luck, then departed with the security guards.

"This room is free of surveillance cameras," Fabio said. "You've been invited here, because your churches selected you as their most scrupulously honest members. That's important to me, especially since I have a severe visual impairment and a million dollars in gambling chips are stacked on this table. As a reward for your honesty, the casino has declared each chip as having a value of one thousand dollars. They'll cost you only a dollar each."

"Did you say we only have to pay a dollar for a thousand dollar chip?"

"That's correct."

"What's the gimmick?"

"There isn't any. The casino owner believes honest people should be well rewarded, just as he believes the dishonest should be severely punished. He asks you to donate forty percent of your winnings to battered women's shelters. May I assume you'll honor his wishes?"

The players were shocked at such a preposterous idea. Honesty was one thing, but charity was quite another. Nevertheless, all agreed.

"Each of you is allowed to bet on only one number. If you win, yell BINGO! I'll pay fifty-to-one for every chip you've wagered."

"That's the highest payout I ever heard of," Chaz said.

"Highest in the world," said Fabio. "A suitable reward for your wonderful honesty. Now, I'll sell you playing chips. Since I can't see, please tell me how much money you're giving me."

"Here's a twenty," said Brad.

Fabio grabbed a pile of gray chips and slid them toward Brad.

Brad, a man of outstanding integrity, noticed he'd received seventeen too many. He was already $17,000 richer. "Hey, Fabio," he called.

"What?"

"You, uh, never mind."

"Here's a fifty," Anna said. Fabio pushed sixty-one chips in her direction. Though extremely honest, she didn't bother to correct Fabio's error. If she pocketed the extra chips he'd erroneously given her, she could pay off her credit card and take a trip to Tahiti. After all, the croupier represented the casino, and the casino had just handed her a gift. Nothing wrong in accepting a gift, she reasoned.

Chaz passed a five-dollar bill to Fabio. "Here's a twenty," he said. Fabio slid thirty-seven chips toward Chaz.

A man of superior honor, Chaz had done this to prove how botched up everything was. He was about to ask Fabio to stop everything and call a casino manager. Suddenly realizing he actually possessed $37,000 in gray, cashable playing chips—more money than he'd ever had at one time—Chaz changed his mind. "This is really great," he said.

Anna was alarmed by Chaz's deceit. But she kept quiet. Why make a stink? If she complained, they might shutdown the game.

"Place your bets," Fabio said.

Each player put a chip on a number.

The ball rolled and fell into the 31 pocket. "Number 14 is the winner," Fabio erroneously proclaimed in his best croupier's voice.

The players couldn't believe it. The implications of what'd just happened were enormous. Palms got sweaty. The smell of easy money made hearts beat faster.

Brad had a chip on number 14. "Bingo!" he yelled.

"How many chips did you put on the number?" the croupier asked.

"One."

Fabio pushed a pile of chips toward the winner's voice. The pile contained seven more chips than the winner deserved. But Brad said nothing about the $7,000 overpayment.

On the next spin, bets were placed on numbers 13, 17, and 24. The ball felt into the 33 pocket. "Number 6," Fabio called out. Any winners?"

Nobody spoke up.

"House wins," Fabio exclaimed. "Please push the losing chips toward me."

Each player quickly retrieved a chip from their losing bets, and pushed the rest toward the croupier.

Removing a small notepad from her purse, Anna scribbled, "Let's take turns winning and split everything three ways." She passed it to Brad and Chaz.

Heads nodded.

Number 15 came up next, but Fabio proclaimed 25 as the winning number.

"Bingo!" yelled Anna.

The players strained to keep from laughing out loud. None had even bothered to place any chips on any numbers.

"How many chips did you have on 25?"

"Three."

"Push the loosing bets toward me," Fabio said. Brad and Chaz were only too happy to push a chip his way, considering they'd just won $150,000 without betting."

And so it went, until they'd won all the chips.

"Congratulations. The House is busted. Game is over. Don't forget to donate forty percent to charity.

"Right."

"For sure."

"Can't wait."

The exit door wouldn't open. They turned to tell Fabio.

Fabio jammed a dagger into Brad's chest, then Chaz's gut.

Anna screamed, "You can see!"

"Yes. Very clearly. You asked the Lord to strike you dead if you stole. I'm Fabio Lord, owner of this casino. I'm pleased to grant your wish."

The next evening, three new players arrived.

"I hear this is a great game," said one.

"It's fabulous," the greeter said. "Especially if you're honest."

FLUIDS

After dropping off my last passenger for the night in Manhattan, I headed for the taxi barn. Feeling restless I decided to drop off the cab and head across the Hudson River to Jersey. Overlooking the river was a great all night place. Owned by the Mob, it catered to Latins. I'd have a few rum and cokes and ogle the incredible Hispanic broads. I loved the hot music. I loved how those babes moved their tight rumps to the intricate rhythms. But most of all, I loved the odor of pungent sweat dripping from their sizzling Latin bodies.

Cruising down 9th Avenue, I didn't see any cars on either side of the road. Typical for 3:00 AM in Manhattan. Best time of the entire day. Peace and quiet. No people. No sounds. Nothing.

As I approached 27th Street, a black Caddie zoomed through a red light. Just missed slamming my passenger side by a couple feet.

I slammed my horn and hollered every cuss word I ever learned while fighting in Iraq.

The bastard slammed his brakes. You coulda heard the tires screeching for a mile.

He backed up in a way that only a Hollywood stunt driver coulda done. Put that damn Caddie right next to my taxi.

"What did you call me?" a woman's voice said from the driver's window.

I couldn't see her face in the dark. But the fact that it was a woman made me even madder.

I repeated my cuss words.

"Is that something good or bad?" the voice asked.

"Get outta the car, and I'll show you," I screamed, grabbing the tire iron I kept for self-defense. I opened my door to confront her. Her car was so close, I coughed up a wad of phlegm and spit toward the voice.

"Umm. You got me right in the mouth. How delicious. Are all your body fluids so scrumptious?"

"What the hell are you talking about? Cut the bull crap and step outside. I got a nice surprise for you." I raised the tire iron to flatten her skull the moment she stepped out. But she didn't move. I tried to make out her face, but it was too dark.

"I think you're cute," the voice said. "Otherwise, you'd be dead by now. I'm going to give you something to hold your wonderful body fluid. Fill it and I'll let you go." An arm extended a small cup.

Her idiotic words completely disarmed me.

"You want me to spit into a cup? For you to drink? Phew, you are one sick bastard." Then it struck me: who said I had to fill it with spit?

"Okay," I said. "I'll fill your stupid cup." I turned away, opened my fly, and let loose into the cup. As I unloaded my bladder, I made sounds in my throat as if I were coughing up half a lung and spitting it into the cup.

The best part about this was that I was being treated for venereal disease.

Extending the cup, I told her to drink it immediately, that it was best while steaming hot.

I jumped into my cab, and slammed the gas pedal. I laughed all the way to the taxi barn.

* * * *

A week later, I went to see a priest. "Father, help me. The Devil's after me."

"He's after us all," the padre said. "He wants everybody's soul. Remember what the Scriptures say: 'resist the Devil and he will flee from you.' Are you resisting him?"

"With all my might. But he...well, it's not a he, it's a she. She shows up every night when my shift's over. When I'm heading to the taxi barn, her car cuts me off and blocks my way. And every time, she just misses slamming into me. She hands me a cup. Asks me to fill it with one of my vital juices."

"What do you mean by vital juices?"

"She wants me to spit into the cup."

"And do you?"

"No. I pee into it. I'm ashamed to say this, but I caught a sexually transmitted disease. It happened one night when I was drunk. But the thing is, she drinks whatever I put into the cup. Every time I do it I feel like I'm getting revenge."

"No need to explain further, my son. Take this bottle of holy water. Next time she stops you, pour it into the cup. One swig of that, and she'll never block your taxi again."

"Really?"

"Yes. She's known as The Juicer. This is one of the worst listed in the Book of Exorcisms. Has she asked you to ejaculate into the cup?"

"No, Father."

"Good. But unless you dispel her, she soon will. And she'll use your seed to commit the most unspeakable blasphemies in demonic rituals."

That night, when the Caddie cut me off, I poured the blessed water into the cup. I heard her gulping.

I bet her screams could be heard for miles.

Next day, I read in the paper that the cops rushed to the scene where a woman was heard screaming, as if she was being massacred. But they didn't find anybody.

The next night, I made it all the way to the barn without interference. What a relief! To celebrate the removal of the unholy entity, I headed to Jersey to watch the Hispanic women dance their asses off.

One of them was so hot, I found myself breaking into a sweat. When I ordered another cold beer to cool down, a gorgeous coffee-and-cream broad slid into the bar stool next to me.

"Hi, Handsome," she said. "Would you get me something to drink?"

"Sure. What'll you have?"

"Some of your luscious fluids," she said, handing me a cup.

THE ULTIMATE PLEASURE

Arcus, a galley slave, was working midnight shift on the first sea trials of the new Roman galley, Romulus. Suddenly, "Pssst!" shattered the silence of the moonlit Mediterranean.

The sound couldn't have come from within the ship, he reasoned. None of the other three slaves rowing through the gentle waves would have dared risk making any sound—even if a wooden splinter suddenly rammed under their fingernails and shot halfway to the bone. To wake the galley's captain would lead to ten lashes at the hands of the fiend, Octavius Valoris, plus a handful of salt thrown in to the raw, gaping flesh. Not to mention forfeiture of two day's rations. If provoked, the bastard might go crazy and toss the offending slave to the sharks. He'd already thrown five to those dreaded predators.

Arcus decided he was imagining things. He remembered old sailors saying everyone who traveled the Mediterranean heard strange sounds during the night, especially when the moon was full.

When he lowered his oar for another sweep of the water, Arcus heard another "Pssst!"

He noticed the oar seemed heavier. He loosened his grip while the other slaves continued to row like automatons.

"Who's there?" he whispered, risking death for the transgressions of not rowing and speaking without permission.

"Shantara," a soft voice said. "My hair's stuck in your oar. Don't row until I can work it loose."

Shocked at hearing a voice from the sea, he prayed to the gods for protection.

"Thank you," she said. "I'm loose. You can start rowing again. I'm coming aboard. I want to see you up close. I've seen your face when you dumped things over the side. You're very handsome. I've been following you for two days, hoping to glimpse more of your wondrous countenance and magnificent body." She sounded sheepish when she added, "I've fallen in love with you."

"Stay away for your own good. If they catch you, they'll beat you and throw you to the sharks."

"Sharks are my friends. They'll come aboard and defend me."

The next thing he knew, the silhouette of a shapely female stood in front of him. He didn't know how she managed to stand erect while poised on her wide, fan-shaped tail. Though extremely tired, he found himself powerfully aroused.

He'd heard that mermaids' voices could arouse men to where they'd burst through their loincloths. Arcus discovered this old, Roman seafarer's legend was true.

"I can't see your face in the dark," he said.

"It doesn't matter. I'm exceedingly beautiful," she said. "And even if I weren't, would you care, considering the pleasure I'm about to give you?"

"What kind of pleasure?"

"You'll soon see," she whispered, as he rowed. "But first, I'm going to summon dolphins to push the oars for you. When you feel their pressure, take your hands off the oar, and press them against me."

"Against you? Where?" he asked wondering what a mermaid's body would feel like.

"The place with no name. Once you touch me, you can give your own name to that which you feel."

He heard the wind of her voice rise slightly then dissipate, as she summoned dolphins. Within seconds, he felt massive force against the part of the oar that was in the water, as dolphins pushed his oar forward.

Releasing his grip, Arcus extended his hands toward the mermaid. She grasped his hands and pressed them against her.

"Mmm," she sighed. "Your hands are warm, strong, comforting. You're making me love you more deeply. Press just a bit harder."

He wasn't sure what he was touching, but he jumped when she returned the favor.

'Oh God!" he yelled. She anticipated his outburst by causing the wind to blow louder than his outcry.

"Was that pleasure you just gave me?" he asked, panting.

"Yes, my Love."

"Something's running down my neck," he said, as the wind rose again to cover his speech.

"Yes… it's the elixir that bursts forth from your neck when you feel extreme pleasure. Would you like to feel it even more intensely?"

"Yes."

She bit into his neck a second time, her lips drawing against his skin with great force.

He felt himself being moved toward the edge of the galley. The next thing he knew, he was covered by cold seawater. He didn't care. Pleasure continued to overwhelm him.

"Come drink, my Children," she called, as a dozen shark fins headed toward them.

Kissing Arcus's eyes, she said, "And now comes the ultimate pleasure."

MOM THE UNKNOWN

I spun the Rolodex, looking for my pukey sister's phone number.

"Hello, Gloria?"

"Is this who I think it is?" she asked. "Well, well. To what goddess do I owe burnt offerings for inspiring my baby brother to call?"

"Mom died. The hospital called. Heart attack."

"Oh."

I knew what'd come next.

"Is there a will?"

"Don't know."

"You coming to Maryland for the funeral?" she asked.

"My flight arrives at Baltimore, 9:00 tonight. I'll get a car and go directly to Parsons Corners."

"Forget the car. I'll pick you up."

"How can you when you have to take care of your three kids and Sam? The funeral service won't be for three days. I'll handle things until you get there."

"Dammit! I said I'll meet you at the airport!"

Of course she would, the greedy rat. She didn't want me alone in mom's house. Afraid I'd grab something she didn't know about.

We argued. She won. She met me at the baggage counter.

"You really don't know about a will, Charlie?" she asked, as we drove through Who-Knows-Where, Maryland.

"Nope."

"Well, you were her widdle baby. I figured she'd tell her favorite about a will."

"C'mon, Gloria. Lay off, already."

She'd never kept in touch with mom. Their personalities had never meshed. The same with Sam, the boozing lout Gloria had married. Shotgun wedding. Gloria and mom had never kissed and made up.

Of course, she'd wail the loudest at the funeral. No doubt she'd pull the gonna-throw-myself-into-the-grave routine.

"Well, there oughta be plenty there," she said. "Mom never owned a car. Think of what she saved and stashed away just from that."

"I doubt she made millions waiting tables over at that roadside diner."

"Tips can add up. And mom, being so damn cheap could have a hundred-thou hanging around, somewhere. I honest-to-god hope so. I want an SUV. Jimmy needs braces, and Sam wants..."

Sam wants to go on a month's binge in Las Vegas, I thought.

When we arrived at Parsons Corners, she asked, "How are we gonna get in the place?"

"I have a key," I said.

"Figures. She never gave me one."

"Maybe she would've, if you'd ever called and asked her."

Once inside, I said, "I'm dead. I'm gonna crash on the sofa."

Gloria didn't respond. She'd already raced to the kitchen. She called our mother, "Stupid woman," as things crashed to the floor.

I yelled, "Can't we look for the will tomorrow?"

"You can, but I'm gonna stay up all night, if I have to."

I don't know how I managed to sleep through the tumult of a crazed woman rifling through the bungalow's contents.

Next thing I knew, Gloria was nudging my shoulder.

"I found the will. It says half of everything is to be split evenly between us. Except for the house, which she left to a church. Well, this dump ain't worth anything, anyway. Let the church pay the death taxes. Hmm. I wonder why she gave this to a church, and not us?"

"Can't imagine."

"Oh, I found this money taped underneath a bread board," she said. "Three hundred dollars. Here's a hundred. I'll give you the other fifty soon as I get change."

She'd probably found at least double that, and it was already stashed in her purse.

The kitchen was a disaster. Gloria had searched inch by inch. She'd even pulled up the linoleum. Remnants of her treasure hunt were piled in the middle of the room.

"Where was the will?" I asked.

"In a shoe box, in her bedroom closet."

I checked the closet. The box was on the floor under mom's chintzy clothes. Thrift store rejects, but they'd belonged to her. I ran my hand across the sleeve of a faded blouse. My eyes moistened. I wished I could've run my hand across her withered arm in that sleeve just one more time.

The box contained faded photos and stacks of Rolodex cards. I examined the bunch marked F.

"Gloria, look at this! I found a Rolodex card with Fidel Castro's name and telephone number."

She grabbed the card from my hand. "His name should be on a C card, not under F. Cripes, she couldn't even do that right! Wait a minute. There's a bunch of dates under Castro's name. And dollar amounts next to each one. You don't suppose she donated to Castro's revolution?"

"Nah," I said. "Maybe she called him."

"The dates go back to 1960. And look at the dollar amounts. Sonovabitch! She kept track of what she spent calling him. It looks like there's... let's see... over $5,000 worth of calls. Why did mom call a communist dictator? Was she a freakin' spy?"

I was too busy examining the D stack to answer. The first three cards had Dalai Lama marked in red. I counted ninety-seven calls. Each was priced. If this were truly a record of long distance charges, mom had spent almost $8,000 chatting with him. One entry said, "Person-to-person collect call received from D.L. $250."

I found cards for J. Edgar Hoover, Queen Elizabeth, Ernest Hemmingway, Clark Gable, all presidents since John Kennedy, and hundreds of other luminaries. Each had numerous dates and dollar amounts.

Gloria pulled a calculator from her purse. "My God! She spent over $100,000 on phone calls. My legacy. All gone. What a loon. I'm going home!"

She stormed out and never returned.

I examined the cards for hours, realizing I knew so little about my mother.

I called every living person listed on mom's Rolodex cards to tell of her passing. Pope John Paul II spoke fondly of when they'd lunched together. Madonna wept. Willy Nelson said he'd write a song in her memory. Ten state governors said they'd lower their flags to half-mast.

I ensured that mom, her phone, and precious Rolodex cards were cremated together.

I was flabbergasted when *The London Times* and *The New York Times* used a full page for her obituary. Both attributed the fall of the Berlin Wall to her down-home telephone diplomacy.

A HELLISH THING

Stanton found a suitcase in a trash container. When opening it, he saw something so frightening he called 911.

Stunned by Stanton's description, the emergency operator made sacred gestures to prevent word contamination.

"Where did you find the suitcase?" asked the operator.

"Corner of Tenth and Elm."

The operator dialed an ultra-emergency number to notify a Decontamination Battalion.

"Don't hang up," the operator told Stanton. "I have purification instructions. You must perform each step within thirty minutes. Do you understand what'll happen if you don't follow them perfectly and in the correct sequence?"

"Yes," he said. "I'll disintegrate into tiny pieces. The ground will open and each piece will fall into the Pits of Gehenna."

While the operator gave Stanton instructions, 500 troops of the First Decontamination Battalion rushed to Tenth and Elm. Knocking down apartment doors, they asked occupants, "Did you put a suitcase in the trash container?"

Everyone denied the dastardly deed.

"They're all lying," said the Battalion Commander. "Punish them with Blaster Bombs."

Every trooper shot Blaster Bombs into the apartment complexes. Within minutes, the entire block blazed. The bodies of eight hundred residents disintegrated into tiny pieces.

While the occupants burned, the entire Battalion fell to their knees and chanted a cleansing ritual. The ground opened and every shred of burned tissue fell into the Pits of Gehenna.

Troops from the Second Decontamination Battalion burst into Stanton's apartment, as he completed the last step of his purification ritual. They fired lasers at the dastardly thing Stanton had found, until it disintegrated into tiny pieces.

Stanton knelt with the Battalion and chanted thanks to the gods for purging the city's impurities. The Ground opened and every piece of the sacrilegious thing descended into the Pits of Gehenna.

Scanning Stanton's thumb, the Battalion Commander said, "You're purified, but not fully degrobilized from the trauma of your horrible discovery."

The commander committed Stanton to the Degrobilization Institute where he underwent daily treatments for two years.

When satisfied that the incident was terminated, and no impurities remained, the Battalion Chief entered the name of the horrid object into a case file. He shuddered as he typed the words: BOOK OF POEMS.

PEST REMOVAL

"Hi, Fred. How's the gun business?"

"Brisk. Every time there's another house invasion by illegal aliens, we're good for a couple dozen pistol sales."

"I got my own invasion, but it ain't illegals," Sam said.

"Hmm. Let me guess. Your brother-in-law, Jeb, from Phoenix."

"Yep. He's visiting for a whole month. Real pain in the neck."

"So, whadda ya have in mind?" Fred asked. "I got a sweet, little, nine-shot, semi-automatic on sale."

"I don't wanna shoot the bastard," Sam said. "Of course, if I knew I could get away with it—"

"Hey, I was only kidding. But seriously, there are ways to get rid of pests without suffering consequences. Nice, clean ways. Ways that the law will never find out about."

"Such as?"

"You may not believe this," Fred said, "but I supply pistols to a bunch of little green guys who come from Mars every week. They're loading up for an impending civil war. Their weapons were confiscated. So, they come to Earth looking for anything that shoots. They're so grateful, they said they'd help me out if I ever needed a favor. I could ask them to abduct Jeb. They'll be here next Monday. I'll ask and see what they say."

"Sounds good to me," Sam said, trying to humor Fred. He remembered when Fred used to see green spiders, bugs, and snakes before he dried out in the Alcoholic Rehabilitation Institute. Maybe he was hitting the bottle again and seeing little green men.

A week later, Fred called Sam. "Hey, is your brother-in-law still bugging you?"

"Yep. He's driving me nuts. He wants to run my house, when he can't even take care of his own. And my wife goes along with whatever he says. When he's here, it's as if I don't even exist. I'm fed up."

"Well, I wanted you to know I talked to the greenies. They'd be happy to take him off your hands. Won't cost you a cent."

Sam wondered again about Fred's sanity. "Fred, I hate to ask this, but did you fall off the wagon?"

"Hell no! I'm as dry as the Sahara. I don't ever wanna to go through anything like that institute program again. Learned my lesson. This is on the level, Sam. You said you wanted to get rid of Jeb, and now's your chance. Don't throw it away."

Fred sounded so genuine, Sam began to feel as if some of what he said might be true.

"So how would this work?" asked Sam.

"They gave me a little gadget for you to stick on top of Jeb's bedroom door. It'll give off a signal that'll guide them right to him. It's very tiny. Something he or your wife will never notice."

"I suppose it's green," Sam remarked.

"How'd you know?"

"Just guessing. OK. Give me the damn thing. I'll give it a try. When can they come and grab him?"

"Tomorrow night."

"I suppose they'll drive up at midnight dressed in black, sneak into the house, knock him out, and carry Jeb away." Sam said.

"Nah, it's simpler than that. They'll park their disc on your roof and come down the chimney."

"I hope it ain't too heavy," Sam said. "The roof has some storm damage. I don't want the whole thing to collapse."

"I'll tell them about the damage," Fred said. "Maybe they can hover over your roof instead of landing on it."

"Oh… did you by any chance ask them what they'll do with Jeb?"

"Yeah. They said some crop circle jobs just opened on Jupiter. They said the weather up there's good most of the year. Don't worry, Jeb will love it. The pay and bennies are great. They even have an overabundance of five-legged, eager females."

"I'll stop by your shop and get the signal thingee tomorrow afternoon," Sam said.

After Sam picked up the gadget at Fred's gun store, he headed home. When he arrived, his wife complained about the unmowed grass out back. Jeb made snide remarks about how buggy the back yard was with the grass being so high. He even complained of a mosquito bite he'd received while lying in a hammock, out back. It wouldn't have happened if Sam had kept the grass trimmed to the proper height.

Sam said nothing, while humming a happy tune.

That evening, Sam put the signal device above the bedroom door.

Everything went smoothly. The kidnapping went without a hitch. Three days later, the victim was on Mars attending crop circle cutting classes.

A week later, while he carved a crop circle in a wheat field on Jupiter, a dozen five-legged beauties headed toward him. "Time for a coffee break," they called, while disrobing.

"I think I'm gonna love it here." Sam said.

HUMBLE PIE

"Where the hell have you been, Harry?" a woman yelled in the dumpy coffee shop.

Daydreaming, Harry almost answered, as he took a counter seat.

"Ignoring me ain't gonna get you off the hook, Harry."

He figured poor Harry Whoever was either trying to exit quickly, or was sitting red-faced at a table. He glanced around trying to spot the poor guy.

"Why the hell don't you answer me?" the voice insisted, a few feet from his ear. A redheaded waitress behind the counter stared at him.

"Huh?"

"Don't give me that. I need more than a damn huh. You're a day late. I oughta make you eat humble pie!"

Harry put on his glasses for a better look. Fiftyish. Frumpy. Excessive makeup. Earrings he could run a fist through. Nametag said, "Clara."

"Well? Is that all you're gonna do? Just stare at me?"

"Sorry," he said. "Didn't mean to stare. How come you know my first name?"

"Oh, so now you wanna play dumb. You stand me up on my birthday, then come waltzing in here like nothing happened."

"I don't know what the hell you're talking about. By the way, is Clara short for Clarabelle?"

"Cut it out, Harry, or I'll have Eddie burn your stupid ham and eggs."

"What ham and eggs? I just got here. I didn't order anything."

"I ordered your usual when I saw your car pull up. Why are you acting so squirrelly? Been boozing again? Let me smell your breath."

Leaning over the counter, she stuck her nose in his face. "C'mon open up. Give me a whiff."

He had enough. He started to rise, but she grabbed his wrist and dug her nails in.

"You leave here, and I'll have the sheriff on your ass. Now breathe out."

Harry almost punched her. But his angry flash gave way to restraint, figuring if he smashed a middle-aged woman's face, they'd throw the book at him.

"All right," he said, and exhaled forcefully into her face.

"You sonovabitch! You're crocked. Your breath stinks ten times worse than stale beer. Didn't the doctor tell you to lay off the sauce?" She yelled to the fry cook, "Hey Eddie, burn his ham and eggs."

"Will do," a voice said from the kitchen.

"You do, Eddie, and I'll come back there bust your mouth!" Harry yelled. *Geez. What the hell am I saying? I don't even know these people. I hate ham and eggs. I want a cheeseburger.*

"Chill out, Harry, everything's cool." The cook set a plate on the pickup counter.

"You're a freakin' wimp, Eddie!" the waitress yelled. She grabbed the plate of food and threw it at Harry.

He ducked and ran. Jumping his car, he gunned it.

Whew. What the hell was that all about?

A piercing siren jolted him. The rearview mirror was filled with flashing lights.

Harry pulled over.

"Turn the engine off, Harry. Get out of the car. Clara called. She said you're drunk and that you just tried to kill her again. This time she's signing a complaint. I gotta take you in."

"But—"

"You have the right to remain silent."

Numbed, Harry didn't hear the rest.

Nobody listened when he yelled, "Mistaken identity." He told them to compare his fingerprints with the real Harry, whoever the hell he was. "If you don't release me immediately, I'll sue you for false arrest."

They ignored him.

An ambulance-chasing lawyer came to Harry's cell. "Looks grim," he said. "Attempted murder is tough to defend. There are lots of witnesses this time. I'll need a $5,000 retainer to take your case."

When Harry tried to explain, the lawyer's only response was, "You should've eaten humble pie, Harry. You know how Clara is. By the way, your breath stinks worse than stale beer."

When Harry said he didn't have $5,000, the lawyer left in a huff.

That night, Harry got sick. They called a doctor.

"Dammit, you're pressure's off the charts," the doctor said. "I hear you've been drinking again. I told you last week that liquor doesn't mix with the meds I prescribed. What are you trying to do? Kill yourself?"

"No. I don't wanna die. I just retired."

"Well, you have one foot in the grave right now. Your heart doesn't sound right. I'm putting you in the hospital."

"Please, help me, Doctor. Ask the sheriff for my wallet. Look at the picture and name on my Arizona license."

"Sheriff," the doc called, "Mind showing Harry his driver's license?"

"What've you done?" Harry hollered. "This is a Missouri license. You stuck my picture on it and changed the name. I don't know anybody named Harry Betendorfer. I'm Harry Peterson from Phoenix, Arizona!"

They looked at him gravely. When they left the cell, Harry heard the doctor and sheriff buzzing that he should have eaten humble pie, apologized to Clara, and all of this could've been avoided.

When an ambulance arrived to take Harry to the hospital, they strapped him to a gurney, and shoved him inside. A deputy sat up front trying to hustle the big-busted, blonde driver. An acne-pitted paramedic sat in the back with Harry.

"Nice to see you again, Harry," the paramedic said. "Heard you're in bad trouble. You should've eaten humble pie and apologized to Clara." Then he yelled to the driver, "Did you call Smitty to see if everything's ready?"

"Yep," the driver replied.

When they removed him from the ambulance, Harry said, "What's going on? This don't look like a hospital."

"It ain't," said the medic.

When they turned Harry over to Smitty, he said, "You're really dumb, Harry. It would've been a helluva lot easier to swallow your pride and eat humble pie—instead of becoming one."

Harry screamed when Smitty rolled him toward the largest oven in his bakery.

ROSWELL RED

"Howdy." said the used car salesman. "I'm Roswell Red. I got the best used cars in all of New Mexico. You looking for something in particular?"

"Yeah. A blue Pinto hatchback," Jim said.

"Ford stopped making them years ago." the salesman said, replying to the secret passwords. "Who sent you?"

"Carlos."

"I don't know any Carlos."

"Well he knows you. He's the one who gave me the password. I brought cash. I want to buy one of your—"

"Shhh! This lot might be bugged. Let's go to my trailer. I have it electronically swept every day to make sure there's no bugs inside."

Once inside the sales trailer, Jim asked, "Can I see one of your special artifacts?"

"Depends on how much cash you brought."

Jim removed $50,000 from his briefcase and dropped it on the salesman's desk. "There's plenty more in the trunk of my car."

Red donned heavy gloves, opened a freezer, and removed a thin, transparent plastic container. "Don't touch the plastic without gloves," he said. "You'll get instant frost bite."

Jim removed a magnifying glass from his case and scrutinized the thing inside the container. "Creepy. Looks like a blue hot dog. Is this their original color?"

"Yep. That's what the Air Force medic said who stole this from the slop buckets at Roswell's morgue back in '47."

"How much do you want for it? My client is quite motivated."

"A million."

"Will you accept the $50,000 as earnest money? I'll have the balance in your hands in an hour."

"Yep."

"Give me a receipt for the $50,000 and I'll go get the rest."

"Sure."

While the salesman prepared the receipt, Jim called someone on his cell phone

"Here's your receipt," said the salesman.

Jim glanced at it and said, "Carlos wants to know what else you have along the same lines."

"Three more blue fingers like the one you're getting. Two blue, ear-like things. One blue head."

Jim mumbled into the cell phone, then asked, "How much is the head?"

"Ten million."

Jim spoke into the cell phone again. "Carlos wants to know if the brains are still intact?"

"Nope. The head's hollow. Everything was removed during the autopsy. Nobody knows what happened to the stuff they pulled out. But they say it was as blue as the head."

"Can I see it? I want to describe it to Carlos. He may be interested."

Red placed another large, transparent container on the desk.

"Phew! Ugly bastard," Jim said into the phone. "Carlos wants to know if this from a male?"

"Nobody knows. But I do know that it's the only one on Earth."

"How long will it last after it's defrosted? Carlos is thinking about having it mounted so he can display it along with the unicorn and dragon heads he owns."

"I don't know. Tell him this thing has been frozen since 1947. If he defrosts it and it rots, I can't be liable. Same with the alien finger."

"Well, when I come back in an hour with the rest of the cash for the finger," Jim said, "I may buy the head as well."

"Remember the head costs ten million. Payable in cash."

"No sweat. My client has plenty."

"Before you leave," the salesman said, "Can I interest you in a nice pre-owned car? Roswell Red offers the hottest deals in New Mexico."

"I'm not interested in a car. But I wouldn't mind having a wallet made from the skin of a Reptilian or a Gray."

"You and everybody else. Well, just be patient. One of these days another UFO will crash somewhere, and we'll skin the bastards. Then I'll have a nice selection of key chains, cuff links, lamp shades, wallets, and other doodads. Meanwhile, give me your business card, and I'll put your name on the waiting list."

THE GOLD BUTTON

It's tougher than ever to find a decent cigarette butt in the gutter. I'd just spent the better part of an hour looking. Nothing. Pissed me off.

Damn do-gooders. Wish they'd lay off with the don't smoke crap. Makes for less pickings these days. It's making life miserable. I need a smoke real bad.

So far, I've spotted candy wrappers, a banana peel, assorted unidentifiable junk, and a stupid button. But no smokes. Dammit! Where the hell does a guy go to complain?

The button looked pretty fancy. I don't know why I bothered to pick it up. Can't smoke a stupid button.

I exhaled on it, rubbed it against my jeans, and it got pretty shiny. I checked the back hoping it'd say "14 carat." Nope. Figures. All it said was, "555-2279." Like somebody scratched it on the back with a pin, or something.

If I had a quarter, I'd go to a payphone and dial those seven numbers. If I didn't get one of those sorry-the-number-you-have-dialed-is-not messages, I'd say, "This is Joe. I found your button. Is there a reward?"

So now I was curious. All of a sudden, the button seemed more important than a cigarette.

"Hey Ma'am, can you spare a quarter? Well, if you ain't got a quarter, can I borrow a cigarette? No I ain't getting fresh. No need to call a cop!"

Damn! Why is it so hard to bum a quarter from old ladies, anymore?

"Mister. I ain't a boozer or doper. I need to call my mom. She's sick, and—"

"Hey kid. Got a quarter so's I can get a cup of coffee? Well, a dime is good. Thanks. God bless you sonny. Know where I can get fifteen more cents?"

"Sir, can you spare a quarter? I'll give you a dime. Yeah, that's the idea...like an instant rebate. Here's the dime. Thanks. Glad I made you laugh. God bless you, Sir."

I dialed 555-2279. It rang. Oh man. It's my lucky day.

"Five five five, two two seven nine," said a man's voice.

"Hi. This is Joe. I found your button."

"How did you get this number?"

"It was on the button."

"What button?"

"A gold one, but not real gold. I was hoping there was a reward. Like a carton of Marlboro."

"Where are you Joe?"

"Can't see the sign. Hold on. I'm gonna put the phone down and take a look. Back in a minute."

"Corner of 7th and Chestnut."

"What are you wearing?"

"Blue jeans. Red and white checkered shirt."

"Hang up now, and wait beside the phone booth. We'll send somebody to get the button."

"Don't forget my reward."

"Hang up *now*!"

So I did. Real quick. Guy sounded like somebody you don't wanna mess around with.

I waited.

A Dodge drove up. Two guys in dark suits got out.

"You Joe?"

"Yeah."

"Let's see the button."

"Here. See the numbers on the back?"

The two guys mumbled something to each other.

"We'll take it. How much?"

"Figure it might be worth a carton of Marlboros. I could use a smoke now though, in the meantime."

"Here's a Camel."

Oh man, they're too strong for me. But a smoke is a smoke. "Thanks. So, how do I get my Marlboros?"

"Get in the car, we'll find a place."

I ain't stupid. I was in the Army. I even got a good conduct medal.

"I get car sick real easy. You don't want me puking all over the minute you put it in gear. Right?"

They threw me in the car. A couple people were around, but they didn't do nothing.

One of them leaned against me real hard so I couldn't move. I turned my head and stuck two fingers down my throat. Began to heave. Didn't matter. He bopped me.

I didn't know where I was.

"So, you say your name is Joe Swarnasky. Age 61. No address. Tell us again how you found the button."

"It was in the gutter. I was looking for ciggies. Who are you guys?"

"Doesn't matter. What matters is who you are. Have you ever been inside the Russian Embassy?"

"Hell, I don't even know where it is. I couldn't care less. Think they'd let me in dressed like this?"

Somebody walked in and handed a folder to the mean-looking guy asking all the questions. He shut up and looked inside.

"Says here your middle name is Stanislaus. You prefer to eat with your left hand. Well, Joe, it looks like you're in trouble."

"What? Over a stupid button? Because I eat with my left hand? Forget the Marlboros. Let me go. I got things to do, people to see."

"You got people to see all right. FBI counterintelligence. People don't find buttons with our telephone number in the street."

It took the FBI a couple hours to realize I was nobody, never been nobody, never will be nobody. They apologized. Even chipped in enough for a carton of Marlboro.

One of them drove me back to the phone booth. Nice guy. Gave me a couple bucks for a burger and fries.

When the Marlboros ran out, I went back to my daily search for smokes in the gutter. That's all I pick up now. Learned my lesson. A guy's gotta know his place and keep his routines.

Since then, I've found other buttons. I wouldn't touch them with a ten-foot pole. Even if one of them happens to be 14 carat gold.

COPY CATS

Unlike our planet," said the Martian astronaut," Earth's inhabitants live above ground."

"What do their structures look like?" asked Mars' Emperor.

"Here are some photos."

"Hmm. Many look alike." Pointing to a building, he added, "Okay, let's build all our structures to look exactly like this one. After 5-million years, radioactivity from ancient wars has finally dissipated from our surface. Time to move our citizens out of caves."

Soon, 10-billion identical structures covered Mars.

When an American astronaut circled Mars, he couldn't believe his eyes.

"Houston Control," he said. "I think we should rename the planet Mars."

"To What?"

"Starbucks."

A QUICK TRIP

Liz shuddered, as Dr. Zangara approached with a huge syringe. Though she agreed to participate in an experiment, she didn't know it meant getting a ten inch needle rammed into her flesh.

"Do you really have to stick me with that awful looking thing?" she asked.

"It's a necessary step so you can go backward in time. However, the needle to go forward in time is much smaller. Do you prefer to travel into the future?"

"No. I want to go back five years and change things so I can marry the guy I threw away."

"Then you must get the injection, and lay down on this rotating table."

"But I thought you had a time machine."

The needle and table will have to do until the time machine I'm building is finished. Which will take ten more years. Do you want to wait that long to resolve your problem from the past?"

"No."

"Then let's proceed. My time is very valuable."

"Okay," she said.

She screamed when he jammed the needle in her forehead. "You said it wouldn't hurt."

"It shouldn't. When I tested it on lab mice, they didn't complain. Okay, I'm going to start the countdown from ten. When I reach one, my assistant will start the rotating table. You may have the sensation that you'll fly off. It's only an illusion. The straps will hold you very securely. Okay, I'm starting the countdown now. Ten...nine...eight..."

Closing her eyes, she thought of what she'd do when she was transported five years into the past. She couldn't wait to find herself sitting in a fancy restaurant with Harry, at the point where he offered her an engagement ring. This time when he offered the ring, she'd scream, "Yes!" and throw herself into his arms. Then two minutes later she'd be transported back to Zangara's lab.

"...three...two...one."

The table began to rotate. In no time, it was spinning at ten revolutions per second.

Suddenly, Zangara heard a loud pop.

"Oh hell!" he said. "She disappeared."

"That makes twenty-three that have disappeared this month," said his assistant. "Perhaps we should terminate the experiment before the authorities find out."

"Never!" Zangara shouted. "I intend to win a Nobel Prize. Bring in the next woman."

Meanwhile, Liz returned to the present. Instead of showing up on the rotating table, as Zangara promised, she ended up inside a cage at the city zoo. She no longer knew her name was Liz. And she didn't even stir when a male gorilla within the cage approached and stroked her furry body.

That evening, a courier delivered an envelope to Zangara. Inside was a fat check and a note of thanks.

The note said, "We really appreciate your latest addition to our collection of endangered species. At the rate you are supplying us, we'll soon have the largest and finest collection of female gorillas in the world."

GREEN DUST

Harry stood in the mall yelling through a bullhorn. "Attention, everyone! Save yourselves and your children. Put a stop to alien abductions, right now. These pink sheets tell you how! Take as many as you want! They're free."

Shoppers ignored him.

"You fools! You're putting yourselves and your families in jeopardy!"

Security guards grabbed Harry. They took away his bullhorn and tossed his pink sheets into a trashcan.

"Let me go, you fools. Do you realize the number of abductions is increasing every day? You may be next. I can tell you how to stop them. If you don't listen to me, you'll end up as mindless robots on Mars."

"Calm down, Mister. We're just gonna escort you to your car. You gotta leave mall property right now. Don't ever come back unless you're just gonna shop. If you ever try this again, we'll hafta call the Sheriff and have you arrested."

"But you gotta listen. Last night, a bunch of little green men tried to abduct me. When they were yanking me from bed, somehow my arm hit the start button on my CD alarm clock. A polka disk was loaded. It started playing the *Beer Barrel Polka* real loud. The aliens started to scream. They covered their ears and ran away. Then they jumped in a flying saucer and took off so fast, they left a greenie behind. I wrestled him to the ground and tied him up. I brought him into the house, put my alarm clock against his ear, and kept playing polkas. Before I knew it, he turned into a pile of green dust."

"Green dust?"

"Yeah. I can prove it. I vacuumed it. If you come to my house right now and empty the vacuum cleaner bag, you'll see for yourself."

"What else is in there? Pink dinosaur dust?"

The guards laughed.

"Go ahead, have your big laugh. You won't be laughing when the Martians come and grab you."

"I'm quaking in my boots," a guard said.

As Harry got into his old, battered car, a guard asked, "So how do I make sure that humongous Martian monsters don't kidnap me?"

"Buy all the polka music you can find. Play polka music everyday without letup. No matter where you are. At home, in the car, even in church. And when you go to bed, turn up the volume even higher."

The guards laughed so hard, they almost fell over.

When they told their supervisor about the old nutcase, she went to the trash bin, removed one of the pink sheets, and read it.

That night, she opened a hidden wall safe in her apartment and removed a small box. Holding it close to her mouth, she said in a strange language, "Come in Central Command.. .come in Central Command."

"This is Central Command."

"We have a potentially serious problem," she said. "Someone may have discovered a way to interfere with our abductions. Check last night's records to see if our Collectors reached their quota."

"Hmm. That's odd. Says here that one got away. A male. First time that's ever happened!"

"And it might not be the last. He was in the mall, trying to tell everyone."

"Did anybody listen?"

"No. I think he's the only one who knows so far. We're okay for now. But, he's very aggressive. He may call talk radio shows. Who knows where that could lead? We'll have to change our procedures, or we might not achieve this year's abduction goals. And you know what that means."

"Yes. No year-end bonus. We can't let that happen. Have any ideas?"

"Yes. Here's what I want you to transmit to all Collectors, immediately..."

Two days later, a small article appeared in newspapers: "Music stores all over the world have reported a string of bizarre robberies. Curiously, thieves have stolen only CDs that contain polka music. Stores not stocking polka music have suffered no losses. In fact, total worldwide losses are valued at only several thousand dollars. Store owners say, at most, they carry one or two polka albums, because the market for polka music has virtually disappeared."

"Nobody wants to listen to cheerful, upbeat music anymore," said a storeowner, "except for the crooks who robbed what may be the last copies of the world's polka albums."

From then on, all aliens abducting Earthlings wore thick earmuffs. Also, during abductions, the aliens asked Earthlings if they owned polka CDs.

Most had no idea what the aliens were talking about.

INSTRUCTIONS

We were exploring the Moon's surface, when I tripped over something.

"Hey, Harry," I said. "Look at this. Reminds me of a Coke bottle."

"A Coke bottle on the Moon? Get real."

I picked the object up. "Okay, so it isn't a Coke bottle. It just reminds me of one. Hmm. I'm gonna wipe the dust off. Hey! It has a cork on top. And I can see something inside. It looks like a piece of paper."

"Yeah, I see what you mean. How the hell did this get here? Why don't you pull the cork?"

"I better tell Houston about this and get their permission," I said.

"Forget them. I asked for one measly moon rock as a souvenir from our moonwalk back in 2009. They said I wasn't allowed to keep anything I picked up. Everything we found was the property of the US government. Screw them. Pull the cork. Let's see what's inside."

"Damn, it's tight. I'm gonna go back to the capsule and get pliers. Hold this until I get back. I'm not sure it can take the atmospheric pressure if we bring it inside the capsule."

When I returned, I asked Harry to hold the thing while I grabbed the cork and pulled. I had to yank on it pretty hard to work it loose. When it popped out, red sparks flew. Scared us.

I shook the container until the thing inside fell out.

"Holy cow! It *is* paper," I said, unfolding it. "And something's written in English. Man, this is creepy. I don't know if I should read it."

"Give it to me," Harry said, "I'll read it."

When I passed it, he read out loud: "If you follow these instructions, detail by detail, I guarantee you will find a pot at the end of the rainbow. It's signed The Man In The Moon."

"Somebody's pulling our chain," I said. "Somebody from last year's spacewalk must've left it here."

"I'm not so sure," Harry said. "None of our astronauts would be fool enough to contaminate the Moon's surface with something like this. Maybe the Russians did it during their moon walk."

"Regardless of who did it, it's stupid. There aren't any rainbows on the Moon. How can there be, if there isn't any precipitation?"

I no sooner said those words when a rainbow appeared over a hill, about half a mile away.

"Geez," Harry said. "Would you look at that? I wonder how that happened?"

"We better turn on our radios and notify Houston."

"Wait. Stop and think for a moment. What if there really is a pot at the end of the rainbow? They aren't supposed to appear here. But now we see one. If that can happen, who's to say there isn't a pot at one end?"

"I think we better get back to the capsule," I said. "We've been out over an hour. Remember what Parkins said about hallucinations as a possible side effect from our new oxygen system?"

"I'm not going back until I check out that pot. Are you with me?"

"Yeah. But I found this thing. So, whatever's there belongs to me."

"But we're a team, and if you hadn't found it, I probably would've. We should split everything fifty-fifty."

"No way. I'll go seventy-five, twenty five. If you don't agree, I'll tell Houston about this thing."

"All right," said Harry. "Let's get going. In another twenty-three minutes we have to check in with Houston."

We headed for the rainbow. The closer we got, the brighter it got. Strangest thing I ever saw.

Harry let out a yell when he spotted a pot at one end of the rainbow. It looked big enough to cook for a hundred.

"Look, it has a lid," he said. "And there's a fire underneath. What the hell's going on?"

"Damned if I know." I looked around as if I expected to see somebody. "How the hell can there be a fire when there's no oxygen? We better leave this alone and tell Houston. This is too weird."

"What a wimp. This is the tenth time you mentioned Huston. The very people who'd confiscate anything valuable we might find here. If you aren't going to pick up that lid to see what's inside, I will."

"Go ahead."

Harry used both hands to lift the lid. He stuck his head inside the pot. "Come here and take a look," he said.

"Not until you tell me what's there."

"One of the neatest cocktail lounges I ever saw. There's beautiful paintings on the walls. You should see what's at the bar. Wow! What beautiful women. Hey, one of the babes is waving at me like she wants me to come inside."

"Don't go!" I yelled as Harry raised his leg to get into the pot. But it was too late.

I looked inside, and saw nothing. Screaming, I raced back to the capsule.

"Houston, come in. Something terrible just happened. Harry disappeared."

"What do you mean by disappeared."

"He stepped inside something."

"What do you mean something? What was it?"

"A pot. With a lid. And a fire underneath."

I heard some buzzing in the background at Houston, which I couldn't make out.

"Return to Earth immediately," the Mission Chief yelled.

"I can't leave without Harry," I yelled back.

"Return now. That's an order."

I was about to throw the switches to ignite the engines when I decided to go back and take one last look. Maybe I'd spot Harry, and tell him Houston wanted us back immediately.

I disconnected all communication with Houston. I could see in my mind's eye how they'd be jumping around and yelling about my insubordination and endangering the mission.

The rainbow was still there. And so was the pot. I lifted the lid and looked inside. I saw the cocktail lounge Harry mentioned. Like he said, the paintings on the walls were beautiful. And so were the women who waved their hands inviting me in.

When I saw what was left of Harry, I raced to the capsule, and threw the ignition switches.

"There really is green cheese on the Moon, like legends say," I told Huston Control. "But it's shaped like a man that looks a lot like Harry. And the Moon creatures are eating it."

ONE MILLION JEBOOLAS

William was alone in the farmhouse that stormy night when someone knocked.

"Who's there?" he hollered.

"Hungry," a voice gurgled. It sounded as if somebody were talking from inside a fish tank.

William's mother told him to always help folks in need. But she also told him never to let strangers into the house.

"Would you like some crackers?" William asked.

"Hungry," the voice replied.

William spread gobs of peanut butter on crackers, then put them into a plastic sandwich bag. Without removing the chain lock, he opened the door slightly and pushed the bag outward. A purple, furry paw with two little stumps for fingers grabbed the bag.

Startled, William slammed the door. He wished his mother were home. He hoped she wasn't stuck in the storm.

Another knock.

"What do you want?" William asked.

"Thirsty," the voice said.

William filled a cup with water and passed it to the paws that came through the narrow opening.

Moments later, the voice said, "Nice." Then it said, "Paper."

Tearing a sheet from a notebook, William passed it outside.

"Name?"

"William Lane."

"Spell."

He pronounced each letter slowly.

Another knock. "Finished," the voice gurgled.

William opened the door slightly and grabbed the paper. He couldn't believe his eyes. It was full of beautiful, geometric designs, with more colors than he'd ever seen. He figured Mr. Purple Paws had to be very intelligent to draw so well. Suddenly, William wasn't scared anymore. Especially when he saw his name on the paper. It came right after the words, "Pay To The Order Of."

"What is this?" he asked.

No answer.

"It's very nice. What do the words One Million Jeboolas mean after my name?"

Silence.

"I can't wait to show this to my mother and all my friends. Want some cookies and milk?"

No response.

He waited for the next knock, but it never came. Nor did he ever hear that odd, gurgling voice again.

William told his mother the moment she got home. At first, she was angry that he opened the door even a tiny bit. But when he explained how he helped somebody, she said she was proud of him.

She didn't know what to make of the fancy drawing. "Oh my. I never saw anything so beautiful. The designs remind me of crop circles we saw on TV. But these are much fancier."

"What does this mean?" he asked, pointing to the words that said "Pay to the Order of William Lane: One Million Jeboolas."

"I'm not sure," she said. "If I didn't know better, I'd say this is a check. But I don't see a bank's name anywhere. And I never heard of jeboolas. Well, look at it this way. Your visitor was a wonderful artist who made something very nice for you. But it's nothing more than a very fancy drawing. I'll frame it and hang it in your room."

William's mother asked her friends about jaboolas. None had ever heard of them. But, everybody who saw the drawing agreed on that it was a beautiful work of art. It had more colors than they'd ever seen, and the crop circle designs were fabulous. Some people suggested she show it to the Space Agency, but she never did.

* * * *

When he grew up, William went to college and studied Journalism. He was hired to write for a newspaper near the Interplanetary Expedition Center. His job was to interview astronauts returning from different planets. When he interviewed the first astronauts ever to return from Mars, he asked, "What do Martians call their money?"

"Marsogs," said the Mission Commander.

William asked the same question of astronauts returning from Mercury.

"Mercosogs," they said.

The crew returning from exploring Saturn said, "Satursogs."

For fifty years, he asked astronauts if they'd run across anything in outer space called jeboolas, or if they'd seen creatures with purple, furry paws. All said no.

* * * *

One day, instead of waking up on Earth, William found himself floating on a puffy cloud heading for a distant star. Many others rode clouds that moved in the same direction.

When they arrived on the star, William and the other cloud riders saw a sign that said, "All Travelers From Earth Line Up Here." Behind the sign, ancient-looking people consulted huge books and asked questions of every person who arrived. After answering, the people were directed to golden gates. When passing through the gates, they disappeared into glowing mists that emitted wonderful music and laughter.

"What's the price of entry into one of those gates?" William asked.

"It depends," an ancient man said while searching for William's name.

"Depends on what?"

"The number of jeboolas you've accumulated."

"I have a million," William said.

"That's quite odd. I've never seen anyone with more than a thousand."

William pulled the drawing from his pocket. "Look. It says right here."

Suddenly, William was a boy again, surrounded by beautiful creatures who lifted him overhead with their purple paws. "William Lane's here!" they shouted.

A diamond-encrusted path appeared on which stood a magnificent, purple being. "Welcome, William. What's your favorite game?"

"Baseball. I'd play it all day long if it were possible."

A purple paw handed William an emerald bat, and a ruby ball.

"Come along," the creature said. "Let's go play... forever. By the way, what do you call that delicious brown substance you spread on the crackers?"

CRAZY JOEY

I moved three times to get away from Joey. But somehow he discovered where I was.

I dreaded the idea of moving again to avoid that psycho bastard. He thought I was his reincarnated wife. When I didn't respond to his amorous advances, he threatened me.

A restraining order didn't discourage him. I moved to another city.

I was tired of running. If only there was a way to spot Joey sneaking up on me, I could bash his skull.

Then I got an idea. I went to an auto parts store and bought a rear view mirror. I mounted it on my head, but it kept falling off. Next, I strapped it to my shoulder, but I still couldn't stabilize the damn thing. It was even worse on my buttocks.

Terribly discouraged, I saw an advertisement that offered hope: "Bod Mod, a specialist in body modifications, announces a new facility in Chicago."

The ad included several testimonials. One in particular caught my eye: it showed a picture of a man with three arms. His testimonial said, "Now I can do almost twice the work. My company is so pleased with my increased performance, they gave me a huge raise. Now I can make more widgets than ever. And when I play baseball, I never miss a catch. Thanks, Bod-Mod."

I made an appointment.

"How can we help you?" asked a Body Modification Designer.

I told her about Crazy Joey and my fears. When she proposed a fantastic resolution, I signed a contract and underwent surgery.

After my recovery, Joey tried to jump me from behind while I was walking my dog at night in the park. They buried him a couple days later.

Absolutely delighted with my new abilities, I decided to go into business for myself. I became so successful, I wrote Bod Mod a testimonial, which they've included in their latest TV ads.

The ads show me with a bald spot on the back of my head. An eye sits in the center. As the camera zooms in on my new eye, I smile and say: "I'm Lisa Snerd. I sure love my third eye. It's changed my life. I'm now a successful detective with a seven-figure annual income. I can do far more surveillance than any of my competitors. My caseload is ten times the national average since Bod Mod added the extra eye to my head."

Then I approach the Chief Surgeon of Bod Mod and say, "Thanks for including little extras, like making a special floppy hat with a slit in the back. It's very stylish."

At that moment the camera zooms to show the hat.

"Plus, this hat helps me see everything that's going on behind me without anyone noticing. And a very special thanks for installing .30 caliber, sawed-off machine guns in both shoulder blades. Now I don't fear anybody, including terrorists. I'll be back next year for another modification. I love you guys. You're the best!"

FLASH FROZEN

"Don't try to stop me!" Shelly yelled, as she headed for the mall exit with a flame thrower.

"You don't have to do this," a coworker said. "The Army should arrive in an hour. Let them handle the problem."

"Those beasts may invade before the Army arrives. I can't let that happen. I took an oath to defend shoppers, regardless of race, color, creed, political preference, or country of origin."

"At least wear a football helmet. They can't bite through helmets to get at your brains."

"I'm allergic to helmets," she said.

Opening the exit door, Shelly saw a dozen zombies heading her way.

"Take that, you mangy bastards," she hollered, firing a ten-foot stream of napalm.

The zombies screamed as they burst into flames. All fell to the ground and disintegrated.

"Hey lady. What the hell are you doing?" a voice called.

"Killing zombies."

"But they're your friends. They're here to help you."

"What? Everybody knows they like to attack people in shopping malls."

"Did you ever wonder why?"

"Because they wanna eat everybody's brains," she said.

"Not anymore," said the voice that came from behind some cars. "These zombies are different."

"In what way?"

"They're programmed to differentiate between ordinary people and werewolves. Do you realize they came here to save everyone in the mall from a werewolf attack?"

"That's nuts. Zombies are nothing but a bunch of mindless, head-biting brain eaters."

"If you don't believe me, let some of them into the mall. They'll sniff out the werewolves right away. I promise they won't touch anybody who isn't a werewolf. You better hurry. The sun is setting. The full moon will rise soon. Then everybody in the mall will be in jeopardy. Our intelligence indicates that fifteen werewolves are in the mall right now, just waiting for the moon to rise."

"Your intelligence? Who are you?"

"Dr. Dumont, of the Haitian Zombie Institute. I programmed these zombies to hunt werewolves. I'll prove they're not brain eaters. I have some slices of flash frozen pepperoni pizza. I'll come out into the open and lay on the ground. I'll put the pizza slices around my head. Then when I press a key on my cell phone, six zombies will surround me. If they aren't what I said they are, they'll bite my head open and devour my brains. So, I'm asking you to hold your fire. I'm coming out. I'll lay down about fifty feet from where you're standing."

"Okay," said Shelly.

A man in a white lab coat lay on the ground, put slices of pepperoni pizza around his head, and pressed a key on his phone. Immediately, six zombies came out of an SUV and moved toward him. When they reached Dumont, they put their putrid mouths near his head and gobbled all the pizza. None bit Dumont's head.

Amazed, Shelly said, "I believe you. So what happens next?"

"I want you to let these six zombies inside the mall. They'll quickly identify all fifteen werewolves prowling inside. When they spot one, use your flame thrower to destroy it."

"You mean you want me to go with the zombies?"

"Yes. Walk in the middle of them."

"How will I know when they find a werewolf?"

"Since zombies can't talk, the tallest one will spit on it. I'll give you a flashlight with a special lens. When you shine it on the targeted person, the gob of spit will turn bright purple."

"Are you sure your zombies are completely pacified, and won't go nuts and attack me?"

"Guaranteed. But to calm your fears, I'll give you some pepperoni pizza. If one gets a little rambunctious, which shouldn't happen, just shove the pizza into its mouth, and all will be okay. Look, you'll be a hero. Wouldn't that be nice? Think of all the great publicity. I can just see the headlines right now: INCREDIBLY BRAVE WOMAN SAVES MALL SHOPPERS FROM WEREWOLVES. I'll bet you'll be on Oprah's show within a week."

"Sounds great. I'll do it."

"Smart move," Dumont said, pressing a key on his cell phone. The zombies gathered around him.

Shelly wished she could hear what Dumont was telling them.

"Okay," Dumont said. "They understand their instructions and are good to go."

The zombies formed a circle, putting Shelly in the middle.

When they entered the mall, the tallest zombie spat on somebody.

Shelly shined the light on the target. Sure enough, she saw purple goop on the guy's face. She roasted him with her flamethrower.

Before long, they worked their way toward Macy's. By the time they reached the store's entrance, Shelly realized she'd torched at least thirty potential werewolves. Then it struck her: Dumont claimed fifteen were inside. Bewildered, she wanted to consult Dumont, but didn't know how to contact him. She felt nervous about leaving the zombies behind. But then she couldn't keep killing everybody the zombies spat upon.

Suddenly, the tall zombie spat on her. Another wrestled away the flame thrower and torched her.

Within minutes they torched everyone else in the mall.

Dumont went inside and surveyed the carnage. "Nice work," he said to his zombies, as he threw them a dozen slices of pizza.

After Dumont emptied all the mall's cash registers, he checked his map to see which mall he'd rob next. Then he realized his supply of freeze dried pepperoni pizza had run dangerously low. That meant he'd have to forestall the next mall robbery until he raided a Wal-mart warehouse and stole their supply of his zombies' favorite snack.

On the way to the warehouse, he wondered if any of the guards had flame throwers. If so, he wondered if the same goofy story about fifteen werewolves would work like it did with the female guard at the mall. Then he remembered what a famous man had said, "A sucker is born every minute."

He found those words pacifying, as he approached a Wal-mart warehouse.

THE RED PHONE

The back cover of the fantasy paperback at Barnes and Noble said, "Inside this book is a miniature telephone. Don't let the size fool you. It works. Pick it up and see."

Frank tried to open the book, but couldn't. That's when he noticed a keyhole in the binding.

"Hey, lady. How come you have books that are locked?" he asked a clerk.

"Whadda ya mean?"

"This book is locked. I can't open either cover. See this keyhole?"

She took the book, examined it, and without saying a thing returned it to the shelf. Her glance implied Frank was a colossal jerk.

After she left to assist other customers, he grabbed the book. Damned if it didn't have a keyhole in the binding. And double-damn, he still couldn't open either cover. Once again, he read the words saying a phone was inside.

When scrutinizing the keyhole, Frank saw tiny printing. Unable to read it, he went to the Accessories Section, found a magnifying glass and held it over the keyhole. The words said, "Use your car keys."

When he inserted the key to his Yugo, the cover popped open! Sure enough, a tiny red phone sat inside.

He pressed the phone to his ear. After three rings, a high pitched voice broke in. "You've reached the Martian Central Employment Agency. All operators are either busy or at lunch. Please try again in an hour."

Frank shelved the book and went to Denny's for lunch.

He could hardly wait for the hour to pass. But when he returned to the fantasy shelves, the book was gone.

He hurried around the store checking to see if somebody had it. Sure enough, a ditzy-looking teenage girl was sipping coffee and reading it.

"Excuse me," Frank said. "Are you gonna buy this book?"

"Maybe. What's it to you?"

"Well, I was gonna buy it. It's the last copy. Do you mind giving it to me? I'm in a hurry."

"You gotta be kidding. Get outta here before I call the manager."

"Listen... that book's very important to me. If you give it to me, I'll treat you to a Double-Whammy Super-Duper Chocolate Muffin Delight and a whole pot of Delicio Maximo Olay Latte.

The muffin and coffee cost fifteen bucks.

Frank found a spot where he couldn't be easily noticed, opened the lock, lifted the phone, and listened.

"Mars Central Employment Agency. Glixa speaking. How may I help you?"

He gave his name and told the voice about the book and phone.

"Oh Yes, Mr. Brown," she said. "You were highly recommended. Do you need a job?"

"Not at the moment. Though maybe I will in a few weeks. There's rumors of downsizing. What kinda jobs do you got?"

"Our client has a huge contract to carve crop circles on Jupiter and all its moons. Pays very highly. Housing and food are provided. The assignment should last at least a hundred years. Interested?"

"Sure. But I don't know how to make crop circles."

"Our client is highly motivated and will pay you to go to crop circle carving school."

"I assume there's oxygen on Jupiter," he said.

"Yes. Besides that, the company has installed every convenience. Frankly, you'll love it there. I went a few weeks ago to check out some of the job sites. The weather is wonderful every day. This situation is the best in the Universe. Are you interested? The company is offering 100,000 Interplanetary Monetary Units as a sign-up bonus, if you accept their offer today."

"Hmm. Actually, I'd be even more interested if they have females on Jupiter."

"Not to worry. The ratio of females to males is a hundred to one. And they're considered the most gorgeous in the universe."

Following instructions, Frank flew to Florida and paid a boat owner to take him to an island in the middle of the Bermuda Triangle. The owner kept asking Frank why he wanted to go to a deserted island in the middle of nowhere. Frank said he was going to survey the island for potential purchase. That didn't stop the owner from scratching his head when he dropped Frank on the beach and departed.

The Martian shuttle descended that night as planned. When Frank boarded, they led him to a room and locked the door behind them.

"What the hell's going on?" he yelled, banging on the door. "Is this how you treat new employees?"

That's when he noticed a book on a cot. It looked like the one he'd seen at Barnes and Noble. Only this one wasn't locked. When he opened the cover, he saw a tiny phone inside.

After three rings, Frank heard a recorded message from the Emperor of Mars. The Emperor apologized profusely for the complex tactics used to entice Frank aboard. He said none of that would have been necessary if Earth's news outlets and radio talk shows hadn't alerted Earthlings about abductions. To avoid further negative publicity, it was necessary for the Emperor's agents to jump through hoops to obtain fresh Earthmen for important medical experiments.

When the phone went dead, the door opened. Two Martians rolled in a table. The third had a huge saw in one hand, a scalpel in the second, and a blowtorch in the third.

GOOD TIME CHARLIE

"We're really gonna miss him," said General Smith, as the interstellar vehicle rose from Area 51. "He was a Good Time Charlie."

"Really?" asked the President of the United States.

"Yes, Sir. When we determined he wasn't a security risk, I took him to Las Vegas a few times. Put him in a Disney character costume, so nobody'd get frightened by his appearance. Didn't take him long to get the hang of life on Earth. He was quite the lady's man, you know?"

"None of the CIA and NASA reports mentioned that."

"Well he was. Used to pick women up six at a time in the casinos. I guess they flocked to him because he was exotic. Kids loved him too. They'd gather around and ask for his autograph when he visited schools in Vegas. He'd draw crop circles telling them that's how his name was written in Martian. Besides that, he used to go to bars around town and buy drinks for everybody. Yeah, he was a real Good Time Charlie. He even used to buy things for my kids for Christmas."

"Well, he's gone. And hopefully, he'll deliver my message of condolence to the highest authority on Mars.

"Condolence? I don't understand what you mean, Mr. President."

"I sent a note of sympathy for their fallen comrades—that bunch of green, freaky-looking things that were found dead when their saucer crashed in 1947 at Roswell, New Mexico."

"None of that ever happened, Sir. It was just a story released by the Roswell public information officer who was going nuts from boredom in the boonies of New Mexico. After all, they didn't have a thing to do after the war with Japan ended. And the Russians hadn't yet become a full blown threat."

"Well, when did this one arrive?"

"1975."

"Really? I don't recall seeing that in any of the reports."

"That's because the early reports were destroyed by order of the President at the time."

"I see. Where did they find this one?"

"Disneyland."

"What was he doing there?"

"Scouting for potential abductees."

"Didn't anybody notice him?"

"No, Sir. He broke into one of their warehouses, and put on a Donald Duck costume. So, he had the run of the park, completely free of detection. He did that for over two years. God only knows how many people he marked for abduction before we apprehended him. Meanwhile, hanging around Disneyland for so long helped him learn English and Spanish."

"Do you think he was responsible for the rash of abductions in the mid-70's?"

"Hard to tell. We asked him about that when we caught him in '77. We offered him immunity from prosecution if he'd confess. But, he refused to incriminate himself or anybody else. He said he was going to, but began to feel a certain fondness for Earthlings. He'd discovered we weren't as awful as he'd been told while growing up on Mars. So, he told his contacts on Mars to abduct farm animals instead, making Martians believe that they were really the human species on Earth."

"If I'd have known that, I would've given him a medal," said the President. "And granted him instant citizenship."

"He'll be back in a few months. I'm sure he'll be more than willing to accept both."

"Better yet, I think the American people should show their gratitude by buying him a Starbucks franchise. Or a McDonald's franchise."

"Actually, he mentioned a few times how he wished he had a liquor license," said the general. "Perhaps you can arrange for him to have a liquor store in Los Angeles. That way, he won't have to wear costumes to hide his appearance. Nobody in LA will notice anyway, considering how zonked they always are."

"Great idea. I'll have my aides work on it so everything will be ready when he returns."

"I'm sure he'll appreciate that, Sir."

"If nothing else, it'll help him remain a Good Time Charlie," said the President. "You know—drinks on the house for everybody. He'll have all the liquor on hand he wants."

"If you don't mind, I'd like to tell him about your offer of giving him a liquor store when I communicate with him, this afternoon."

"It's fine with me. And while you're talking to him, could you find out what it takes to get on election ballots up there? I might run for election. Wouldn't mind being the first human President of Mars. Especially since we have term limitations here."

"Sir, I doubt that'd go over big on Mars."

"Why?"

"They have an Emperor who serves for life. Only his offspring can succeed him."

"Hmm. I'll have to let the Emperor know I'm available for adoption."

THE VICTIM

"**W**here is it?" a paramedic asked, as he rushed through the front door.

"In the kitchen," Harry replied.

"Oh man! This is the bloodiest mess I've ever seen."

"It ain't blood. It's jelly."

"Yeah, sure," the medic said. Reaching for his phone he dialed. "Police Dispatch—I wanna report a 787. The victim's at 123 Oak Street. There's an awful mess here. Looks like a massacre."

"What's a 787?" Harry asked when the medic hung up.

"Homicide."

Before Harry knew what happened, another paramedic had him in a choke hold. "You're under citizen's arrest. The cops will be here in a few minutes to take you away."

"Wait," Harry gurgled. "I killed it in self-defense."

"Yeah, sure. That's what they all say."

He tied Harry's hands behind his back and shoved him into a chair.

"Listen, guys. You're making a terrible mistake. I swear if you don't untie me, I'll sue you bastards. I can prove I'm innocent, if you'll just run a finger through what you think is blood, and taste it."

"Quiet, you crazy loon, or I'll tape your mouth shut!"

"Wait a minute," said the paramedic who was checking the victim for signs of life. "This puddle is too thick to be blood." He stuck his finger into the red mass, then put it in his mouth. "Well, I'll be damned. It tastes like strawberry jelly. Mmm. It's Delicious! Come here and try some."

"Geez, you're right," said his partner. "It's even better than Smucker's and Knott's. Talk about full-bodied flavor."

Soon, both medics were on all fours lapping jelly from the linoleum.

"If you guys don't mind," Harry said, "I'll join you. I didn't get a chance to eat breakfast. This freakin' giant, powdered jelly donut attacked me while I was pouring corn flakes."

They were so engrossed, they didn't bother to respond.

"Now that you know this ain't blood, how about untying my hands."

They were lapping so ferociously they ignored Harry, as he fell to his knees and slurped along with them.

"Hey, what the hell's going on here?" asked a cop, waving a pistol.

"We're having dessert," said a medic with red-stained face. "Have some. It's terrific. Best strawberry jelly I ever tasted."

"Don't mind if I do. I'm nuts about jelly."

When they lapped up all the jelly that'd poured out of the donut's multiple stab wounds—all of which were inflicted by Harry—they untied him and apologized.

He explained how the giant, powdered jelly donut appeared from nowhere and pounced on him. Powdered sugar paw prints on his neck were further proof of the donut's dastardly intentions.

Harry showed them the butcher knife he used in self-defense.

"Well, since it's a jelly donut," the cop said, "it won't have to be buried. Actually, there's no sense letting it go to waste. But I gotta admit, I never ate a six-foot jelly donut before."

"But it's dead," said a medic. "Wouldn't it be a crime or a sin against Nature to consume a dead body."

"Yeah, if it was a human corpse. But it ain't." The cop squeezed the donut. "Hey, it feels nice and squishy. It's super fresh, like right out of the bakery. Even though all the jelly's poured out, it should be scrumptious. Anybody wanna help me devour this puppy?"

Even famished vampires had never attacked victims with such gusto.

They found the donut's doughy remains exceptionally delicious—especially the parts on which powdered sugar remained.

Before long, the entire donut was gone.

The cop, used to a daily diet of free donuts, ate far more than his share. That's because he threatened the others with his pistol when they complained about his gargantuan portions.

After a loud burp, the cop said, "Nothing really happened here. Understand? I'll report it as a minor domestic dispute to clear the books."

"But somebody will have to pay for the ambulance service," a medic said. "We just can't go back and say it was a domestic dispute and nobody got hurt. Hey, we're on piece work. We get paid so much per head by the ambulance service for every injured person we deliver to the hospital. Plus we get a bonus from the hospital for every new patient with insurance that we bring to the Emergency Room.

"No sweat," the cop said, as he slammed Harry's head with the butt of his pistol. "Now you got a paying customer. Oh hell, I forgot to ask him if he had insurance."

They checked Harry's wallet and found a Blue Cross membership card.

Relieved, the medics carried him away on a stretcher.

The cop caught up to them. "Here's my card. If you run across any other giant jelly donuts, don't report it to the department. Just call me. Night or day. Got it?"

"Yeah," said a medic. "And what do we get in return?"

"If you or anybody in your family gets parking tickets, I'll take care of them."

"That plus a jar of jelly from giant jelly donuts, every month," said a medic. "One for each of us."

"Agreed."

* * * *

None of them ever had the same pleasure again. But they would have, if they liked crème filled donuts. Especially since dozens of crème-filled donuts were killed while attacking citizens the very next night.

BEST WAY TO LOS BANOS

"Where are you going, Senor?" asked the Mexican bartender, as he poured a second tequila.

"Los Banos," said Joe.

"This is not a good night to take the highway. The moon is full. The demons are restless."

"What do demons have to do with anything?"

"They prowl the highway seeking the unwary."

"And what happens when they find them?"

"They tear them apart and devour them."

"Sounds like silly superstition to me. I thought you folks in this part of Mexico were educated."

"This is not superstition. You can go to the church and ask the priest."

"I don't need a priest to get directions or tell me what road to take. The map says the only way to Los Banos, other than the highway, is a primitive road. It would add another hundred miles to my trip. Even worse, I hear it's full of vicious bandits. I don't want my motorcycle robbed, nor do I wanna get my ass shot off."

I cannot in good conscience allow you to take the highway to Los Banos," said the bartender.

"Oh really? So what are you gonna do to stop me?" Joe pulled a switchblade from his pocket and snapped it open.

The sight of the ugly, narrow blade made the bartender back away from the bar.

"Just as I figured," Joe said. "You ain't nothin' but a big bag of wind."

"Please, Senor, for your mother's sake, do not take the highway tonight. Go tomorrow after the sun rises and the demons are sleeping."

Snickering, Joe threw pesos on the bar and hurried out.

What a terrific night for riding a Harley. The air was calm, clear, crisp. The only sound came from the purring of his bike.

Joe tuned Mexican party music on his radio. The tequila, cruising at 80 mph, and the music made him joyous. The thought of meeting Teresa in Los Banos increased his exuberance. Soon they'd ride to the farthest regions of the heavens on a mattress.

Suddenly, lightening flashed across the road. An earthquake struck so hard, Joe was thrown from his Harley. He tumbled and slid down the road, stopping inches from a fissure.

Bleeding and barely conscious, the last things he remembered were a horrible stench, searing flames, and a weird voice that said, "You should have taken the other road, Joe."

THE TATTERED MAN

"So what happened after the zombie bit the guy's head and ate his brains?" a kid asked.

"Nothing," said the camp counselor. "That's the end of the story. By the way, I never said the bad guy was a zombie."

"He hadda be."

"Not necessarily. He coulda been a Head Eater."

"What's that?"

"A monster ten times worse than a zombie. Zombies only eat your brains. Head Eaters yank your head right off your body. First they put the neck of your severed head over their lips and drink whatever blood's inside your head. Then they jam their hand through the neck like it was the opening of a cookie jar, pull out everything, and eat every scrap. For desert, they rip out your eyeballs, jam them onto lollypop sticks, and lick them."

"Ewww!"

One of the kids said, "My dad told me about them. Only he called them Camp Monsters. He saw one when he was at summer camp when they were around a campfire telling scary stories. All of a sudden, they heard a terrible scream. Then a weird looking guy ran out of the bushes. Everybody ran away, except for a girl who sprained her ankle. The monster grabbed her head and tore it off. Then he jammed his hand up through the neck, pulled out all the gunk inside her head and ate it."

"How did your dad know he ate the stuff in her skull if he ran away?" a kid asked.

"When the cops came, one of them stuck a flashlight inside her head and took a look. My dad said the cop puked his guts out for a whole hour."

"Were her eyes gone?"

"Yep. The monster musta ate one of them, because the other one was only half-eaten. It was on a stick. It still had lotsa blood on it."

A kid threw up.

"OK," the counselor said. "One more story and that's it for the night. This one's about Bloody Bones."

"Is that another kind of monster?"

"Yeah. Some say this one's worse than Head Eaters. Anyway, there was this beautiful princess who lived in Transylvania who useta take long walks in the woods. One day, she got lost. And it got dark. As dark as it is now. Suddenly, she heard—"

A blood-curdling scream interrupted the story. As the kids looked in the direction of the noise, they saw a tattered man running toward them. Panicked, the kids scattered.

Jim sprang to his feet. "Hey jerk! You're late. You were supposta scare them when I was telling them about the zombie who ate a guy's brains. What happened? And why are you wearing that stupid mask?"

Instead of answering, the man threw a backpack that landed at Jim's feet.

"What's this?" Jim asked.

No response.

"C'mon, Sam. Cut the crap."

The man remained silent.

When the counselor picked up the backpack, a baby's head fell out.

"What the hell are you doing with a doll's head? Is that how you were gonna scare the kids? With a stupid doll? That woulda never worked. Gimme the five bucks back I paid you to scare the kids."

When Jim extended his hand for the money, the man grabbed it and ripped it from the socket. The shock threw Jim to the ground. He landed with his face close to the doll's head. He uttered feral grunts when he realized it looked like his infant son.

The kids returned with the cops. A sergeant picked up Jim's severed, eyeless head, turned on a flashlight, and stuck it inside. Another cop looked inside the baby's severed, eyeless head. Gagging, he said, "I thought we caught all the Head Eaters."

"We did. This was done by a Camp Monster. They like to tear off arms and munch on them like corn on the cob. Like an appetizer before the main course."

Suddenly, everyone heard a horrible scream. When they looked in the direction of the noise, another tattered man rushed toward them.

The kids panicked and scattered. But the cops pulled their pistols and fired a dozen times.

The wallet they found on the body contained five dollars.

BEYOND BELIEF

"**Me** and Charlie crashed a weird party," Willie said. "You wouldn't believe who was there. Or maybe I should say WHAT was there. Scared the hell out of us. After our eyes got used to the lights and looked around, we ran out of there. But not before Charlie reached out and touched one of those creepy things."

"What did you see?" asked Jim.

"Very strange beings. None had had more than two legs. And get this: they all had two arms. Even worse, their freakin' heads were sitting above their arms on top of their bodies—if bodies is even the right word."

"C'mon. Nothing has a head on top. Not even Gribblesnatchers on Saturn. What the hell you been smoking?"

"Nothing. I swear. None of them had heads on their backs like us. In fact, they only had one head. They were the ugliest looking things I've ever seen anywhere in the universe."

"Aw, nothing could be that awful," Jim said.

"I'll take you there so you can see for yourself."

"Okay, let's go. By the way, what happened to Charlie?"

"He got so scared, he jumped in his ship and headed home. You should've seen the look on his face. He said he was going to tell the Interstellar Protector Patrol about what he saw. If they believe him, they ought to show up any minute to exterminate those freaks. So, if you want to see something beyond belief before they get wiped out, we better get there fast."

Willie and Jim arrived too late. The Interstellar Protector Patrol had already torched the building.

"Hey, Officer," Jim yelled. "What was inside?"

"Ugliest bastards we ever saw. We captured one and killed the rest."

"Can I have a look at the prisoner?" Jim asked.

"That's against the rules until it gets processed through the Species Identification Center."

"How long will that take?"

"Hard to say. Something this weird might take a dozen or more sun rotations to classify."

"Is it true that they only had one head, two arms, and two legs?"

"Yes."

"Just like I told you," Willie said.

"You've seen them?" asked the Officer.

"Yes. Me and my friend Charlie. He's the guy who reported this thing to you guys."

"Hmm. You better come with me."

"Why?" Willie asked.

"For psychological reorientation. You've suffered a terrible trauma. You might start babbling like your friend."

"But I feel fine. Just got a bit scared, that's all."

"You sure?"

"Fiblee biblee kiblee boop."

INCREDIBLE NEWS

"Ladies and Gentlemen, I have incredible news," said the Illustrious Pooh-bah. "Our scientists have discovered that the Moon's surface is composed of a substance similar to cream cheese. Soon, we'll be able to end global hunger forever."

"Your Excellency, how will we get the cheese from there to here?" asked a reporter.

"Through a polymer tube that stretches from the Moon to Washington."

"How will the Moon Cheese affect those who are intolerant to dairy products?"

"Tests show it is easily digested by anyone."

"My pet boa constrictor doesn't have digestive problems," said a reporter, "as long as I feed it white mice fourteen times a day. Will Moon Cheese be an adequate substitute?"

"Yes. Tests with boa constrictors show they only need one Moon Cheese feeding per week. Once they get a taste, they refuse everything else. Think of the savings in pet food you and other boa constrictors owners will realize. Susan, I see you jumping up and down in the back."

"Thank you, Excellency. "If everyone ends up eating Moon Cheese, will it affect waste elimination?"

"I'm glad you asked. Tests have shown that elimination will cease permanently in humans, animals, birds, fish, and insects. This means untold trillions will be saved when we shut down the world's waste management systems."

"Illustrious Pooh-Bah," said another reporter, "can you tell us what happens after all the nutrients are extracted from Moon Cheese by our digestive systems?"

"Yes. A few drops of a sticky, green substance will ooze from everyone's forehead. In fact, I have samples of the ooze. My assistants will distribute them at the end of this news conference."

"Does the substance have any odor?"

"Yes. The aroma is similar to a combination of decayed whale blubber, methane, and pig snout. I'm going to be frank with the people of the Amalgamated States of America. For a while, the entire nation will have to stay indoors once everybody eats Moon Cheese. We know this will be an inconvenience. But it won't be forever. Our scientists are working on the aroma problem right now. Look, if we can get the Moon Cheese here, end global hunger, and end the daily accumulation of millions of cubic yards of body waste, I think the American People will put up with a bit of readjustment while we figure how to handle a few drops of forehead ooze. I'll take one more question."

"When will the first supply of Moon Cheese be available?"

"Next year. I know you're all eager to try it. I already have. It's absolutely delicious. I had two heaping platefuls for breakfast."

Just then, some in the audience noticed a green substance oozing from Pooh-Bahs' forehead.

In seconds, the room was empty.

"Hey, y'all," hollered the Pooh-Bah. Come back! Don't you want your samples?"

THE COMPLAINER

"Hey, waiter!" Harry yelled, "There's a fly in my coffee!"

"Not to worry," said the waiter, peering into Harry's cup. "It's Horace. He belongs to the owner. He's training for the Olympics. Man, look at him go. He's in great form this morning."

"What? Get this cup outta here and give me a fresh one."

"Shhh. Horace is very sensitive. If he hears you, he may think you don't like him."

"Cut the crap!" Harry yelled. "Give me a fresh cup of coffee, or I want my money back."

"Do you hear that, Horace?" asked the waiter.

"Yeah," the fly said, as it looked up at Harry, while doing a slow backstroke. What's your problem, Mister?"

Harry laughed. "Oh, I get it. You're a ventriloquist. Pretty neat trick making it seem like the fly's talking."

"I ain't a ventriloquist," the waiter said. "Horace *is* talking. He just asked what your problem was. You better answer. He don't like it when somebody don't answer him."

"I ain't talking to no damn, stupid fly. Gimme my money back."

The fly leapt from the cup and karate chopped Harry's nose. The impact knocked Harry off the chair. His face was blood-soaked when he hit the floor.

"You hit him pretty hard," the waiter said. "He ain't getting up."

The fly flew to Harry, lit on his chest, and put its ear against Harry's shirt. "No heartbeat," it said.

"Aw hell. Why'd you hafta hit him so hard?"

"He deserved it for not answering my question. Let's put him out back in a garbage can."

The waiter grabbed Harry under the shoulders, while the fly grabbed Harry's feet. Carrying the corpse to the back alley, they dropped it into a dumpster.

"Leave the lid open," the fly said, as it began to whistle into the wind.

Before long, the sky was black with flies.

"Free, fresh chow," Horace called, pointing to Harry's body.

As thousands of famished flies dined on Harry's corpse, the waiter and Horace returned to the coffee shop.

Fifteen minutes later, a patron complained about a fly in his coffee. He too didn't talk nice to Horace.

"Hey, I got an idea," Horace said, while he and the waiter carried the second body to a garbage can. "Instead of letting all these flies dine on corpses for free, we could charge them each a dollar."

"Sounds like a good idea. But where are we gonna get extra corpses for them to munch on after this one's gone?"

"No problem. If I keep swimming in customers' coffee cups, I'll bet they'll complain like these two guys did. When they do, I'll slam their noses right into their brains. Then all we'll have to do is carry their dead bodies outside, drop them in garbage cans, let the flies know dinner is served, and collect a buck from each one that wants to eat."

Horace and the waiter got rich.

Unfortunately, they invested all their earnings in the Stock Market. They lost everything during the great Market Crash of 2008. Worse, a customer didn't see Horace swimming in his coffee, and drank the whole cup in a single gulp.

REALITY TEST

"Billy, your dad was on a rampage again last night."

"I know," said the eight-year old.

"The cops came just when he was gonna hit me. When they threatened to jail him, he calmed down. Now he'll probably punch one of the neighbors for calling the cops. I wonder who did? The Smiths and Browns are the only ones on the block with a telephone."

"They didn't call the police," Billy said. "I did."

"Stop talking nonsense."

"It's true, Mom."

"Baloney. You were in bed when it happened. You better go to confession and tell the priest you're telling lies again."

"I ain't lying. I went out the upstairs window and called the cops. All you gotta do is ask Aunt Teresa. I ran to her house, woke her and she let me use her phone."

"Stop, or I'll wash your mouth out with soap."

"I really did, Mom."

"How?"

"I took out the screen, and went out the window. I stood on something sticking out of the building. It was so dark, I couldn't see what it was. I jumped off there and landed on top of the fence. I walked across the fence, with my arms out like the guys do in the circus. Then I grabbed the top of the fence and hung until I could see how far away the pavement was. After that, I ran over and woke up Aunt Teresa."

"It ain't possible," she said. "Come outside and I'll show you why. Shame on you for making up such fibs."

Grabbing a step stool, she put it on the ground in the narrow alley behind their apartment.

"Stand on this and look at the top of the fence. What do you see?"

"Barbed wire."

"Right. Now, I'm gonna pick you up. I want you to reach out very carefully and touch one of those metal pieces sticking out. Be careful, they're sharp."

"Ouch! It cut me."

"That's what barbed wire does. Look how the strand of barbed wire stretches across the top of the whole fence. Now, are you gonna stand there and tell me you jumped from the 2nd floor, hit the top of the fence with all your weight, walked across the top in your bare feet, and then hung from it by your bare hands?"

"That's what happened, Mom." Billy said, as he rushed to the sink to run water over his finger.

His mom remained silent while pouring peroxide over his finger and covering it with a band-aid.

"Billy, open your hands and look at your palms. What do you see?"

"Nothing. Just bare skin."

"Right."

"Now, take your shoes and socks off and look at your feet."

He did.

"OK, tell me what you see."

"Nothing."

"Right again. This is what we call a reality test. When people make something up, there's always a way to prove it didn't happen."

"But it really happened, Mom. Just the way I said."

"Then why ain't your hands and feet gashed? And why ain't you in the hospital full of stitches?"

"I don't know. Maybe it happened because of the light they shined on me from the flying saucer."

"Oh, so now we're back to that one again. Billy, listen to me. You have to stop telling fibs. It makes people nervous. They're talking about you. When I go to the store, people look at me funny, like I'm an alien or something."

"But you are an alien, Mom."

She stared at him. "This is a new one. I swear, I don't know what to do. My husband's a terrible drunk, and my only son is becoming a terrible liar. Have you told anybody I'm an alien?"

"Just God."

"Let's keep it that way. Otherwise, people will come for you and take you away. They'll put you somewhere—a place you won't like, I guarantee you. You may never be able to come home again."

Somebody knocked.

Billy opened the door. Aunt Teresa said, "Go play for a while. I wanna talk to your mom."

Walking toward the nearby hills, he muttered, "Nobody ever believes me."

He went to the spot where he'd first seen them. The little men. With the funny-looking green skin.

Within the cluster of trees that hid Billy from view, he took a stick and started to draw something in the soft soil the little men had cleared. They said it was a communications center. They told him to use it whenever he wanted them to come for a talk.

When Billy finished drawing, the image was like a tiny version of an exquisitely beautiful crop circle. It was more intricate than anything he'd ever seen on those hokey TV shows about crop circles.

Within minutes, two green men entered his hideout.

Billy told them what'd happened the night before. They said it proved his skin was getting tougher and was getting more like them every day. They assured that they'd remove his drunken dad from his midst, forever. Then they examined him.

While munching a sandwich, his mom said, "Aunt Teresa told me you really went there last night. How did you get past your father, slip through the front door and get back in without him seeing you?"

"I didn't use the door."

"Okay. I give up. Let's forget this. It's just too spooky. My nerves can take only so much."

"Don't worry Mom. Things are gonna change."

"Yeah. When I'm six feet under. Here, have some milk."

"I'm not supposed to drink milk," Billy said.

"Why not?"

"They said it will hurt the eggs they put in my stomach."

His mom didn't answer. She dropped her head and prayed for strength.

Something deep inside told her not to worry. That her son would not end up institutionalized for what she suspected was childhood schizophrenia. Something told her to rejoice, for soon her only son would become the mother of a new and glorious species.

She didn't understand why the words *giant sea monsters* came to mind.

THE WHITE DRAGON

An artillery shell wiped out the command post. The roar was deafening. I ducked to avoid the shower of dirt, rock, and debris.

After a minute I looked around. I didn't see anybody. I called to my buddy, Smitty. No answer. I yelled for Staff Sergeant Nevins. No answer. I called out for anybody. No answer.

They're all dead! Oh no. It can't be! They can't leave me all alone on this hill surrounded by Chinese troops.

My hair stood on edge.

Static. A radio was around somewhere. More static and a voice. I crawled toward the sound. I found the radio buried under rocks and wood pilings where the command post had been only minutes before. Damn thing was bent almost in half.

A voice faded in and out. "Shady Lady… this is Colonel Crow. Come in! Martin, hold that hill! You must hold—"

"Colonel, this is Private Smith. Lieutenant Martin's dead. Everybody's dead. Do you read me?"

No answer.

The radio spit more static, then died. I shook it a few times.

Nothing.

I cursed and flung it.

We had been under continuous attack for three days. That was not supposed to happen. We were supposed to be relieved a few days ago. Then the Chinese People's Army went crazy and a gazillion of them crossed the Yalu River from Manchuria. We were in their path.

My body ached. My brain reeled from lack of sleep. I had a fever.

An explosion brought me around. I felt my head. It seemed hotter. I had to do something, but wasn't sure what. I didn't want to die. I was only nineteen. I hadn't even lived yet. I wanted to marry my girl. I wanted to see my mom and dad again.

I heard somebody walking toward me. "Oh my God! Dad! Get down before you get shot. There's a million of them out there."

"Hell, they don't scare me," he said standing ramrod straight. "So what's your problem?"

"I'm surrounded. Everybody's dead. I'm here alone. I don't know what to do."

"Same thing happened to me in the jungle at Guadalcanal. Know what I did? I fought like a Marine. And that's what you're gonna do right now!"

Mom interrupted. "Be quiet, Harry. He'll get killed." Looking at me with soft eyes, she said, "Surrender, Billy. That way I'll see you again when this war's over. And when you get home I'll make you a nice apple pie."

Her smiling face faded.

"Forget apple pie," Dad yelled. "Do what I said. Attack the bastards. Make me proud."

I could feel his arm gripping my shoulder.

Then things started to go black.

Another explosion brought me around. Glancing around, I realized I was still on Hill 203, North Korea. Close to the Yalu. Surrounded by enemy troops.

I whimpered.

Dad shouted, "Get control of yourself. They're gonna attack. Get ready. Semper Fi!"

I checked my ammo. Only two clips left for my rifle. Sixteen rounds.

I heard my dad yell, "Fix bayonets!"

I tried to lift my rifle. Damn. It felt like it weighed a hundred pounds. *Why did they give me something so heavy? How'd I ever lug it up this steep hill?*

"Dad, I can't even lift my rifle. I'll hafta surrender."

Dad didn't answer.

I looked around for something white. Lt. Martin used white towels when he shaved. Where the hell were they?

I spotted one stuck between some rocks. I crawled toward it.

All my bones ached. My head spun when I stood up for the first time in two days. Staggering to the edge of the hill, I waved the towel with my last bit of energy.

Peering over the edge, I saw... fog parting... the Golden Gate Bridge... sailboats in San Francisco Bay... beautiful flowers. I was at the top of Lombard Street, the most crooked street in the world. How neat! I'd always wanted to play there.

Stretching out my arms like wings, I hollered, "Let's play airplane."

Imitating an aircraft engine, I ran down Lombard, spinning the towel like a propeller. In seconds I was airborne. It was glorious!

I landed in Chinatown. Firecrackers exploded all around. I wound my way down Grant Street, wearing a hideous dragon hood, while a dozen people snaked and swayed behind me like a twisted Slinky. Children shrieked. Women blanched. Men backed away with frightful looks.

What fun!

At the bottom of the hill, I collapsed from laughter.

* * * *

Everything was out of focus. Someone touched my shoulder.

"Son, I'm General Brown. Can you hear me?"

I couldn't form words to tell him. I laughed.

"General," someone said. "He has a very high fever."

But he just laughed. Didn't you hear him laugh?"

"He's delirious. 105 temperature. We'll bring him to you when he snaps out of it."

"I can't wait that long. I've got to know what really happened up there. Intelligence says Hill 203 has no Chinese troops on it, whatsoever. That makes no sense. They took hundreds of casualties trying to get it. They killed all our guys up there—except this one. Then they ran away from it—just like that?"

"Interrogators told us a crazy story they got from a Chinese prisoner. When he was captured, he was babbling about a white, demon dragon. Said he saw it on Hill 203. He swore the thing came racing down the hill, screeching in an ungodly voice. Huge monster. Zigzagged in and out of their positions. Scared away all their troops. They dropped their weapons and ran like hell."

"Dragon? Ridiculous! Next it'll be Martians."

Nervous laughter filled the field hospital.

"There's more. He said it spun a white cloth like a propeller. He insisted the monster decapitated heads from some of their troops. Scared the living hell out of him. He was only too glad to surrender."

"Dragons? Monsters? Cloth propellers? Decapitations? Crack Chinese troops dropping their weapons and running away? This war gets more bizarre every damn day! Well, when you get this Marine on his feet, send him to see me. Maybe he saw the damn thing. Hell, now you have me talking as if I believe it!"

"General, there's something even stranger."

"Now what?"

"When the medics found this Marine at the bottom of Hill 203, he was clutching a bloody white towel and a severed head."

A GOOD EDUCATION IS IMPORTANT

"**G**imme a break! All you ever do is criticize," Fred said to his parrot. "I should never have spent five thousand bucks sending you to charm school. What did I get for my money? You're as charming as a rancid dish rag."

"Bitch, bitch, bitch," said the bird. "That's all you ever do!"

"Look, Jerk-O, I spent ten thousand sending you to school to learn the King's English. So, I expect to hear refined speech, not five-letter, nasty words."

"Yakety-yak," the bird said, swinging on its perch.

"Better watch your mouth," Fred said, "or I'll feed you to the neighbor's cat."

"Oh yeah? You and what army?"

Enraged, Fred opened the cage door and rammed his hand inside to strangle the bird. Before he could grab the parrot, it jumped off the perch and slammed Fred's wrist with a karate chop. Fred's wrist bone broke in six places.

Screaming in agony, Fred tried to remove his shattered limb. The bird grabbed his arm and twisted it until Fred fell to his knees.

Rushing through the open cage door, the parrot pounced on Fred and broke his neck with a single blow. "You forgot to mention the two thousand you spent on Karate lessons," the parrot said, kicking him in the ribs for good measure.

The bird checked Fred's pulse. "Well, I'll be damned. He's dead. I wonder if he mentioned me in his will?"

Ransacking the house, the bird found nothing. Ripping paintings from the wall, he discovered a safe hidden behind an original Van Gough. Within minutes the bird cracked the safe. "Thanks for paying seven thousand to send me to safe cracking school," it said to Fred's corpse.

The parrot read the will. "Dammit! The jerk didn't leave me a penny. But he left ten million to that two-bit strumpet, Elsie Marrot."

Raging, the bird trashed Fred's mansion. When surveying the horrendous damage, it was struck with an idea. Grabbing a pen and some correction fluid, it erased "M" in Elsie's last name and inserted "P." Next, it scribbled Fred's initials to authenticate the change, put the pen into Fred's hand, and wiped off claw prints.

"That makes it official. All I gotta do now is put this will in Fred's hand, call 911 to report a house invasion, and wait for the legal process to run its course."

A few months later, the parrot was lollygagging in a luxurious beach house on the Mexican Riviera, sipping mint juleps—or whatever parrot's drink when they're fabulously wealthy.

MIRTH

"Sixty seconds until air time," said the producer of the *Morning News Show*. "You look tense, Sarah. C'mon, loosen up. The audience knows this is your first day as a newsreader. They'll give you some slack. Nobody out there bites."

"Sorry," said the network's newest and most stunning newsreader. "I don't know what's come over me. Maybe I'm getting the flu or something."

She didn't want to tell the producer she was grieving over her beloved poodle that died hours earlier.

"Fifty seconds," the producer said, then added, "You're face is still tight. Take a few deep breaths. Did you ever hear the one about the salesman and farmer's daughter who hated pepperoni pizza?"

In twenty-seven seconds, the producer told the funniest joke Sarah had ever heard. She laughed so hard, she almost fell off her chair.

"That's better," the producer said. "Ten seconds to air time. Nine...eight..."

Sarah was still chuckling when she looked squarely at the teleprompter mounted just below the TV camera.

"...Three...two...one..."

"Good morning, America," Sarah said in an upbeat voice, her face still full of mirth. "I'm Sarah Scott. Here's the news. Bubonic plague still rages in China. A government spokeswoman said fewer than a million people have survived in the entire country. Here in our own back yard, California, Oregon, and Washington sank beneath the Pacific last night during a violent earthquake that lasted thirty minutes and measured at 15 on the Richter scale. Meanwhile, most of Chicago burned down overnight. Three million are homeless."

Still smiling at the memory of the joke's punch line, she added, "Locusts have attacked early morning commuters in the nation's capital. Thousands are feared dead. We switch now to the White House and President Higgenlooper."

The word LIVE appeared on TV screens to the upper left of the President's head. Appearing confident, he peered directly into the TV camera lens and said, "There's nothing to fear but fear itself."

The picture switched back to Sarah at the news desk. Still feeling high spirited, she said, "Meanwhile, in Rome, the Pope was abducted by

Martians who are demanding the world's entire food supply as ransom. All flea market food stands, farmer's markets, grocery stores, supermarkets, food banks, and soup kitchens around the globe are closed until further notice. More after these words from our sponsor."

The screen filled with a graying man wearing a physician's white jacket. "Hi. I'm Doctor Zober. Are you feeling hassled? Worried? Oppressed? Remember this: there's no problem so bad that it can't be run away from. That's why I developed the ultimate solution: Doctor Zober's Instant Suicide Pills. Maybe you're fourteen and just discovered you're pregnant for the third time in three years. Or your heroin pusher hasn't received his shipment, and you're heaving all over the place. Or maybe you have fifteen kids and your job just got permanently outsourced to a third world country. Or maybe your pet poodle just died. Why suffer? In one second, and for just one penny, you can have a permanent and lasting solution. No matter how broke you are, everybody can always find a penny somewhere to put into one of Doctor Zober's Instant Suicide Pill vending machines. And if by some remote chance you don't have a penny, steal one. Our pills now come in ten delightful colors. What's more, vending machines are now installed on every light pole in the nation. So remember: when things get real, real bad, you can always run away from your problems… for just a penny. Doctor Zober's Instant Suicide Pills. Available at every light pole in the nation. Guaranteed to work instantly and every time, or double your money back."

When the camera switched back to the news desk, Sarah was gone.

They found her body below one of Dr. Zober's vending machines.

YOU GOTTA BE KIDDING

I opened the letter from Nifty Swifty Credit Corporation. Sonovabitch! A bill for twenty-nine bucks. Damn jerks made a mistake. I always paid my credit card bills in full, every month.

"Late Penalty," it said. "One dollar charge for each day payment is late."

"You gotta be kidding!" I yelled. They were fining me more than the full amount of the bill I'd already paid. Yeah, I sent the payment late, but it wasn't my fault. The damn thing got lost in the mail before it reached me.

I dialed the number for Nifty Swifty. Their main office was right here in Santa Buffoona.

A shrill, highly accented, recorded voice answered. "Thank you for calling Nifty Swifty Credit Corporation. Please note the following important information. The City Council of Santa Buffoona, California has passed a law making the English language illegal. Kofufu, a dialect of Esperanto, will replace English as the official language of the City of Santa Buffoona. This law will take effect at noon on April fifteenth, two-oh-oh-eight."

"You gotta be kidding," I said, noting it was ten minutes to noon, and today was April 15th.

The voice continued. "One minute past noon, and thereafter, anyone dialing this number will hear our message in Kofufu. To repeat this message, press 998877, or press one of the following:

For Chinese, press 1.
For Latin, press 2.
For Aramaic, press 3.
For Transylvanian, press 4.
For South Vietnamese, press 5.
For North Vietnamese, press 6.
For East Vietnamese, press 7.
For West Vietnamese, press 8.
For Ebonics, press 9.
For all other languages, press 10."
I pressed 10.

A voice said, "The following menu provides access to three hundred languages, except English. If you wish to hear directions in English until the April seventh cutoff, dial the Amalgamated Nations English-to-Kofufu Translation Department. That number is... that number is... that number is...."

Click. Dial Tone.

Damn. Only five minutes left to get someone in Customer Service who speaks English.

I dialed Nifty Swifty again. Had to listen to the whole damn mishmash before it would let me press 10. This time I got an 800 number for the Amalgamated Nations.

I dialed.

"Amalgamated Nations Headquarters. How may I direct your call?"

"Are you real? I mean, is this a real human voice?"

"Certainly, Sir. I am a real live human bean. Homo Say-pee-unz. Of the male persuasion. From whence are you calling?"

"Santa Buffoona, California."

"Wonderfully progressive city. The Secretary General just approved Santa Buffoona's request to join the AN as a sovereign anarchistic republic. We're thrilled."

"Quick! Connect me with the English-to-Kofufu Translation Department."

"You can dial that directly, Sir."

"I'm running out of time. This is an emergency."

"Sir, The Amalgamated Nations does not consider your emergency to be a *fluega montegra desonato*."

Damn. The clock had struck noon! Kofufu was now in effect.

"Y-G-B-K," I yelled.

"Eh? Y-G-B-K? *Shatasa puba?*"

"It means you gotta be kidding, you jerk."

"*Engras ista graduata!*"

"Same to you, Pal."

I'd fix Nifty Swifty's ass. Then I'd do something about the stupid city council.

I went to a bank in the next town, where they still spoke something akin to near-Pidgin English. Got a money order for twenty-nine dollars worth of Eskimo shekels. "Choke on this, Nifty Swifty Credit!" I said, dropping it into an envelope.

On the back of the envelope in huge letters, I wrote in Pig Latin, "REW-SCAY OO-YAY."

I took a white bath towel, and sprayed BRAZY CASTARDS in large black letters. Attached it to the TV antenna on the roof for all to see.

Then I called every number in the city directory, yelling the same two words to everyone who answered.

The next day, I was arrested. *Was it because of the Pig Latin I'd written on the Nifty Swifty return envelope? Had that too become an illegal language? Was it the financial transaction I'd made in Eskimo shekels? Or was it the English spoonerism on my towel-flag?*

Never found out.

The charges were read in Kofufu. I was tried in that language after swearing in with my erect middle finger touching the AN flag. Not sure what I swore to. Just repeated what the big guy with the flamethrower said.

Then I was sentenced by a judge in guttural Kofufu.

"You gotta be kidding!" I screamed when he sentenced me to *torella* years in the pokey, with chance for early parole after *bragliozee* years. Unfortunately, early release depended on my being a good *wamalaki*.

If you think I ain't gonna be the best *wamalaki* in the universe, you gotta be kidding.

NASTY RUMORS

"What's your name, Sonny?" asked Santa.

"Jimmy."

"What would you like me to bring you for Christmas?"

"An AK-47, ten thousand rounds of ammunition, a box of hand grenades, and one of those Israeli guns. I forget the name."

"Uzi."

"Oh yeah. And an Uzi."

"Hmm. Do Mommy and Daddy know about your Christmas list?"

"Yep."

"Did they say you could have these things?"

"Not exactly."

"What exactly did they say you could have?"

"Roller blades, soccer ball, and a chemistry set."

"I see. Well, I have lots of those, ho, ho, ho. But, I'm all out of the other things."

"That's not what I heard."

"What've you heard?" Santa asked.

"That you have an Uzi. And you're gonna use it to kill the Easter Bunny."

Santa almost fell off his throne in the shopping mall. He strained to prevent himself from exploding and whacking the kid across the face.

The kid's mom was beaming, as she waved. Santa waved back, cursing under his breath. *Who's responsible for ramming this nonsense into the child's brain? Home? Movies? TV? Video games? Comic books, texting?*

"Kill the Easter Bunny? Ho, ho, ho. Santa would never do that. Why we're great friends. He visits me at the North Pole every year. We go skiing, sleigh riding, and build snow forts. His bunny helpers and my elves make big snowmen together. In fact, my elves have the contract to make all his jellybeans. Where did you hear about me and the Easter Bunny?"

"At school."

"I see. This is what we call a rumor, Jimmy. Rumors are never true. People say them to make trouble. Now listen. You must forget this rumor, because it's a lie. Will you do that for Santa?"

"I guess. But you first have to promise me you won't hurt the Easter Bunny."

"I promise. Now run along. And have a Merry Christmas."

Sighing, Santa wondered what the world was coming to.

A shabbily dressed blonde girl came toward him, then stopped. She turned and ran back to her mother. The mother said something, then nudged the girl back toward Santa.

"Hello young lady. My, what pretty blue eyes you have. I'm soooo happy to see you. What's your name?"

"Cindy."

"That's a pretty name. And what would you like from Santa?"

"I only want one thing," she said, eyes filling.

Santa was touched. He hated to see little girls cry. He figured the poor child was economically deprived and painfully aware of the life's harsh realities. No doubt downsizing and outsourcing jobs were severely affecting this family. He'd fill her stocking with nutritious, extra-high-protein granola bars.

"And what's the one thing you want?"

"For you to not kill the Easter Bunny. I'd miss him so much. Why do you want to do that, Santa? I thought you were nice."

Santa went into a coughing spasm. The photographer elf dashed over with a bottle of water. After a few swigs, the hacking stopped.

"Don't cry, Cindy. Santa would never do anything like that. I love everybody. The Easter Bunny is my best friend. Do people hurt their best friends?"

"Sometimes they do," she sniffled. "My best friend hurt me."

"Oh, my. What'd she do?" he asked, taking a mental note to put some coal into the nasty best friend's stocking.

"She laughed at the shoes Mommy got me from the Goodwill store."

He wanted to hug the poor little thing. But, if he did, somebody might misinterpret his intentions and call the police.

"Don't cry, Honey. I promise you I won't hurt the Easter Bunny. He'll be hopping over to your house next Easter with a huge basket full of the best chocolates money can buy. I'm going to call him during my break and make sure he does. You live on Elm Street, right?"

"Yes."

"Look at me, and listen to Santa. I love everybody. I think you've heard some bad rumors. Rumors by bad people who hate good people. They're trying to make good people seem foolish, or evil. Things like this happen at times. If I promise to put a hundred toys, games, and dolls under your tree, will you forget that ugly rumor?"

"Oh, yes. Thank you, Santa."

She almost broke his heart when she kissed his cheek and hugged him.

Santa called home during his break. "Hello, Sweetheart? How are you? Yes, I'm fine. I miss you too. Are the elves and reindeer well? Listen, Dear, something awful has developed…"

Three more hours of hearing upset children repeating the same horrible rumor, exhausted Santa. He'd spent more time pacifying than listening. He had no idea what he could do to eliminate this abominable rumor. It was worse than the time Nietzsche had declared God dead. Without belief in a Supreme Being, there was no need to believe in lesser beings. It took tremendous effort from Santa to bring children of the 19th Century back to the wonderful world of belief.

But now it was worse. Cell phones, 24-hour newscasts, and the Internet could spread filthy lies at lightning speed. Oh, he'd devise a strategy to put the kibosh on this horrid lie. But Christmas was only five days away—too late to crush the canard. Many children were already ruined.

Feeling dejected, Santa went to his dressing room.

The moment he opened the door, the Easter Bunny shot him three times with a silenced pistol.

Santa's Kevlar vest protected him. But, the impact stung his chest and knocked him to the floor.

"Why?" Santa gasped.

"*CNN* reported you were gonna kill me. Getting selfish? Thinking about merging Easter with Christmas, are you? Trying to downsize me? I heard you and the Tooth Fairy are in cahoots."

"Wait. It's just a horrible rumor."

"Liar!" the Easter Bunny yelled, firing a shot into Santa's face.

Fox News reported that Santa Claus and the Tooth Fairy had been gunned down. The commentator said officials were investigating to determine if it were a hate-crime.

Within minutes, the entire planet buzzed with sordid rumors.

The Tooth Fairy survived. Santa didn't.

Children everywhere wept when Christmas was canceled until further notice.

SWITCHEROO

"Frank the Walrus is smoking again," said the trainer to the odds maker at the Las Vegas casino.

"Oh man!" said the odds maker. "I figured he'd last another day to make it 100 days without smoking. Thanks for letting me know. We're gonna take a bath on this one, considering we gotta pay 1,000 to 1 if his nicotine fast doesn't last until tomorrow."

"I thought he'd last myself. But some jerk snuck two cartons of Marlboro 100's into his den overnight. Frank's favorite brand. When I went to feed him a few minutes ago, he was flat on his back in a nicotine stupor. And his den was filled with smoke."

"Can you dry him out and get rid of the smoke before the press arrives? We'd make it worth your while. Say, a hundred thousand."

"Well, I only got an hour before that guy from *The Times* shows up for his daily inspection of Frank's den and checks the results of our daily nicotine tests. I can get rid of the smoke in time, but there's no way to drain the nicotine from Frank's blubber in time."

"How about this: is there another walrus there that looks like Frank? I mean, to me, all walruses look alike. Maybe you can play switcheroo. Hide Frank somewhere. Then stick a walrus in his den that never smoked in its entire life."

"That wouldn't be fair."

"Fair? Who cares about fair? We stand to lose millions. I'll give you two-hundred thousand if you pull this off."

"We only got one more walrus," said the trainer. "His name is Charlie. He's not a smoker. He likes Hershey bars. Maybe if I give him a few, he'll take Frank's place and keep his mouth shut. Like I said, nobody will know the difference."

"You tell Charlie if he cooperates, a grateful patron from Las Vegas will supply him with all the Hershey bars he can eat for the rest of his life."

"Okay, hold the phone. I'll check with him. Back in a minute."

The trainer went into Charlie's den, told the walrus about the situation, and the Las Vegas offer.

Three minutes later, the trainer said to the odds maker, "Charlie wants to know if he can get Hershey bars with almonds."

"Yeah. Anything he wants."

"I'll let him know. Back in a minute."

After a quick discussion with the walrus, the trainer said on the phone, "We got a bit of a problem. Charlie has another demand for his services. He wants a hundred pounds of Reese's Pieces every day, besides fifty each of the milk chocolate and almond Hershey bars. The giant sized ones that cost a dollar each. What'll I tell him?"

"Agreed. Hurry up. Time's running out."

The trainer talked to Charlie again and told the odds maker, "Now he wants a free suite at your casino for a whole year, free chips to play roulette every day, plus a dozen show girls in his room every night. All platinum blondes."

"Damn! That walrus is a real shrewd bastard. I can swing the suite, but I don't know about the girls. What does he have in mind?"

"It's so foul I don't even wanna say."

"Hmm. Well, tell him I agree. As long as what happens in Vegas stays in Vegas. Know what I mean?"

The trainer told the walrus. Then he informed the odds maker, "Okay, it's a deal. I'm gonna switch the walruses right now."

Frank was taken to a basement and chained to a wall. Then Charlie was placed in Frank's den as a secret substitute.

The ploy worked.

The casino reaped hundreds of millions in winning bets. The trainer got his two-hundred thousand. Charlie got his Hershey bars, Reese's pieces, and year's stay at the casino, complete with fabulous presidential suite, tons of roulette chips, and twelve of the most beautiful platinum blonde show girls in Nevada.

While the trainer cleaned out Frank's den before putting Frank back into it, he found a crumpled VISA receipt from Wal-mart for two cartons of Marlboro 100's. He figured it was left behind by the jerk was who snuck cigarettes into Frank's den to make sure Frank broke his smoking fast.

Holding the receipt up to the light he saw it was signed by… Charlie the Walrus.

THE BLUE THING

"Governor Smith, what are you doing, like, to thwart the impending Martian invasion?"

"Who said that?" Smith asked dozens of journalists in the conference room.

"Over here," said a petite blonde. "Susan Sands. Channel 655 News."

"Who's the tasty tidbit?" the governor mumbled to an aide.

"Summer intern. College student."

"Is she eighteen?"

"I don't know."

"Find out."

"To answer your question, Ms. Sands, I've directed the National Guard to distribute specially-coated pocket-sized mirrors to every citizen of our magnificent state—illegal aliens included."

"Why mirrors?"

"In the interest of national security, I'm not at liberty to discuss this in public. When you get your mirror two days from now, you'll find instructions etched on the back."

"Thank you, Ladies and Gentlemen," said the governor's Chief of Staff."

As they departed the conference room, the governor said, "I want to see that sweet little thing in my office right now. Do whatever it takes to get her there. Then make damn sure nobody disturbs me for an hour."

"What if she won't come?"

"Tell her I've decided to give her the very first mirror and discuss how it works."

The five-foot girl was agog when ushered into the governor's opulent office. The aide said he found out she was eighteen.

"Geeez. This is, like, beautiful," the girl said.

"Yes, it certainly is," Smith said, visualizing how she'd look during the sexual delirium she'd experience on his leather sofa.

"Please make yourself comfortable. Try the sofa."

"Oh wow. It's, like, really really comfortable."

"Tell me, Ms. Sands, do you believe in evolution, or the big bang theory?"

"Oh, like, the big bang. Like it all happened at once."

"Me too," he said. "I've often visualized it as two objects in space, ramming into each other. Fitting so nicely together. Then vibrating intensely until—wham! The big bang. Maybe even two or three big bangs."

"I, like, never thought about it that way. Do you, like, have any jobs for somebody like me?"

"We have a number of spots. But so many qualified girls have already applied. The competition is very tough. But there are ways around that. Do you have any special…talents?"

"I, like, can twirl a baton. I know how to use, like, a microwave."

"Hmm. Impressive. I'll see what I can do."

"Can I have, like, my mirror now?"

"I thought we'd probe deeper into the big bang, first" he said, brushing his hand lightly against her backside. "Ooops. Sorry,"

"It's, like, okay. Actually, I was, like, hoping you'd do that. You can, like, do it some more, if you, like, want to. With, like, both hands."

Smith pulled her to him and reached down to caress her bulbous flesh with both hands. In a split second, a vacuum pulled his hands into a vortex.

"What the hell! What's going on? I can't get my hands loose." He tried to scream for help, but a fleshy blue mass covered his mouth.

"Didn't you want to merge your body with mine?" said a deep, metallic-sounding voice. Rejoice! You've succeeded! Listen closely. I'm going to remove the blue glixer gagging your mouth. When I do, I want you to whisper. If you call out, you'll die instantly in a most horrible way."

"What do you want?" Smith asked.

"I want to know how the mirrors work."

"Never. I don't care if you kill me."

Another blue mass pierced the governor's brain and massaged its pleasure center.

The governor's body thrashed with pleasure for thirty seconds. Then it stopped.

"Wow!" said the governor. "I can't believe how intense that was. Whew."

"If you want more, tell me everything you know about the mirror. You'll get more of this every fifty words."

An hour later, an aide entered the office. The girl was nowhere to be found. The governor was on the sofa. He looked depleted, relaxed, with a smile the likes of which the aide had never seen.

"Was it that good?" the aide asked.

"Unbelievable. Listen… there's nothing to fear. Tell the National Guard to stand down. Don't distribute the mirrors. Let the Martians come. They bring wonderful benefits for mankind. In fact, I can't wait until they arrive. They have this blue thing that…"

THE ARROW

Joe was so battered by the economic turndown, he went to a store and had them make a T-shirt with large letters that glowed in the dark. It said: PLEASE ABDUCT ME.

That night, he put on the shirt, climbed his roof, lay on his back, and waited for Martians to whisk him away. But nothing happened. That didn't stop Joe from repeating this behavior night after night.

Joe's next-door neighbor, Larry, heard about this. Larry thought Joe's abduction by anybody was a great idea, considering what an obnoxious bastard he was. So, Larry went to the same store and had them make a T-shirt with even larger letters that read: PLEASE ABDUCT. However, Larry's shirt included a big arrow that pointed to the right.

When he was sure Joe was on the roof and lying down, Larry put on his new shirt and climbed onto his roof. He lay on his back and made sure the arrow on his shirt pointed to Joe's house.

An hour passed. Nothing happened.

Soon, Larry began to beseech the god of the Martians to grant Joe's wish. He reminded the Martian deity what a pain in the ass Joe was and how great life would be if Joe was removed from the planet.

Larry figured his fervent prayers had been answered when a flying saucer appeared. It hovered over Larry's roof, while the craft's commander read the message on his glowing T-Shirt. Seconds later, Larry was abducted.

Heading toward Mars at warp speed, Larry asked the saucer's alien pilot what the hell was going on.

"Aren't you wearing a T-shirt that says please abduct?"

"Yes. But you weren't supposed to abduct me. You were supposed to grab my next-door neighbor. Didn't you see the arrow on my shirt pointing to his house?"

"What's an arrow?" asked the pilot.

COMPARING PRICES

"**W**hat can I do for you, Mr. Glixi?" asked Sam Burns, Roswell's only private investigator.

"I want you to find my spacecraft."

"Look, I got no time for jokers."

"I'm not joking," Glixi said. "I'm a business man here on a special project. I'm willing to pay you ten gold bricks to find my spacecraft."

"How big are the gold bricks?"

"As big as your chair."

"Hmm. Tell you what, make it twenty bricks and I'll get to work on it right away."

"Agreed."

"Okay, let's start from the beginning. Where were you when you last saw your space ship?" Burns asked.

"In the Safeway parking lot, near the Roswell Army Air Force Base."

"What were you doing there?"

"I was inside the store checking their prices."

"You came here in a spacecraft to check supermarket prices?"

"Yes. I work for Cheap-O, the biggest chain of discount stores on Mars. We're thinking of expanding our operations to Earth. Safeway's our biggest potential competitor. We need to know their prices before we can determine if we can compete."

"So what happens if you can't beat their prices?"

"We'll forget Earth and head for Jupiter. It'd be a shame if we had to do that. The Emperor of Mars, the biggest stockholder of Cheap-O, might get angry and destroy your planet."

"Well, we wouldn't want that to happen now, would we?" Burns said, playing along with what he considered the biggest nutcase he'd ever run into.

"Yes it'd be a terrible shame. You have beautiful females on this planet. Hate to see them all vaporized. Look, I'm in a hurry. I must finish my work in Safeway and leave tonight. I'm due at a meeting early tomorrow morning to report my findings. But if I don't have my spacecraft, there's no way I can get back in time. And if I'm not back, the Emperor might think I was a victim of foul play. He'd get real mad and destroy your planet."

"Okay. I'm going to call my associates and get them over to Safeway right away."

Burns picked up the phone and asked the operator to get him Harry Jones. Jones, a police detective, answered the phone. Burns explained how he had an important Martian executive in his office, and the purpose of the Martian's visit. He figured Jones would ensure some cops would soon show up to haul Glixi—or whatever his name was—off to the nearest psychiatric hospital.

Stalling for time, Burns asked, "So what does your spacecraft look like?"

"Just like one of your planet's Ford station wagons."

"This year's model?"

"I'm not sure," said Glixi. "What year is this on Earth?"

"1947."

"How strange. On my planet it's 135,948."

"I see," Burns said, wishing the cops would hurry. "So how come your planet decided to make your spacecraft look like 1947 Ford station wagons?"

"Our research indicates that it's the most commonly seen Earthling movers in Safeway parking lots," Glixi said.

"No wonder somebody stole your car—uh—spacecraft. In this part of Earth, the Ford wagon is the car that's most often stolen. That's one thing you guys on Mars forgot to research."

"Oh dear. I sure hope the thieves change their minds and bring it back."

Cops arrived, listened to some of what Glixi had to say, and whisked him away for mental examination.

The next morning, two hours after Glixi was supposed to have presented his cost comparison briefing to the Emperor of Mars, a stolen Ford station wagon crossed the border into Mexico.

While Sam Burns listened to the marital woes of a beautiful blonde client, and three Mexicans counted their pesos for delivering a stolen Ford station wagon, the Emperor of Mars suspected Glixi was a victim of foul play.

He reached for a button marked, DESTROY EARTH, and pressed hard.

THE RUBY IDOL

Ed checked the old Portuguese treasure map to make sure he'd taken the right path. He'd come too far down the Amazon to make a mistake now.

The map showed a lone towering spire of granite. Ed found himself standing directly in front of it. The spire's very presence in the middle of the Brazilian jungle didn't add up. But neither did the fact that a huge bull elephant was standing behind the spire and blocking the path.

"What's the password?" the beast asked.

Ed was taken aback. Everybody knew elephants couldn't speak, much less converse in English.

"I'll ask you one more time. What's the password? If you don't tell me in the next few seconds, I'll smash you into a thousand pieces."

"Wait," Ed exclaimed. "Nobody told me about a password. Let me check my map. Maybe there's one here. Aw hell, I don't see one. Look, give me a break. I came thousands of miles to find the Ruby Idol. It can't be more than two miles from this very spot. Let me pass, and when I find the idol, I'll give you a million dollars—after I auction all the other ancient artifacts in the Cave of Treasures."

"Promises, promises," said the elephant. "Do you think I was born yesterday? Do you know how many guys showed up here with maps expecting to find the idol? They all promised to pay me once they found it."

"You mean others have been here looking for the same thing?"

"Yep. Those maps are a running joke throughout Brazil. I'll bet yours is like all the others. Where did you get yours? As a bonus for subscribing to *People Magazine*? From the Sears catalog? Or did McDonald's give you one when you super-sized your Big Mac?"

"No. I didn't even know they were offered through the mail or from Sears and McDonalds. I got this one from eBay. I bid ten thousand dollars and won. So what happened to all the other treasure hunters? Did you stomp them?"

"Nah. Didn't want to get grease all over my feet. I let them pass. Then snakes got 'em. There's lotsa nasty serpents all over the place in this jungle. Some are as big as the Empire State Building."

"I think you're giving me a line of baloney," Ed said. "How do I know you ain't on your way to find the idol, yourself? Maybe I oughta put a few bullets in your skull."

The elephant let out a horrible noise. Within seconds, Ed was surrounded by vicious vipers. Several bit him. He was dead before he knew what hit him."

"Thanks, guys," the elephant said to the departing vipers. "Come back in a couple hours. I'm gonna roast him for dinner. Bring the wife and kids."

Whistling a merry tune, the elephant removed all of Ed's valuables. Then he put Ed on a spit and placed the corpse over a barbeque pit. After he sprinkled his own special formula barbeque sauce over Ed, he pulled out a notebook computer and logged onto the Internet.

Minutes later, he completed the description of a new treasure map that promised to show the way to the Ruby Idol in the Amazon Jungle. When he pressed ENTER, he got a note from eBay verifying his item was up for bids around the globe.

"The best lesson I ever learned when I worked for Barnum and Bailey's Circus," the elephant said, "was that a sucker's born every minute. Because of that fundamental truism, I figure I'll be able to retire on the French Riviera in another year—from auctioning my phony treasure maps."

SAHARA

"Thanks for your help, Ms. Jones," I said to the gorgeous bank clerk. "It was nice to meet you. Actually, you're the first person who I've had a chance to talk to since I arrived yesterday. All this rain kept me inside the hotel—I'm not used to it."

"Not used to rain? Where were you that you didn't see rain?"

"The Sahara Desert. I just came back from spending three years at a monastery."

"The desert? A monastery? You mean with monks and all?

I nodded.

"Are you a monk, Mr. Walsh?"

"No."

"May I ask why you went to the Sahara Desert and for so long?" she said in a sarcastic tone.

It was impossible for me in a few sentences to describe the complex emotions, tragedies, and mystical reasons that drove me from the world and into an isolated monastery. On the other hand, her question gave me the opening I needed to ask her out.

"Well, I went as a visitor. And I decided to stay. It's quite complicated. Maybe I could explain it over dinner."

I'm not sure how I sounded. Searching her eyes, I saw what I didn't want to see.

"No, I don't think so."

"Uh... well, thanks for your help."

Intellectually, I was ready for a rebuff, but not emotionally. My feelings ganged up on me. I felt so stupid. I'd made a fool of myself by mentioning the monastery.

Suddenly, a vision of Jones and her boyfriend flashed through my mind's eye. "He'll never marry you," I said. "He's going to leave you. He's going to break your engagement tonight."

I felt worse than before. Strong intuitions always upset me. My hands trembled as I hurried from the bank.

Across the street was a coffee shop. The rain pelted my face with a force that made me wonder if the elements were urging to leave that town before I even got settled, and never come back.

I entered the shop, sat in a booth, and dropped my head into my hands. I was staring at a spot on the table when rain pounded even louder on the windows.

Rainy days. Nothing good ever happened to me on rainy days. My mother said that I was born on a rainy day—a painful breech birth that she never let me forget. My father deserted on a rainy day. The day they buried my fiancée, it poured.

"Coffee?" someone asked.

I didn't even look up. "Yes, please."

The next thing I knew, Ms. Jones from the bank was facing me. She was soaking wet.

"Why did you say such a terrible thing to me?" she asked. "Who the hell are you?"

"You know who I am. You saw my driver's license. You cashed my cashier's check for $50,000 and deposited some in my new savings account and some in my new checking account. Look, I didn't mean to say what I did. It just came out of me. Sometimes I can't help it. Especially when I'm around people I like who I can't stand to see get hurt."

"You like me? You don't even know me, Mr. Walsh. You just met me. How can you possibly like me?"

"I'm going to marry you," I said. "In six months."

My face stung from the hardest slap I'd ever felt.

When I recovered from the blow, she'd disappeared.

"Look, Mister," said a guy with a Manager's name tag. "I don't want any trouble. I don't like it when customers insult others in my coffee shop. It ain't good for business."

"I didn't insult her," I said. "I just told her something she wasn't prepared to hear."

I left immediately.

The next day, after a brisk three mile walk, I decided to go to the bank and tell Jones I was sorry. I wasn't sure what I was sorry for, because deep inside I know my intuition was true.

Jones wasn't there. When I inquired about her, a co-worker said she was ill.

Searching the phone book in my hotel room, I found her number. If she were going to be my wife, I figured I should call her. Maybe something I'd say could help her get over the hurt.

Her voice sounded weak when she answered. She started to weep when I gave my name.

"I know it hurts," I said. "I've been there. Just wanted you to know somebody's in your corner. Did he break up with you?"

"Yes. Listen to me, Mr. Walsh. I don't ever want to see you or speak to you again. This is too weird. And this stuff about marrying you—you couldn't be more wrong. If you try to see me or call me again, I'll talk to the police. I don't know what you really want, but you frighten me."

"The fright will pass," I said before she hung up.

Six months to the day I first mentioned it, she became my wife. She was radiant. I was overjoyed.

I blessed the day I walked into that bank to deposit my money.

SOCIAL CLIMBERS

"That woman they call Marcia is a snake," Stokes said.

"Hold on," said Rolf. "That woman you're insulting is my wife!"

"Look, I'm telling you the truth. She's a *real* snake in disguise. A cobra from India. I should know. I've hunted and killed dozens of cobras. I can spot one a mile away, even when they try to disguise themselves."

Rolf punched Stokes in the face. Several women screamed when he flew backward into their midst.

Rubbing his jaw, Stokes raised himself from the floor. "Busting my face isn't going to change a thing. When you wake up dead one morning from her bite, you'll see what I mean."

Rolf kicked Stokes in the ribs.

Back at their apartment, Marcia yelled at Rolf. "Why did you attack that man? You made such a terrible scene, we'll never get invited to the Mayor's Christmas party again. Do you realize the amount of ass kissing I had to do to wrangle that invitation for us?"

"He deserved it," Rolf said. "He called you a name. He's lucky I didn't cave his skull in."

"What did he call me?"

"A snake."

"Really? What do you suppose he meant by that?"

"Exactly what he said. He claimed you were a real snake. From India."

"Geez. I wonder where he ever got such a bizarre idea. Must be schizoid or something. What kind of snake did he say I was?"

"Cobra."

"Unbelievable," she said. "Look, I'll call the Mayor's aide tomorrow and apologize for you. I'll tell them you heard the guy saying sleazy things about the Mayor fooling around with a teenage girl. And you got so mad you slugged him. Hopefully, you'll become a hero for punching somebody who tried to defame our magnificent Mayor. If I can make you sound like a defender of his good name, maybe we'll get invited to His Honor's New Year's Eve bash. And if I succeed, I want you to promise me you'll control yourself, no matter what anybody says."

"I can't promise I won't belt the next jerk who calls you a name."

"Oh, Rolf. That's so sweet of you. But, stop and think of the implications for your business by if we hobnob with the elite of this city. All you gotta do is just take things on the chin without exploding. Just leave all the conniving to me, and you'll wear a tuxedo more times in one month than you've ever done in your entire life."

They kissed passionately and headed for bed.

During the night, Rolf woke to horrible screams coming from downstairs.

Racing downstairs with a pistol, he found blood everywhere. Entering the kitchen, he found a dead cobra.

He ran through the house yelling Marcia's name. But she didn't answer.

Rolf's 911 call brought a SWAT team.

SWAT found a severely wounded mongoose—a cobra's worst enemy—on Rolf's front lawn. Even stranger, the animal had a college ring on one its paws. Engraved inside was the name Stokes.

No one ever saw Marcia again.

A CHANGE OF PACE

"Hey you, get out of the way!" a cop yelled. "Let the medics through."

Jason realized the cop was pointing a baton in his direction. He moved aside quickly when he saw paramedics carrying a stretcher. As they passed him, he almost threw up at the shocking sight of the bloody, mangled mass that used to be a face.

"Looks like the Face Ripper struck again," said a stranger. "Another beautiful woman bites the dust. If this keeps up, there won't be any good looking women left in this town."

"Geez. I didn't know you guys had a serial killer problem. Otherwise, I never woulda turned off the Interstate to grab a meal."

"Doesn't matter if you did. He only attacks females."

"How many did he kill so far?"

"Twenty-seven."

"What? How come I didn't hear about this on *Fox News*, or see it in the papers?"

"The politicians keep it quiet. Otherwise, nobody would come here. That'd put lotsa people outta work. The unemployment level is already bad enough in this burg."

Though the bloody sight should have killed his appetite, Jason found himself excited and hungrier.

"Is there a half-decent restaurant near here?" he asked.

"Minnie's Hash House is pretty good. It's just two blocks from here."

While eating meatloaf, Jason realized that the Ripper might be the answer to his problems. Though he loved his stunning wife, Marcia, he was sick of her nagging. Plus, he was certain she was having a fling with a lawyer ten years his junior.

Returning home, he went to Wal-Mart and bought a dozen, hand-cranked LED lights. Then he drugged Marcia, put her and the lights in the car, and headed for the Face Ripper's town.

Arriving at the woods just outside town, he laid her on the ground, cranked the lights, placed them around her to illuminate her form, and headed back to his car. As he approached his Mustang, he heard footsteps crunching autumn leaves.

"Who's there?" he called.

"Police. What's going on here?"

"I was driving by and saw strange lights in the woods. See them over there? I went to take a look. There's a woman lying on the ground. I think she's dead. I was just going to jump in my car and drive to town to report it."

The cop pulled his pistol. "Put your hands over your head and walk slowly toward your car. Now, put your palms against the car and spread your legs real wide."

"But I didn't do anything wrong," Jason said.

"I'll be the judge of that," the cop said, slapping cuffs on Jason's wrists. "Now turn around."

The cop shinned a high-powered flashlight in Jason's face. "Hmm. Anybody ever tell you you're good looking?"

The next day, word spread quickly through town. A man was found dead in the woods with his face ripped apart, though a nearby, beautiful, unconscious woman wasn't touched.

Nobody knew what to make of it.

They didn't realize until four more good-looking men were killed that the Face Ripper was bored and needed a change of pace.

JACOB IS MISSING

"Jacob! Where have you been for three days? Everybody's been going crazy looking for you."

"Away," he said.

"I thought you were dead."

"Dead? Nah. I feel more alive than ever."

"The cops said they found your metal detector and your shoes on the beach. But couldn't find you. I thought you got too close to the water and a big wave pulled you into the ocean. I was afraid the sharks got you."

"He told me to take my shoes off."

"He who? You got lots of explaining to do. You didn't even take your heart medicine or thyroid pills, or your—"

"I don't need them anymore."

"Don't talk crazy. An eighty-year-old man needs his medicine. I'm gonna call Dr. Rothman right after I tell the cops you're back."

"Ruth, I'm tired. I've been up for three days and nights straight. I'm going to bed."

"Don't you wanna eat first? Maybe a bagel. Or some borscht."

"Nothing. I'm still stuffed. The food was great."

"Are you telling me in the middle of strolling on the beach with your metal detector, you dropped it, took your shoes off, went to the Greyhound Depot, and took a bus 200 miles to see your sister just to eat her gourmet cooking? Without even calling me?"

"I didn't go to my sister's."

"You better tell me where you were, before I bop you with this pot."

"Later," he said. "But I'll say this: we were wrong. God exists."

Then he headed to the bedroom.

Ruth called the cops to say Jacob was back. She agreed when they mentioned Alzheimer's.

Next, she called Dr. Rothman.

"Jacob's back. Says he doesn't need medicine anymore."

"Oy," Rothman said. "He'll be dead in a week. Bring him to see me this afternoon. What else did he say?"

"Something stupid. That God exists."

"Hmm. Bad sign. Maybe dementia."

"All our lives we've been hard working Communists," Ruth said. "Suddenly he disappears four days then comes back and talks God."

"Don't worry. I'll give him something to focus his mind."

When she hung up the phone, Ruth went to the bedroom. "Jacob. Wake up. I can't wait any longer. Where the hell were you?"

"First you gotta promise to believe everything I say."

"Yeah, sure," Ruth said flatly.

"I was walking down the beach, waving my detector across the sand. Got a good reading. Figured something gold. Then, suddenly there was a big noise, and this huge whale comes flying right out of the water onto the beach. Ended up just a few feet away from me."

"A whale? Around here?"

"Yeah. Massive. It opens its jaws, and out walks this guy. 'Come with me, Jacob, he says.'"

"Stop this nonsense, already, Jacob." She left the bedroom in a huff. Called Dr. Rothman again and told him what Jacob said.

"Worse than I thought," said Rothman. "Just let him talk. Act like you believe him. Maybe he'll hear how ridiculous he sounds and snap out it."

"So what happened next?" Ruth asked.

"This guy in fancy robes said, 'I'm Jonah.' He invited me in. To go for a ride. For three days and nights."

"Sounds nice. Is he coming back? Maybe I can go along next time. Maybe we can get him to take us to the Bahamas."

"Don't talk stupid, Ruth. Anyway, he says, 'take your shoes off.' I do. We went inside. The place was beautiful, like a ritzy Beverly Hills mansion. Had everything. Crystal Chandeliers. Magnificent furniture. High definition TV. Fantastic stereo. Computers. You name it. Other people were there too."

"Anybody famous?"

"No. Just folks. We stayed up three days and nights talking, eating fabulous food, drinking fine wine."

"What'd you talk about?"

"God, mostly. But we took breaks to watch TV, listen to CD's. Sinatra, Chopin, Ella Fitzgerald. Watched a Woody Allen movie. Looked through a glass bottom and saw everything in the ocean. That whale took us down pretty deep."

"Fascinating," Ruth said, shuddering.

"It was incredibly magnificent!" Jacob said. "Then the whale beached, opened its mouth, Jonah said goodbye, and here I am."

"I'm glad you're back Jacob," she said, kissing his cheek.

"Gotta tell you, Ruth. Nietzsche and Marx were wrong. God is not dead. God exists."

"Do you realize what you're saying Jacob? You've given your life to the Party. To make man the center of the universe, not some ridiculous god. Now you wanna throw all that away?"

"Absolutely. Oh, look at this. Jonah gave me a souvenir. A coin from Nineveh."

Ruth looked askance at the junky-looking piece of discolored metal.

* * * *

Dr. Rothman's physical exam of Jacob left him stupefied. Jacob was in better health than the doctor himself. "I don't understand it. It's a medical anomaly."

"What is?" Ruth asked.

"His heart is perfect. His thyroid is perfect. All his ailments, even his discolored toenails, are gone. If I didn't know he was eighty, I'd say he was thirty-five. This man's gonna outlive everybody."

Days later, Jacob was strolling on a deserted beach waving his detector across the sands. He chuckled when he dug up a diamond engagement ring.

Suddenly, a whirlwind came out of the north, a great cloud, with a fire enfolding itself. It was extremely bright and amber colored. In the midst was a fiery wheel spinning within a wheel. Upon the wheels were four living creatures. Each had four faces and four wings.

Petrified, Jacob dropped his detector and ran. But the fiery object prevented his escape.

"Come hither, Jacob," called a voice.

"Who are you?" Jacob asked, trembling.

"Fear not. Let us soar beyond the heavens. Come see that which is beyond imagination. That which was, is, and will forever be."

"Are you Ezek—?"

"Come."

A search party found Jacob's metal detector and shoes on the beach.

Ruth was certain the sharks really got him this time.

LET'S TRADE

"Can anybody hear me?"

"Yes!" exclaimed the radio operator for SETI (Search For Extraterrestrial Intelligence). "Who are you?"

"I'm the Emperor of Mars. I need your help. We have more dinosaurs than our planet's ecosystem can support. Do you need any on your planet? We'd be happy to send you some."

"Dinosaurs? I don't think so."

"Do you have any on your planet now?" asked the Emperor.

"No, they all died out long ago."

"Then you don't know what you're missing. I'd be eternally grateful, if you'd take some off my hands. In fact, I'd be pleased to offer you an all-expense paid, wonderful vacation on our planet if you accepted a few. This includes lodging at a suite in our best hotel, which is staffed by our most gorgeous and very friendly females."

"Hmm. A vacation on Mars sounds fantastic," SETI said. "What if we make a trade?"

"What do you have to offer?" asked the Emperor.

"Gorgeous rats."

"What are they?"

"The most delightful creatures on Earth. You'll love them. They're quite delicious."

"Sounds great! We'll ship our dinosaurs tomorrow."

The next day, six-billion dinosaurs arrived on Earth in flying saucers. The same day, Earth dispatched six billion rats to Mars via UPS.

Earthlings were thrilled with their new, imported dinosaurs—until they discovered Martian dinosaurs had insatiable, gargantuan appetites. The dinos ate cars, airplanes, people, London, Australia, and everything else in sight. Then they ate each other. In six months, everything on Earth was gone, except for mountains of dinosaur dung.

The Emperor of Mars was ecstatic. He'd conquered Earth without firing a shot. And he'd received enough rats to feed all his subjects for an entire year.

I NEVER FORGET A FAVOR

"**I**'m gonna make the bastard pay," I hollered when cops told me zombies had attacked and one of them had killed my wife at Santa Buffoona Fashion Mall.

"We'll have none of that vigilante talk," said the Chief of Police. "We don't want citizens violating the law by trying to get revenge. Especially when it comes to brain-munching zombies. That's our job. I gotta warn you—if you find the zombie who killed your wife and do anything nasty to it, you'll face hard time."

"You'd jail me because I killed a zombie?" I asked.

"Right. The laws of this town say nobody kills nobody, and that includes vampires, werewolves, ghouls, space aliens, and zombies. They have civil rights and the freedom to live out their existences just like you do."

"This is nuts," I said.

"I agree," the Chief whispered. "But I've sworn to maintain all the laws passed by our idiotic city council. If you don't like the laws they pass, then use the ballot box to vote the bastards out."

When the Chief left, I packed my bags. I wasn't going to live another day in that insane town called Santa Buffoona.

Then I realized that I'd lose everything by leaving, considering I'd had quite a bit of equity in my house.

I stopped packing and drank a double shot of vodka to soothe my nerves. Flopping on my easy chair, I pondered the alternatives. None seemed good, considering how much I'd lose by abandoning my house and quitting my job, especially during a recession.

I decided to stay. I'd hunt and kill the bastard zombie that ate my wife's brains.

Then I remembered the million dollar life insurance policy I'd bought for her. Suddenly, I realized the zombie actually did me a helluva favor. My wife was a royal pain, who constantly bitched about everything. She had a list of honey-do's a mile long, and was always bugging me about them. Plus, she was a lousy cook.

I placed an ad in the *Santa Buffoona Daily Herald* personals column stating that I wanted to get in touch with the zombie who attacked my wife at the mall. Witnesses said the beast was wearing a tattered, brown, short sleeve shirt with a high fashion designer logo over the pocket. I mentioned that in the ad. I included my phone number so he could call me. I said it was important that he contact me, and that he'd be absolutely delighted when he did.

I got a bunch of calls from con artists, none of which were zombies. Damn Jerks!

When the zombie I sought didn't contact me, I checked zombie information sites on the Internet. No wonder he didn't call. Turns out zombies can't read newspapers. That's because their eyes rot out during the first month following their zombification. Plus, some of them couldn't read even when they were alive, before they were changed into zombies.

I figured if they attacked shoppers at Santa Buffoona Mall, they might next raid Westgate Mall, which was five miles away. So far it had never been attacked by zombies. It had been overrun by werewolves a few years ago, but never by zombies.

The question was: when would zombies strike Westgate? Another question was: would they be the same zombies who'd stormed Santa Buffoona Mall? Never know when a whole new bunch of mall-attacking zombies might cross the southern border. Especially since Santa Buffoona was the biggest border crossing town in all of the Southwestern United States.

Doing some statistical analysis, I worked out the probabilities of a potential zombie attack at Westgate. The results suggested it was mostly likely to happen within a week.

I took a room at a motel close to the mall. During the evening of the third day, a newsflash on the TV said Westgate Mall was under siege by marauding zombies.

When I reached the parking lot, dozens of zombies were heading to the main entrance. Cops were blasting them in the head with shotguns as fast as they could pull triggers. The noise was deafening.

The Chief of Police was yelling at the zombies through a bullhorn to cease and desist. I guess he never read the Internet zombie information sites. Otherwise, he'd have known that their eardrums rot within sixty days of zombification, so they couldn't hear a thing.

I tried to reach the Chief to tell him, but a zombie grabbed me from behind. As I fell to the ground with the zombie hanging onto my neck, I heard a shotgun blast. The Chief's shot blew off the zombie's head. I was hit as well. My shoulder stung like hell and was bleeding.

Medics raced toward me, firing flame throwers. They managed to clear a path to an ambulance. Before it sped away with me inside, I noticed the headless zombie who had attacked me was wearing a tattered, brown, short sleeve shirt. Armani was embroidered over the pocket. I kinda felt sorry for the poor bastard, especially since he'd done me a favor. So, I never had a chance to thank him and give him $10,000 I'd put aside from the insurance money to reward him for getting rid of my miserable wife.

While my wounds healed, I called the morgue and asked about the disposition of the dead zombies. I bribed the Medical Examiner to locate the brown shirted body and the head to which it belonged, and put them into a deep freeze unit.

I arranged to have the body placed in Santa Buffoona Shady Oaks Cemetery, after dark.

I dug the grave myself. Dropped in that poor hapless zombie, who couldn't help that he'd been zombified when he died. I figured the dirty deed might've been done by a rogue scientist in Haiti who probably made lotsa money selling zombies to owners of sugar cane fields.

When I laid him to rest, I said some appropriate words. Then I went home to pack and head for the French Riviera with my million.

A GOOD RUBDOWN

"**Alfred**, I want a massage. Right now! My back muscles are so tense."

"Sure thing, Dear. Where's the lotion?"

"In the house! Like everything else is. Where the hell else would lotion be—up my ass?"

"Aw, c'mon, Dear. I was only asking. I thought maybe it was in your purse."

"That's your problem, you boob. Trying to think. Why bother when all your thoughts are stupid. Just like your ideas. For five years now, I've worked so you can stay home all day and screw around with your damn chemicals. And what do you have to show for it? Nothing! You haven't invented a thing, like you promised. You said within five years, we'd be on easy street. Well, if we're on easy street why the hell are we one paycheck away from financial collapse?"

"I'm making slow and steady progress," Alfred said. "I promise I'm gonna invent something spectacular very soon. It will astound the whole world. The Nobel Prize Committee will beg me to accept their prize for the most outstanding scientific achievement of the century."

"That's what you said two years ago, you freakin' moron."

"Lisa, Dear, I'm doing my best. It's very difficult to test all the permutations of my chemical mixtures at home. I really need a full laboratory, like all the big chemical companies have. Since I don't have all the equipment I need, every process takes much longer. But I'm on the verge of an important breakthrough."

"Breakthrough? Here's a breakthrough for you, you damn half-wit!" she screamed, smashing the sharp part of her high heel into his upper arm.

He yelped when the heel pierced his skin. Blood stains appeared on the sleeve of his T-shirt.

"Just because you're bleeding doesn't mean you get a break from giving me a massage. Get the damn lotion and let's get the show on the road!"

"Yes, Dear," Alfred said.

Though his wounded arm ached terribly, he remained silent. Any outburst might mean she'd punish him by purposefully turning his meals into nauseating slop for a month. Just like two months ago, when he'd forgotten to turn on the dishwasher.

"That's nice, Alfred. But then even Stalin did a nice thing or two in his lifetime. You give good massages. Maybe you oughta go to school and get a license to be a masseur. At least you'd bring home a paycheck."

"But I wouldn't have enough time to finish my experiments."

"Screw your experiments!"

"Why don't you turn over," he said, "and I'll do your front."

When she shifted, Alfred applied gobs of lotion to the front of her entire body.

She opened her eyes for the first time. "Alfred! Why in the hell is my skin bright red?"

"Must be the lotion. Might be a bad batch."

"My lotion's light blue. And it turns clear when applied to the body. What the hell did you put on me?"

"My experimental insect repellant."

Lisa screamed the foulest words he'd ever heard. She tried to slam her fist into his face, but found she couldn't move her arms. Trying to kick him, she discovered her legs were numb. "You bastard! What did you do to me?"

"I gave you a nice coating of insect repellant. Soon as it dries, I'll put your lotion on top."

"But I can't move. And I'm getting dizzy. Quick! Call 911!"

"Now how could I possibly do that? You told me last week I didn't have enough brains to figure out how to dial 911. Remember? So perhaps you'd like to remind me how to do that."

Lisa's voice grew weaker until barely audible.

"You'll be okay," he said. "You may pass out for a while. But right now I'm gonna test my latest batch of insect repellent. When the test is over, I'll remove the repellent, and you'll be fine. Okay… I'm gonna start the test."

He opened three large jars containing highly agitated wasps, mosquitoes, and bees.

"Oh dear. I've failed again," Alfred said, as mosquitoes pounced on her eyeballs, bees rammed into her ear canals, and wasps bored into her nasal passages.

GROSS MISINTERPRETATION

"**W**hat do you suppose this Martian robot is saying?" asked the President of the Reorganized States of America. "It hasn't stopped talking since you brought it to my office."

"I don't have the slightest idea, Sir," said the Chief of Staff. "Linguists from the State Department are on the way. They should be here any moment."

Meanwhile, the robot kept babbling.

"Do you think the Martians made this machine to look like them?" asked the President. "If so, I hope the ugly bastards never land. The whole world would panic."

"I have to admit," said the Defense Secretary, "I never figured anything in the universe would have a square head. Or four arms. Not to mention those eight things that are sticking out where legs should be."

At that moment the receptionist buzzed the President. "Sir, the linguists are here."

"Send them in."

A dozen nerdy-looking civil servants entered. One of them said, "That thing just spoke in an obscure Swahili dialect used by only a few hundred African natives."

"What did it say?" asked the President.

"Repeat or die."

"Now it's saying the same words in Southern Chinese," said another linguist.

"Hey, it just said the same thing in Latin," said another.

Within minutes, the robot had repeated the same words in seventy-five languages with which the linguists were fluent: "Repeat or die."

"What's that supposed to mean?" the President asked the Secretary of State.

"Sounds like a death threat. But I don't get why it's saying repeat. Repeat what?"

More linguists were brought in from nearby universities. Within five hours, over 250 languages spoken on Earth, including obscure dialects, had been identified. When the words were translated, all said the same thing: "Repeat or die."

The President's staff contacted London, Paris, Moscow, Beijing. The heads of state from those countries were also scrutinizing similar robots that kept saying, "Repeat or die," in a thousand languages and dialects.

The Secretary General of the Amalgamated Nations convened an emergency session. A robot was taken to the General Assembly Meeting Hall. Representatives from Earth's seven hundred and fifty six nations listened to what the robot said. All confirmed that it was repeating the same words: "Repeat or die."

After two days of the most intense international discussions ever held, the Secretary General asked for advice from the world's religious leaders. Afterward, he requested airtime over all the world's TV and radio stations.

"Citizens of Earth. This is the Secretary General of the Amalgamated Nations. It is my duty to inform you that members of the AN representing every nation, plus leaders of the world's religions have conferred and agreed on the following four points:

One: Talking robots have been dispatched to our planet from Mars. They have been found on every land mass and body of water on our planet.

Two: These robots are repeating a message in every language and dialect known to mankind. The message consists of three words: repeat or die.

Three: We have decided that the three words are a warning informing us that we must repeat everything we do. If we fail to comply, we must assume that Martians will kill everyone on Earth.

Four: To avoid genocide, from now on we must repeat every behavior twice. For example, eat breakfast twice in a row. Brush your teeth twice. Read the newspaper, then read it again immediately. Put a sock on, take it off, and put it on again. And so forth. We believe this is the only way we can save humanity from total annihilation."

Everyone on Earth was notified to repeat their behavior through radio announcements, phone calls, TV newscasts, email, telegrams, loudspeakers, smoke signals, jungle drums, handbills, Morse code, letters, road signs, semaphore, graffiti, theatre marquees, banners, telepathy, sky writing, tweets, and sign language.

The repetition of all behaviors was maddening. Nations were in chaos. People bought SUVs, then bought them again, just seconds later. Babies that stopped crying had to be pinched to make sure they cried again. Commuters caught busses, got off at their destinations, took other busses back to their places of origin, then repeated the trips.

Nevertheless, seven days later, a million Martian spacecraft surrounded Earth and fired death rays. Within hours, everything on Earth was reduced to smoldering ashes.

"Why didn't those stubborn idiots obey?" yelled Mars' fanatically religious Emperor. "They could've saved themselves. I wasted billions manufacturing and shipping robots to their miserable planet to warn them. Why were they so willing to be obliterated?"

He ordered his aides to form a Blue Ribbon Panel and conduct a thorough investigation. Only the best minds on Mars were appointed to the panel.

Three months later, the panel announced their findings.

"Because of budgetary restrictions caused by our ongoing wars with Mercury, Saturn, Neptune, and Uranus, we decided to save money by outsourcing the talking robot project. Goofus, one of Neptune's moons, was low bidder. By outsourcing we saved one billion-trillion jeboolas. However, we didn't know that Goofus does not educate its citizens. Goofonians are hopelessly illiterate. Not familiar with any alphabet, they made a one-character error when installing the robot voice program. This caused the robots to say REPEAT instead of REPENT."

LUCKY CHARM

"I've got one last dirty trick in mind," said Wagner, the outgoing President of the Amalgamated States of Zamboozia.

"What's that?" asked the Attorney General.

"How about rounding up every pickpocket in the nation, transporting them to Washington, and letting them roam through the crowds on Herkimer's inaugural day? Our cut will be twenty percent of the take. It'll make a nice consolation prize, considering how we lost an election because of a stupid, dumbed-down, easily swayed electorate."

"Wonderful idea," said the AG.

While the plan was being prepared, a disgruntled aide to outgoing President Wagner told the Chief of Staff for President-Elect Herkimer.

When advised of the dastardly plan, Herkimer, purported to be the wisest man in all Zamboozia, said, "We can't let this happen to the honorable and wise citizens of this great nation who were smart enough to elect me. Here's what to do. Issue this notice: everyone who attends my inauguration must have all pockets removed from their trousers. This way the brigands won't be able to steal a red cent. Anyone who refuses to comply will lose their healthcare and be investigated by the Internal Revenue Producing Agency."

"Sir, that's a magnificent decision. The people of this nation will love you even more. Consider it done."

Every radio, TV, and internet news outlet broadcast the no-pockets requirement, twenty-four hours a day for two solid weeks.

Even commercials mentioned the no-pockets rule. A commercial appeared on TV in which several men were walking down the parade route on Inauguration Day with cans of Sparky—Herkimer's favorite soft drink—in their pockets. They were confronted by police, who reminded them, that they should've cut off their pockets, and bought the special Sparky cans that came with wrist bands. The cops cut the pockets from the offender's trousers, and gave them complimentary cans of wrist-band Sparky. The happy offenders made comments about always observing the rules made by the soon-to-be President, because he was the wisest man in all of the sixty-seven Amalgamated States of Zamboozia. The commercial closed with the Sparky jingle that some say was adapted from a catchy tune written by Karl Marx, back in the 1800s.

The millions who expected to attend didn't even question the idea. Pockets across the nation were quickly removed from trousers.

When the President-Elect was advised that 17-million surplus pockets were now available for a better use, he told his future head of the Commerce Department to collect them before the inauguration, and send them to grocery stores. They could be used to package very small grocery items; thus, saving the environment, and reducing global warming by at least ten degrees.

When asked how that could lower the overall temperature, Herkimer told them to just do as they were told, because he was smarter than them.

Herkimer was the only person attending the inaugural festivities who had trousers in his pockets. He needed them to carry the good luck charms he'd accumulated, to which he attributed magical powers. And he was right. They'd transformed a bland person, who knew very little about anything, into a super star. No doubt his charms—especially a blessed arrowhead given to him by a shaman— were good juju. They'd caused his incredibly rapid rise to power as well as a landslide election in which he received 99.9% of the vote.

On Inauguration Day, Herkimer mounted the festooned platform, as millions roared approval. He took several bows, as the attendees yelled, "Encore." He wondered what glorious accolades they'd shout after he'd actually spoken the first word of his swearing-in speech.

Suddenly, a lovely woman fainted in the first row.

"Wait. One of our wonderful citizens has just fainted. I certainly understand why. Few can view me in person without doing so. Anybody have some water to give the lovely lady?"

Nobody on the platform had water.

A boy ran toward the stage. "I don't got water, but I got Sparky." He loosened the wrist band holding the soft drink can to his wrist.

"Let that boy through," Herkimer said.

"What's your name, Son?" he asked, wondering why the boy hadn't fainted at hearing his voice.

"Groucho."

"Wonderful name. I assume you are one of our nation's esteemed undocumented emigrant citizens?"

"Yep."

"Fantastic. As you know, as of today, you'll be documented and granted automatic citizenship in fulfillment of one of my campaign promises. How old are you Groucho?"

"Ten and three."

"Well, at exactly one o'clock this afternoon, you'll become ten and eight by Presidential Decree. That will make you old enough to vote, drink, and run for president in the next election. That's another of my campaign promises which will go into effect this very day."

Herkimer then told an aide, "Bring the fainted woman forward."

Leaning toward her, Herkimer put the Sparky to her lips. As he poured some into her mouth, he said, "I baptize you in the name of the President, Senate, and House of Representatives of the Amalgamated States of Zamboozia." Grabbing her nose between two fingers, he squeezed and shouted, "Be healed!"

She sprang to life. As she thanked him profusely, billions around the planet, who were watching TV, wept openly. People as far away as Iceland were joyous that they'd managed to illegally vote for Herkimer, several times each.

Patting Groucho's head, Herkimer promised an extra three grains of rice per person would be added to his family's monthly food allowance.

After kissing Herkimer's hand, Groucho returned to the crowd and disappeared among its great unwashed masses.

Herkimer began his five hour speech that preceded the actual swearing-in ceremony. "Citizens of this great nation. I want to glurp. I mean glop..."

Frantic, Herkimer reached into his pocket to fondle the arrowhead, his most powerful talisman. But it was gone.

On the verge of panic, he yelled "Hiddle-diddle," to the nearest Secret Service officer.

Though he spoke gibberish, the crowds applauded every word. In fact, when he said, "Glop," he received the most thunderous applause of the entire ceremony.

Herkimer was not reelected. The opposing party nominated someone named Groucho who was even more mesmerizing, and made even greater promises.

When Groucho mounted the platform to take the Presidential Oath, the arrowhead he'd picked from Herkimer's pocket four years earlier, was permanently welded to his body.

TASTY TIDBITS

"**W**hat's happening?" asked Zombie One.

"I decided to leave Haiti and go to America," said Zombie Two. "I'm tired of munching on brains of villagers I catch in the jungle. After a while, they all taste alike. I need a big change of diet. I hear American brains taste far different, because they eat lots of pepperoni pizza."

"What's pepperoni pizza?"

"I'm not sure. When I get to America and find out, I'll send you a post card to tell you."

"By the way," said One. "Where is America?"

"Across the ocean."

"So how are you gonna get there?"

"I built a row boat."

"What's that?"

"Something you make out of banana leaves. It floats on water. You get inside, and run your hands through the water real fast to make the boat go wherever you want it to."

"Does it have room for me?" asked One.

"Nope," said Two. "If you wanna go to America, you'll have to build your own boat. There's plenty of banana leaves in the jungle to do that."

Just then, One felt the onset of sharp hunger pangs. He bid goodbye to his friend, and headed deeper into the Haitian jungle. He didn't have to forage for food very long. An unfortunate native from a nearby village, who was heading to a voodoo ceremony, crossed One's path.

While munching on the villager's brains, One realized that what Two had said about the need for a dietary change was quite true. The warm, bloody, mushy, grey matter he spooned from his victim's skull with a sharpened ice-cream scoop tasted as bland as the last batch he'd eaten. He wondered if American brains were truly better from eating so much pepperoni pizza.

As he wiped gray matter from his chin with his tattered sleeve, his calcified brain was struck with an idea. He'd search the jungle to find where Zombie Two kept his row boat, steal it, and head for America.

One searched the jungle that night, but didn't find anything made out of banana leaves. Next, he headed to the beach. After several hours, he found Two's row boat. Pushing it into the water, he jumped inside. Unfortunately, the leaves couldn't support his weight, and the boat sank.

None of this would've happened if Haitian taxpayers hadn't defeated a hotly-contested bond proposition to build schools for zombies. Had the bond passed, Zombie One and Zombie Two would've attended and learned that although banana leaves float, they aren't strong enough to hold passengers or cargo. Especially on the ocean. Also, they would've have learned how far away America actually was. Even more important, they would've learned they could get there easily and quickly by taking an airplane, and exactly what pepperoni pizza was. Further, with a math class or two, zombies who wanted to build row boats would've learned enough to calculate how strong a boat had to be to hold passengers and cargo.

Meanwhile, completely ignorant of all of the above, it was inevitable that when Zombie One stole Zombie Two's row boat and jumped in, the boat sank. When it did, a school of sharks sensed One's presence and tore him to shreds. Afterwards they complained to each other about how bland he tasted. But they didn't complain about blandness nearly as much as Zombie One did. That's because sharks are more pragmatic then zombies. Sharks accept whatever they can get in the way of meals over and above the tasteless fish that comprise the greatest portion of their daily caloric intake.

Hopefully in the near future, Haitian taxpayers will see the error of their ways and do something to educate their zombie population. If not, they should consider setting up schools for sharks to teach them to avoid eating zombies. Another option is to teach sharks about food additives, such as monosodium glutamate, so they can sprinkle it on zombies to make them taste better.

MULTIPLE DIMENSIONS

Harry wandered aimlessly through the park trying to decide if he should shoot or hang himself.

He'd found Lisa's note on the kitchen table an hour earlier. She said not to look for her. She and her new love were leaving the country.

After heaving three times in the bushes, Harry decided to shoot himself.

Spotting a bench in an isolated section of the park, he sat down, removed a pistol from his pocket, and pressed it against his head. As he visualized lovely Lisa for the last time, he was suddenly distracted by the sounds of someone calling for help. The pleas seemed to be coming from a scrunched paper bag at the other end of the bench.

"I must be going nuts," he mumbled. "Lisa often said I was. Maybe she's right. Maybe that's why she found somebody else."

Once again he heard distressful sounds coming from the bag.

Overcome with curiosity, he looked inside.

The sight of a tiny, gorgeous, naked female startled him.

"My lord! She's only a few inches long. What kind of female creature has blue skin and orange pubic hair? Why is she tied up?"

Laying her on the bench, he quickly untied the threads that bound her. He was startled when she levitated to his face and kissed his mouth. The touch of her lips was so electrifying, he found himself closing his eyes and falling into the sweetest emotional abyss he'd ever experienced.

She kissed him again. And again. And again.

Breathless, he panted, "What... are... you... doing... to... me?"

A melodic voice said, "Thanking you. For saving me. I want to feel more of you. Cover me with your hand. Hold onto the bench tightly with your other hand. Now I'm *really* going to thank you."

When he complied, his body convulsed from waves of unspeakable pleasure. His mind's eye was filled with flashes of brilliant, pulsating, swirling colors that dissolved into a peaceful, golden haze.

Regaining consciousness, he checked his watch. Two hours had passed. He wondered what the hell had happened. The last thing he remembered was getting ready to pull the trigger. Then he recalled the cries from a paper bag and the creature he'd found inside.

The bag was there, but the tiny, naked female was nowhere in sight.

"What the hell's going on? Why would I hallucinate just as I was about to kill myself? I must have a damn brain tumor. How rotten can my life get?"

Grabbing the pistol, he raised it to his head. But something pushed it away. That's when she flew to his lips and kissed him again. "I'm here," she said. "And I'm yours if you want me. Don't kill yourself. If you die, then I too will die."

Harry couldn't believe what was happening. Nor could he comprehend the incredible irony of losing Lisa, then suddenly gaining the affections of the strangest, but most beautiful creature he'd ever seen.

"Why do you want to destroy yourself?" she asked in a melodious voice.

Ludicrous as it seemed, he explained his grief. While he spoke, she sat on his shoulder and softly stroked his hair. He found her touch soothing, comforting, enticing.

Speaking to him sweetly, she convinced him to forget suicide. Kissing him again, she swore she'd love him forever, and that he'd never need anyone else.

"Take me home with you," she said so gently, his heart was moved.

Suddenly, it didn't matter who she was, where she came from, and how she came to be tied up inside a paper bag.

When they arrived at his house, he wrapped one of Lisa's scented lace handkerchiefs around her shoulders. Using a ruler, he found she was only three inches long.

* * * *

Inseparable, their love blossomed. During the daytime, she sat on his shoulder, purring. At night, she slept on his pillow, sighing.

He found himself wishing they were the same size so they could drink of love to the fullest.

If only my appendage were minuscule. If she drives me crazy from her kisses, imagine what'd it'd be like if we consummated our love.

His yearnings grew so powerful, he decided to consult a plastic surgeon. Without explaining why, he asked if were possible for the doctor to greatly reduce the size of his appendage.

"You want to be downsized?" asked the doctor. "That's the weirdest thing I ever heard. The entire male population of this planet is looking for ways to upsize. And here you asking for teensy. I suggest you consult with Dr. Brown. He's the best psychiatrist in town."

Instead of a psychiatrist, Harry visited a priest and explained his situation.

"The Almighty has created all creatures," said the priest. "If she's really from another planet, and she has emotions and a body that functions like an Earth women, then she too is a woman. A woman made for man. So what are your intentions?"

"We're deeply in love. We want your blessing. And we want you to marry us."

"I cannot. What you want is illicit. The difference in your dimensions proves it. This love can never be consummated. Do the honorable and moral thing—find a male of her species. Arrange for them to meet. Let nature take its course. She's not right for you, no matter how wonderful she makes you feel."

When Harry told her of the priest's refusal, she wept.

The next day, she disappeared.

Inconsolable, Harry searched everywhere to no avail. Then he found a note under his pillow. He was almost afraid to read it, considering Lisa too had left him a note when she deserted him.

"I've gone back to Mars," it said. "There's a new hormonal treatment. I'll return as soon as I can. Love and kisses forever. Your Glixa."

Three months passed. Harry was miserable beyond description.

Then one night, he was awakened by her scrumptious kisses.

"It worked," she said, crawling in bed, trying to snuggle her twenty-foot body next to his six-foot frame.

A MILLION DOLLAR EXPERIMENT

"**I** promise you, this won't hurt at all," whispered Dr. Zangara, as he sharpened a scalpel. "And even if it did hurt a tiny bit, remember that I'm paying you a million to participate in this experiment."

"Won't you even give me a little hint about what kind of experiment?" Sarah, the patient, asked.

"Let's keep it a surprise. I'm going to ask you to trust me like the nation of Albania did when they awarded me their Sharpest Scalpel In The World Prize."

"Oh my. You should've told me about that sooner. I suppose a little pain here and there won't be so bad. Especially at the hands of such a world famous doctor."

"I assure you, you won't feel a thing. And before you know it, you'll be in Neiman Marcus buying whatever your heart desires with your million. My assistant will now put a little cloth over your nose. You'll smell roses for a few seconds, then you'll drop off into a deep and wonderfully restful sleep. Ready?"

"Yes, Doctor," she said, eager to check out the latest designer shoes and handbags at Neiman Marcus. "Oh, what a wonderful odor," she added before passing out.

Zangara flopped into a Lazy Boy chair, setting it to the most extreme reclining position.

"Okay" he said to Smith, his assistant. "Move the gurney so that her head is exactly four inches from my feet. Use the tape measure I gave you. Good. Now, carefully insert the scalpel between the toes of my left foot, with the sharp end pointed away from my feet. Yes, that's it. Now, as I lean forward, tie my hands behind my back. Ouch! Not so tight."

"Sorry, Doctor," said Smith, a temporary employee provided by the Amalgamated Autoworker's Union. Though he'd never witnessed surgery on a human body before, he was obligated as a member of the union's job bank to take whatever work the union found for him that day.

""Now hold the mirror I gave you over her head," said Zangara. "Turn it toward me a bit. Yes, that's it. You are about to witness medical history. You'll be able to tell your grandchildren that you were involved. You see, I'm about to perform the most delicate brain operation known to mankind. But instead of using my hands, which would be no challenge whatsoever, I'm going to use my left foot—even though I'm a righty. If

I'm successful—and I have no reason to believe otherwise—I should win a Nobel Prize. I'll be honored by every nation in the world. I'll be *Time Magazine's* Man of The Year. I'll be on Oprah, Rush Limbaugh, Jay Leno, *Fox News*, *CNN*, *BBC*, and every major network in the world. The President will have me for dinner, not to mention every world leader. And best of all, I'll be able to charge anything I want for future surgeries. Oh, before I forget. I assume you aren't affected by the sight of blood."

"Makes me puke my guts out," Smith said.

"Aw, hell. I told my receptionist to ensure the union would send somebody with a strong stomach. Well, it's too late to get somebody else. Just look away when I start cutting. At the count of three I'm going to make the first incision. One. Two. Three."

Smith closed his eyes. But when Zangara said, "Three," he got so curious, he opened them just as Zangara sliced the patient's head open.

Blood spurted everywhere.

Horrified, Smith vomited violently, splashing the patient's skull and Zangara's feet.

The sudden onrush of Smith's putrid, undigested chili, onions, and beer startled Zangara, causing his foot to jerk. As a result, the scalpel accidentally slashed the patient's neck. Her head fell to the floor.

"Look what you made me do!" Zangara hollered. "Quick! Untie me! There's still time to save her."

Fumbling with the knot, Smith vomited all over the back of Zangara's surgical gown. The smell was so ghastly, Zangara threw up all over the severed head.

The head's eyes popped open, its nose twitched. Within seconds, the head expelled gobs of green mucous on Smith's shoes. This caused Smith to heave again, which caused Zangara's stomach to lurch and expel more of its contents.

When everybody stopped regurgitating and expelling, Zangara thought to himself, *Eureka! I've found a cure for sinus problems.* "Tell me, Smith, do you have any trouble with your sinuses?"

"Do I ever," Smith replied, as he wiped chunks of chili from his chin. "Why do you ask?"

"I'll cure you for free. And pay you the million she would have received, had she survived. Just imagine what you can do with all that money. You can move to Hollywood. Buy a limo. Live the good life. No more lineups at the union hall. And best of all, no more sinus problems."

"Hmm. What do I gotta do?"

"Just lay down on the gurney. I'll put this nice little cloth over your nose. In a few seconds, you'll smell roses. In an hour or so, you'll wake up fully refreshed with a million to spend. What do you say?"

Smith showered, then climbed onto the gurney. Zangara covered Smith's nose with the cloth.

When Smith passed out, Zangara put a fresh scalpel between his toes and hopped on one foot to the Lazy Boy. When he was fully reclined, he put a mirror between the toes of his left foot, pointing toward Smith's skull.

"This time, nobody will rudely interrupt my experimental brain operation."

He visualized himself on the cover of *Time Magazine*, as he sliced Smith's head open.

At a critical point in the operation, Zangara's left leg suddenly cramped and went into spasms.

While stuffing two severed heads into the garbage disposal, Zangara decided to take the million he would have paid his victims and go shopping at Nieman Marcus for himself.

"There's always tomorrow," he muttered. "And the way the economy's going, it'll be easy to find willing participants. Might even get them to agree for just the cost of a few months' worth of their mortgage payments."

QUESTIONNAIRE

When Charlie left the bakery with a bag full of donuts, he was abducted by Martians. One of them handed him a clipboard and said, "We won't keep you long. Please answer all the questions on the attached form, then you're free to go."

The questions reminded Charlie of a job application, except for the last which asked, "WHAT IS THE STICKIEST STUBSTANCE YOU KNOW OF AND WHY?"

Charlie thought of the bag of donuts in his lap when he wrote, "Jelly donuts, because the gooey stuff inside sticks to everything."

When they released him, Charlie ran home to tell his wife.

That day, a citizen of Neptune was abducted by Martians and asked the same questions, except for the last one, "WHAT IS THE HUNGRIEST THING YOU KNOW OF AND WHY?"

The Neptunian wrote, "Glib-jibbers, because they are always hungry and eat everything in sight. They ate all our buildings, vehicles, trees, pavements, tools, etc. That's why everybody on my planet lives in caves."

When they released the Neptunian, he ran home to tell his wife.

A month later on Earth, reports of missing bakeries flooded the Amalgamated Nations. Before long, every bakery on Earth mysteriously disappeared. Nobody knew what to make of it.

Soon after, residents of Neptune discovered they could leave their caves without being eaten by glib-jibbers for the first time in a thousand years. The entire glib-jibber population had mysteriously disappeared. Nobody knew what to make of it.

* * * *

On December 21, 2012, the last day on Earth's Mayan calendar, some Earthlings awaited impending doom, while others thought the whole Mayan thing was stupid.

A few minutes before midnight, something began to fall from Earth's sky. Everyone who ran outside to witness the event was amazed to find countless jelly donuts falling from above. Parents woke up kids so they could see the strange event. Before long, the kids found they could slide in the jelly that popped out of the donuts when they smashed against trees, roofs, cars, ground.

Unfortunately, donuts fell without letup for forty days, covering the entire globe. On the forty-first day, Martians dropped by parachute the three-billion glib-jibbers they abducted from Neptune.

Within a month, the glib-jibbers gobbled everything on Earth. When they ran out of food, they turned on each other until only one was left.

A passing flying saucer destroyed the last glib-jibber.

"Your highness," said a Martian general to the Emperor of Mars. "We have conquered Earth without losing a single soldier. Your brilliant plan for conquest is an incredible success. This is the greatest achievement in the history of warfare. What's more, you now own 607,865 jelly donut factories that we abducted from Earth. Instead of conquering the rest of the planets in our Solar System, why not declare peace and sell our enemies jelly donuts? You have a total monopoly. Imagine how rich you'll become!"

"Great idea," said the Emperor. "Meanwhile, let's quadruple the calories in each donut and include something that's addictive. That'll make our customers super fat. Then they'll all die from obesity. When that happens, I'll own all the planets in the universe without losing a single soldier."

All worked according to plan. The Emperor became fantastically rich.

When all his customers throughout the Solar System died of obesity, the Emperor ended up with 607,865 idle donut factories with millions of unemployed donut makers. He didn't survive the rebellion and resulting civil war, which destroyed almost every soul on Mars.

Realizing they were the only living beings left in the entire Solar System, the horrified Martian survivors reactivated some donut factories, raised the calorie count of each donut to 20,000, and ate themselves to death.

INVISIBLE MAN

Like most cities in 2012, Santa Buffoona was severely affected by the Great Recession. The city treasury was nearly depleted, and tax collections were way below normal because of a large number of foreclosed and abandoned homes. Consequently, Santa Buffoona was on the verge of laying off city employees, including police and firefighters.

After a secret brainstorming session with the City Council on how to quickly raise desperately needed funds, Mayor Jones announced the capture of the Invisible Man by the city's recently-formed Monster Catcher Squad. An article in Santa Buffoona's only newspaper, *No News Is Good News*, said the Invisible Man was held captive at the courthouse, and citizens could view him for a nominal fee.

"Step right up, ladies and gentlemen," yelled the Mayor, "and see the greatest show on Earth. The one, the only, Invisible Man! Get your tickets now to see the only Invisible Man in captivity."

"Where do you keep him?" asked a woman.

"In the court house right behind me. He's locked in a gorilla cage."

"Why do I have to pay to see him? Wasn't he caught by our police department's Monster Catcher Squad? Don't my taxes pay their salaries?"

"Yes, but it costs a bundle to feed this character. He has a huge appetite. Staying invisible burns lotsa calories. Besides the cost of upkeep, we paid a fortune for the oversize gorilla cage he occupies."

The woman gave the mayor a dollar and went inside. A heavily armed policeman took her ticket and said, "You have three minutes. When your time's up, you'll hear a buzzer."

Entering the room, she saw the gorilla cage and a huge sign proclaiming, PLEASE DO NOT FEED THE INVISIBLE MAN. A bed, chair, table, and TV were inside the cage. The table was covered with candy wrappers, beer bottles, and empty soup cans. The TV was tuned to a baseball game. Standing next to the cage was a member of the Santa Buffoona Monster Catcher Squad, brandishing an assault rifle.

"I can't see The Invisible Man," she said, scanning the cage. "Is this the time of day when he becomes invisible?"

"He's always invisible, Ma'am."

"Oh. Is there any way to tell where he is right now?"

"He usually sits at the table and watches TV when he's awake. Once in a while he lifts a beer bottle to take a swig. That's when things get spooky. The bottle seems to move through the air on its own. Then beer comes out and floats in mid-air as it moves down his invisible throat into his invisible gut."

"How fascinating. When does he usually drink beer?"

"Hard to say. Nobody can predict when he'll get thirsty."

"Do you think he'll eat something in the next few minutes? I'd love to see chicken noodle soup floating in the air."

"He had lunch right before you came," the guard said.

"How come I don't see any soup floating in his invisible stomach right now?"

"He must be in bed under the covers. He usually takes a nap after lunch."

"Can I put my ear next to the bars to see if I can hear him snoring?"

"Sorry. It's against the law to go beyond the yellow line in front of the cage. This guy's very dangerous. If you get too close, he might grab your head and tear it off."

"Oh my. I certainly don't want that to happen. Can I say something to him?"

"Sure. But he won't answer. He's deaf."

She called out anyway. "Hey, Mr. Invisible Man. How you doing in there?"

The buzzer sounded. "Time to leave, Ma'am," the guard said.

The woman was so intrigued, she went back a dozen more times that week. However, she never got there at the right time to see The Invisible Man drink beer or eat soup.

Tens of thousands visited the cage. Soon the city's coffers were overflowing.

An investigative journalist secretly bugged the room. A week later, somebody tipped the mayor that the District Attorney planned to raid the courthouse the next day and prove the Invisible Man wasn't inside the gorilla cage.

The night before the raid, the mayor announced on *CNN*, *Fox News*, and *BBC* that the Invisible Man had escaped. He assured viewers around the world that Santa Buffoona's most highly trained detectives were hot on the culprit's trail. They expected to capture him within twenty-four hours.

Two years later, The Invisible Man was still at large. Meanwhile, tens of millions from every corner of the globe traveled to Santa Buffoona and paid $25 to see the cage in which he'd been held prisoner. For an additional $2, visitors were allowed to sit in the Invisible Man's chair for a few seconds.

372,164 women found themselves irresistibly drawn to the bed in which he'd slept and paid an extra $5 to lay on it for ten seconds. One claimed in the *Weekly Confidential Tattler* she'd become pregnant by doing so. Pictures of her invisible twin babies were published in the same magazine nine months later.

That year, millions of visitors paid $10 to have their pictures taken with the mayor inside the Invisible Man's cage. Millions paid $15 each for invisible souvenirs.

Thousands swore that when they held their photographs at a certain angle, they could see the Invisible Man standing in the background smiling and waving.

When the first year's income from the tourist attraction topped a billion dollars, Jones was appointed mayor for life. In fact, the City Fathers were so happy with the incredible annual income generated by the Invisible Man, they didn't care if the entire citizenry defaulted on their mortgages and failed to pay any taxes whatsoever.

Soon, Santa Buffoona will announce the capture of the Invisible Loch Ness Monster. A huge lake is under construction within city limits. So are gigantic hotels to house the millions of expected visitors.

SNAKE'S ASHES

I couldn't prove that security guards at the movie studio's amusement park murdered my teacup poodle, Snake, because there were no witnesses. The studio insisted he died by his own hand. No way! Snake was strong, vital, with so much to live for.

The awful events began when we boarded the tourist tram at the studio's amusement park in Hollywood. With Snake snuggled comfortably in my camera case, I boarded a tram full of tourists. Once the tour began, we crossed a bridge that almost collapsed, and went through a tunnel that made us seem as if we were turning upside down. Snake liked that. He laughed a lot.

Next we found ourselves inside a darkened building. Suddenly, King Kong attacked the tram. Snake went ballistic. He leapt from the camera case, charged the huge monster, and ripped its head off.

Security cops arrested Snake and took him away in chains. They ignored my frantic explanations about Snake's highly developed protective instincts, calling him a horrendous terrorist.

Snake's attack caused so much damage, the tram portion of the tour, was suspended indefinitely. They said Snake was in big trouble. They threatened me with a 100-million dollar suit for bringing an untamed, savage beast onto their grounds. They were infuriated even more when they discovered I hadn't bought a ticket for Snake.

They told me Snake would be caged at Mother Bates' house, on the studio's back lot until the Los Angeles Police arrived. I hated the idea of him locked up in a place where several bloody murders had occurred.

I slipped a tram operator twenty dollars to take me to that creepy house on the hill above the Bates Motel. When I arrived, an attendant said Snake was dead. He'd managed to escape from the cage, then jumped out Mother Bates' bedroom window. Searching the area, they found him dead in one of the shower stalls at the Bates Motel. They called it suicide, saying he'd sliced his own paws and bled to death. They figured Snake had realized the enormity of his crime and couldn't face up to the hard time he'd get in prison. Upon discovering his corpse, they'd immediately taken it behind the motel and cremated it.

I asked how many people witnessed my dog's cremation.

They said, "None."

What liars! Snake wouldn't kill himself, no matter what. Why did they burn his body before I could arrange an autopsy? And just how many wounds did he have? Did he slit his own paws? Or had somebody done it for him?

I demanded Snake's ashes. Some studio big-wig said they'd already been scattered. He also said now that Snake was gone they'd dropped all charges against Snake and me.

Glad to be off the hook, I immediately left their property.

A few days later, a package arrived from the studio. It contained a small urn and a letter of condolence and apology. The letter said they'd made a terrible error. They'd found Snake's ashes behind the Bates Motel. They collected and placed them in the enclosed urn. They also included a complimentary pass to a nearby Chinese buffet restaurant as a token of their sincerity.

The day before I left to bury Snake's ashes at Daisy Hill Puppy Farm—the place where Snoopy the famous cartoon dog was born— something ate at my gut. What if these weren't Snake's ashes? What if they belonged to some unfortunate, ragged, mongrel pooch they'd found wandering around the Bates Motel? What if this were a conspiracy?

I took the ashes to a lab for a chemical analysis. Result: rodent ashes.

I swore everlasting hatred and vengeance.

I sold my house and bought a recreational vehicle. Consequently, I never stayed longer than one day in the same place. Made it harder for anyone to track me.

* * * *

I chuckled when I read the small story in the *Los Angeles Times*: FIFTH DOG FOUND HACKED TO DEATH IN MOTEL SHOWER.

The story said over the past two months, maids at various Los Angeles motels had found a total of five dogs hacked to death in shower stalls. Curiously, all dogs belonged to movie studio executives. Detectives were investigating. Some feared a serial dog killer was on the loose.

Six months later, the murdered dog story was splashed across the front page of the country's major newspapers. The count was up to fifty-seven. All massacred dogs belonged to executives of the movie studio where Snake died. All doggies had been hacked to death by butcher knives. Every murder occurred in motel room shower stalls. In an act of utter contempt, the killer sent urns containing the cremated ashes of rodents to the dogs' owners.

The article included pitiful quotes from children of movie studio executives, whose doggies had been murdered and cremated. The FBI's

Behavioral Science Department added a few paragraphs discussing the profiles of serial dog killers.

Somebody offered $100,000 for information leading to the arrest and conviction of the dog murderer.

* * * *

I found kidnapping and assassinating dogs owned by top executives of the movie studio quite exhilarating and loads of fun. Unfortunately, like all good things, the thrill began to dissipate. But, the flames of vengeance that seared my soul remained as strong as ever. I decided to kidnap other pets belonging to movie executives and execute them. But first, I bought a bunch of cute doggie costumes.

Over several months, I kidnapped lots of other pets belonging to studio executives. Before I killed them, I dressed them in the costumes that made them look like my beloved Snake.

Let's see, there was Tommy, and Lisa, and Mary, and Billy, and...

THE BONUS

When the New York Transit cop moved to the next subway car, the skinhead with a swastika neck tattoo approached an old woman. She frowned and waved her hand as if shooing a horsefly.

I moved toward him. "What's your problem?" I asked.

"Nothing a few bucks can't fix," he said. "Can you spare some?"

"I don't give money away. But, if you're hungry, I'm good for a burger and fries."

"Yeah, I'm hungry. I ain't et all day."

"I know a good burger place at the next stop," I said.

* * * *

"This country's turning into a Third World toilet," the skinhead said, his mouth full of greasy fries. "Only the Master Race can save it." Popping open a battered wallet and flashing a photograph, he added, "This is one who should be running the country. He'd shut the borders, put up a fence, and get rid of all the mongrel vermin—overnight."

"I knew him well," I said, pointing to his picture of Adolf Hitler.

"You knew the Fuehrer?"

"Yes. Actually I still do."

"Bullcrap. He's been dead over sixty years. And you don't look more than forty."

"You can't tell a book by its cover. I was his personal physician. In fact, I'm twenty years his senior."

"What the hell are you talking about? That'd make you way over a hundred years old."

"Correct. You see, I made a monumental discovery back in 1935. Something the world has been seeking for thousands of years—the Fountain of Youth."

"You're kidding me," skinhead said.

"I can prove it. How'd you like to meet the very man whose picture you have in your wallet—whose symbol is emblazoned on your neck?"

"What? Meet Hitler? Oh, man, I'd give my left nut if that was possible."

"Then get a knife and slice it off, because he's alive, and living right here in Manhattan."

I pressed a key on my cell phone. "Hello? Mein Fuehrer? Do you have a moment to speak to an ardent admirer? He's fallen on hard times, but I think he may be of great service in your plans to resurrect the Third Reich."

I passed the phone to skinhead. When he pressed it to his ear, his scowl changed to awe. His slumped body suddenly stiffened. "Yes, mein Fuehrer. I would gladly lie, cheat, and steal for you." After a pause, he added, "Yes, I'd gladly risk my life for the glorious Reich. What do you want me to do?"

Skinhead listened, said goodbye to his hero, and passed me the phone.

"This is awesome! He actually wants to meet me, outside. He said he'll be here in a few minutes."

"You're tremendously honored," I said. "Very few ever get to meet him. It's too dangerous. Spectacular lies that were spread about him have poisoned the minds of billions."

"He said he'd meet me behind the dumpster. I wonder how he knows one's there?"

"He comes here often. He likes their French fries. Says they remind him of his triumphal entrance into Paris."

"Don't people recognize him?"

"No. Long ago he had plastic surgery. Well, perhaps we should leave. We don't want to keep him waiting."

We went out and waited behind the dumpster.

Skinhead looked from left to right in anticipation of his hero's arrival. Consequently, he didn't see the black form descending from the night sky. The impact knocked skinhead to the ground. Before he could react, the form's teeth pierced his jugular.

"Delicious," said my Master. "The blood of these skinheads is simply divine. I'm shamelessly hooked. I do hope the supply is plentiful."

"From what I've seen in this city, Master, there's enough for years of wonderful feasting."

"You've earned a bonus," he said. "Expect to see two extra mice in your dinner tonight."

I found myself salivating, as I headed for the subway to snare another skinhead.

PEPPERONI PIZZA

"Who the hell are you?" my wife asked when she answered my knock.

"Don't you recognize me?" I asked.

"No. Get off my porch, or I'll call the cops."

"You got a birthmark way up high on your inner thigh," I said.

Her jaw dropped. "How could you possibly know that?"

"Because I saw it enough times."

"Listen, wise guy. My ex-husband coulda told you that in one of his drunken binges."

"I happen to know your husband—which is me—never drank and still don't. Hold on… did you just say ex-husband?"

"Yeah. I divorced him when he deserted me."

Please, Henrietta. I didn't desert you. Remember that morning I left for Luigi's Pizza Palace? That day you said you had a terrible yen for pepperoni pizza, so like I always did to placate your whims, I dropped everything and headed for Luigi's. Even though it was the worst snow storm every recorded."

"Look, Mister. I don't know what your game is, or how you know my name. But you better get the hell outta here."

"Okay, I'm going. But don't you even want to know what happened to me?"

She started to close the door.

"Dammit! I was abducted! I've spent the last fifteen years being transferred from one spacecraft to another. They examined every inch of me. Then they put me to work cleaning their horrible toilets. Let me tell you, you never want to be anywhere near Martian droppings."

"You're a sick man," she said.

"Look at this pizza box." I extended it toward the door. "Inside is the very same pepperoni pizza I went out to get that afternoon, fifteen years ago. Look inside. The sales receipt's still there. The date I bought it is stamped right below where it says Luigi's Pizza Palace. The pizza inside is as fresh as the day I bought it. The Martians put some kind of chemical in it to keep it that way. One piece is missing, though. A Martian ate it and got sick. I don't know why they kept it fresh all these years. Anyway, when they released me a few minutes ago, they gave me this box with pizza inside to give to you."

"Even if this ridiculous story was true, why in the hell would I want to eat fifteen year-old pepperoni pizza that Martians loaded with chemicals?"

"You don't have to. It's just proof to show you what I'm saying is true."

"Look," she said. "My ex was declared legally dead so I could cash in his insurance policy. I have a new husband. Been married to him eight years now."

"Does he run out to get you pepperoni pizza in the middle of the worst snow storm we ever had?"

"None of your business. This conversation has dragged on long enough. Go now, or I swear I'll call the cops."

"Okay. I'm going. But before I go, I want you to know this: Martians are waiting in the park for me. They're playing a stupid game with me. They were flying in the area where they abducted me, and they started talking about my abduction. They made bets with each other about what might happen if they put me on the ground with the box of pizza, and had me confront you. One bunch is betting that you'll take me back. The others say no way. Thing is, if you don't take me into your house right now, they'll take me away until I die. I don't want to clean their nasty toilets for the rest of my life. So, even if I wasn't your missing husband, won't you let me inside for just an hour? That could convince them that you've taken me back. Meanwhile, they'll abduct somebody else to work in my place."

"You're a total nut." She slammed the door. From inside she hollered, "You better run fast, because I'm dialing 911 right now."

Dejected, I walked back to the park where they were waiting.

One bunch of Martians was furious because they lost the bet. In retaliation, they created extra-large piles of their horrid dung for me to clean up.

The others who won the bet told me for being such a good sport, they'd abduct a bride for me the next time we passed Jupiter. That way I'd have some companionship.

Munching on a slice of pizza, I asked what women from Jupiter looked like.

"Something along the lines of what you call giant squids," they said. "But not as cute."

FIRST CONTACT

The scientist for SETI (Search for Extraterrestrial Intelligence) was startled when he received the first-ever message from outer space.

"Hello… Earth?" said an unearthly voice.

"Yes," said the SETI scientist. "This is Earth."

"How's the weather down there?"

"Pretty nice. How about where you are?"

"Ours is extremely violent. Look, we need your help."

"Like how?"

"Our Sun's about to explode. Could we borrow yours for a while?"

"No," said SETI. "All life would cease on our planet."

"If you want to argue, Earth, we'll look elsewhere."

"Wait. Before you go. Where are you?"

"In a land far, far away."

"Will you contact us again?"

"Nope. You guys are too stingy. What a shame, considering we're the only other life forms in the entire universe. Goodbye forever."

Click.

ELIXER 140

When the gorilla saw me heading toward him with a syringe, he went to the corner of his cage and cringed.

"Aw c'mon, Jasper," I said. "This ain't gonna hurt a bit."

"That's what you said the last time," he said, whimpering.

"So, the last one hurt a little bit, but wasn't a bit of pain worth the spectacular results? My Elixir 138 turned you into a talking gorilla. Not to mention the fact that you speak English better than ninety-percent of college graduates in this country. The recording I made of your voice and sent to Harvard for analysis proved it. In fact, when they sent the results of their analysis, they included an offer for you to address next year's graduating class. Of course they didn't know you were a gorilla. But that's the point. They couldn't tell that you weren't human. So don't moan about a little needle that was stuck in your rump, considering the results."

"So what's in that needle you have now?"

"Elixer 139. It'll cure all those aches and pains you've been complaining about. Plus, according to my calculations, it should extend your life another fifty years."

"But what's so good about that?" he asked. "Another fifty years cooped up this cage will be a living hell."

"Not necessarily. If my next elixir, 140, works you'll be transformed into a Neanderthal Man. A Neanderthal with a fabulous command of the English language. Think what that'll mean, considering you'll be the only Neanderthal in existence. You'll be interviewed on every radio talk show in the world. *CNN, Fox, BBC*, Oprah, to mention a few, will break their necks to get you on their TV shows. Hollywood will beg you to sign movie contracts. Random House will advance you a few million just for your biography. The sky will be the limit. You'll end up living in Beverly Hills with beautiful starlets banging on your front door every hour of the day."

"You make it sound real good."

"It'll be good to the max. You've never seen Beverly Hills—well how could you, because right now you're nothing but a stinking gorilla. They aren't too keen on smelly animals out there, especially one as mangy looking as you are. But once you're transformed into a Neanderthal and become rich you'll see it. And Malibu. And a million other fabulous places. Anyway, let's get on with the test, and I'll give you extra bananas."

Entering the cage, I told him to lie on the floor. When he did, I jammed the needle into his snout.

"Damn, that stings," he hollered, as I pressed the plunger to release the elixir's murky yellow fluid.

"Okay. All done. Here's your bananas. Better stay on the floor. You'll probably get real dizzy in a minute or two."

"How will we know if this is going to work?" he asked.

"Your nose will turn blue."

"Aw, hell. I kinda liked my nose the way it was."

"It won't stay that way. It'll only be blue for a few hours. I had to put something in the elixir to let me know if it worked. Well, I'm going back to my lab. I'll check on you in an hour."

When I returned to the lab, I made entries in my journal. Though I told Jasper I was giving him Elixir 139 to extend his age, I lied. I had no such elixir. I'd given him an injection of 140 to transform him into a Neanderthal.

All that baloney about him becoming rich and living in Beverly Hills was a pile of lies. I was the one who'd be on Oprah, get movie contracts, get big advances for books. And he'd be nothing but a stupid, illiterate, grunting Neanderthal, but the only one in the world. And I'd own him. Poor fool.

When I went back to Jasper's cage, he was gone! Lying on the floor was a hairy cockroach, a hundred times normal size, with a blue gorilla snout.

I grabbed a baseball bat and smashed the damn thing. If it had awakened and escaped, it might've wreaked havoc on the city. If the authorities managed to trace it back to me, I'd end up in prison.

For the next few days, I poured over all the formulas and notes I'd written during the development of Elixir 140. Then I spotted the problem. I'd accidentally turned a positive number into a negative one. That was enough to throw off the entire formula.

A month of recalculations also showed I shouldn't have used a gorilla for the experiment. No wonder Jasper turned into an oversized cockroach. My figures showed that I should have injected a human male, instead.

Checking my records, I found the phone number for the *Los Angeles Times* classified section.

"*Los Angeles Times* Classified. How may I help you?" said a pleasant female voice.

"I'd like to place an ad. Here goes...Want to transform your life and become rich? Call 777-8888 for interview if you are young, healthy, male, and are interested in being a very special guest on the Oprah show."

A FABULOUS CURE

"We're gonna be rich," Dr. Zangara told his wife.

"I've heard that one before," she said. "I don't believe a word you say anymore. Why don't you admit you're a failure and that you should've kept your job with Zeta Pharmaceuticals?"

"I told you a hundred times working in their new product development department wasn't challenging enough. They were too narrow in their thinking."

"You mean logical. Who else but you would try to come up with a serum that cures werewolves? You're lucky they didn't fire you when you proposed that to the Board of Directors."

"I figured I'd have the last laugh when I quit and setup my own development lab. You gotta admit, the serum I invented to cure werewolves almost worked. I figured if it cured all of my werewolf lab mice, it'd work on people. But I never counted on their pineal glands secreting hormones that neutralized my serum. Damn! Do you realize I could've charged $50,000 per injection? Considering there are 100,000 registered werewolves in this country, I could've become rich and famous. Plus, I could've have won the Nobel Prize for Medicine. *Time Magazine* would've named me Man of the Year."

"Even if your serum worked, who the hell could afford a $50,000 treatment?"

"Once I demonstrated my success to the world, I'm certain Congress would have approved full payment through Medicare. Anyway, my werewolf serum is history. My new serum to cure vampires really works. Not just on lab mice vampires, but on human vampires."

"How do you know for sure?" she asked.

"Last night while you were playing canasta with your friends, I tested it on a human vampire. Remember that crate UPS delivered this morning—the one I said was a new machine for my laboratory? Well, it really contained an authentic vampire, complete with coffin and burial soil."

"You crazy bastard! You actually brought a vampire into this house? And it was around when my friends were here?"

"Stop shouting. Everything was under control. When he arrived, I opened his coffin and chained him so tight not even King Kong could've escaped. When it got dark, he woke and opened the door of his coffin.

Whew. What an ugly creep. When he realized he couldn't attack, he begged for blood, saying he was famished. That's when I injected him with my serum. In seventy-five seconds he lost his cravings for blood."

"How do you know?"

"Because I pressed my neck against his mouth. Instead of biting it, he begged me for peanut butter."

"Why peanut butter?"

"My serum's made from peanut butter."

"Chunky or smooth?"

"Smooth. So, instead of sucking blood from somebody's neck last night, this nasty vampire sucked peanut butter from jars. Actually it took ten jars to sate his lust. I figure with a little refinement, I can get it down to six. Do you realize what I've done? Do you know how many vampires there are in the world?"

"Wait a minute! Where did you get the peanut butter from?"

"Our pantry," he said.

"No wonder I couldn't find any peanut butter this morning. What a jerk you are. You know how much I enjoy having peanut butter on my bagels for breakfast. I went nuts this morning, rooting through the pantry, looking for some. There wasn't any, because you gave it all to a stinking vampire."

"Sorry, Dear. I didn't expect him to gobble it all."

"I want a divorce! Nobody screws with my peanut butter and gets away with it."

"Hold on. I'm going to Wal-mart to buy a hundred jars. No doubt the vampire will wake up again tonight, and will want more. Anyway, when it comes to having enough peanut butter, do you realize how much I'll be able to buy after treating just one vampire?"

"It might be months before you see a penny. I'll bet if you bought 1,000 jars, you'd give them all to your precious vampire. As far as I'm concerned, that's a form of spousal abuse. What about all the other peanut butter lovers in the world? What'll happen to them once a gazillion vampires start hogging ten jars each, every time they get hungry?"

"I'm sure stocks are more than plentiful," he said. "Last year the government doled out millions of jars to senior citizens. I hear that didn't even put a dent in the supply."

* * * *

Dr. Zangara demonstrated his amazing serum to lawmakers during a joint session of Congress. Not only did he win a Congressional medal for his outstanding work, but also received awards from the UN and every vampire-infested country in the world.

After one million vampires were certified as cured by the World Health Organization, the Nobel Prize Selection Committee declared Zangara's work as the most important discovery of the twenty-first century. *Time Magazine* named him Man of the Year for 2012.

A year later, Zangara was a fugitive.

His fall occurred when cured vampires lusted even greater amounts of peanut butter. Within months, a million vampires were sucking twenty jars every night. Soon, that rose to thirty, something Zangara never anticipated.

The world's peanut butter supplies quickly dwindled. Supermarkets and big box stores ran out. This lead to global rationing and The Great Peanut Butter Riots of 2012, during which millions of peanut-butter-loving citizens were killed and injured, including Zangara's ex-wife.

Even worse, horror movies showing vampires sucking peanut butter from jars were flops. Same with horror novels. Thousands of writers, producers, directors, and actors lost their jobs.

Peanut butter lovers, fans of blood-sucking vampire novels, the Horror Writers Union, and the Association of Horror Movie Producers joined together to demand justice. More riots occurred until Congress ordered Zangara's execution for destroying an entire literary and movie genre, as well as the world's peanut butter manufacturing and distribution systems.

Coming out of hiding, Zangara demonstrated his new serum made from pepperoni pizza that completely reversed the cure. Before long, the world's vampires were once again sucking blood from human necks.

Peanut butter lovers rejoiced. So did fans of blood-sucking vampire novels, the Horror Writer's Union, and the Association of Horror Movie Producers.

However, when global supplies of pepperoni pizza dwindled to zero, Zangara was charged with a crime against humanity and executed by jamming him into a pizza oven.

THE BATTLE

"Circle the wagons," the wagon master shouted. "Get ready to fight for your lives. That's an Indian war party up there on top of that hill."

Within minutes, two dozen wagons formed a circle. Women and children poured out and hid underneath, while men prepared for battle.

Clayton, the Wagon Master, walked around checking their defenses.

"Mr. Clayton," shouted the prettiest woman in the group. "Is there some way we can prevent them from attacking until dark?"

"None that I know of, Miss Elizabeth. Why do you ask such a strange question?"

"Well, if they don't attack until it's dark, I can assure victory with no casualties to our group."

"What makes you say such a foolish thing?" he said to the only single women traveling from Kansas City to California.

"Come closer, and I'll tell you in your ear."

An invitation from such a stunning woman was a gift from heaven. Clayton imagined her lips brushing his ear as she spoke. Maybe she'd even press her body ever so slightly against him as she got close enough to whisper.

His heart pounded as he approached her. The closer he got, the more he could smell lavender—so unlike the aroma of the other ladies who reeked of brown laundry soap.

The delicious, delicate fragrance of Elizabeth's slender form made him think of things forbidden between married men and beautiful single women. Things he craved for ever since waving goodbye to his wife and children back in Kansas City. Things that made him momentarily forget the impending danger from hostile natives.

His blood pressure shot up when her breasts brushed his arm, as she spoke into his ear. But he went cold as she spoke.

"What in the hell are you talking about?" he snapped. "What does that word mean?"

"It means you're saved. All of you."

"Woman, I think the prairie heat softened your brain. Don't waste any more of my time with your crazy talk. Go over to that wagon and stay by Granny Higgins. Do you know how to shoot a pistol?"

"Yep."

"Then take mine," he said, passing the weapon and a handful of cartridges. "And make every shot count. Don't shoot until you—"

"See the whites of their eyes," she said. "My daddy was a captain in Lee's Army. He used to say that all the time when he taught me how to shoot."

The hot afternoon ended without a single attack by the hostiles. Everyone figured the Indians would make their move when the full moon rose.

As it grew dark, Indians imitated coyote yells. The sounds unnerved everyone in the wagon train, except the wagon master who'd fought Plains Indians during previous continental crossings.

"Don't let them get to you," he whispered, as he made the rounds again, reassuring the folks under his care. "We're lucky the moon is full. Keep a sharp eye out for moving shadows. They'll sneak up on us in groups of two or three. If you hear a sound, shoot at it."

He kept Granny Higgins' wagon for last, hoping to speak a while with Elizabeth. He felt the need to inhale her aroma and hear her soft voice before the battle began.

"How you doing, Granny," he said.

"I was fine until she left me here by myself."

"What do you mean she left?"

"Five minutes ago, she said she'd be back later on. Next thing I knew, she was flat on her belly and crawling in the direction of the Injuns."

"What! You sure?"

"Yep. Left me this here pistol. Told me how to use it."

"Give it to me," he said. "You might end up shooting yourself. Follow me. I'll put you in with the Fiddler family. You'll be safer with them. Mr. Fiddler told me he won medals in the war."

After settling Higgins, Clayton went back to his own wagon. That's when the howling began. Terrible night sounds that the fifty year old had never heard before. Sounds that made his blood curdle.

An hour passed. Still no attack.

Once again, Clayton made the rounds. "Just because you ain't seen them yet, don't mean they ain't coming. They're hoping you'll get real tired and fall asleep. Don't even let yourself close your eyes for a second. The minute you do, one of them will sneak up on you and slice your throat."

When he reached Higgins' wagon, he was surprised to smell lavender.

"What the hell's going on, Miss Elizabeth," he whispered. "I looked all over and didn't see you anywhere. Why did you leave Granny? Where'd you go?"

"For a walk. Everything's fine now. You can tell everybody to relax. Tell them to build fires and make supper."

"I never ran into such a crazy women like you before. You smell good and look good, but your brain is soft as corn mush."

"I swear on my mother's grave, they're dead. All forty-seven of them."

"How can you say such a thing?"

"Because I killed them."

Clayton spat and went back to his wagon.

The night passed without an attack.

At dawn, Clayton and three others rode toward the hill where he'd first spotted the Indians. Well before he arrived, he found bodies torn to pieces and scattered everywhere. He counted forty-seven decapitated heads.

"What on God's Earth happened to these varmints?" he said aloud, covered with chills. He'd never seen such horrendous destruction, even during the most savage battles against the Confederates.

Returning to the wagon train, he ordered everybody to resume their journey.

"What happened?" some asked.

"They're all dead. Thank the Lord. We were saved by warriors greater than the Indians. Hopefully those brave souls are up ahead. Maybe we'll spot them so we can thank them for saving us."

As the wagons headed toward the Rocky Mountains, Clayton pondered what Elizabeth had whispered in his ear the day before. And once again he wondered what the word meant.

Going from wagon to wagon, he asked if anybody had a book that told the meaning of words.

"We got one," said Fiddler.

"Can your missus read?" asked Clayton.

"She reads pretty good."

"How about asking her to look up a word for me."

"What's the word?"

"Come to think of it, it might even be two words: where and wolf."

BAD GENES

"**I** wish I was an Ozgur Mylar Wiener," Harry sang with gusto, as he strolled on Main Street.

Suddenly, his fairy godmother appeared. She was a member of the board of directors of the Ozgur Mylar Corporation. "Is that a real wish you have? Or are you singing that inane little ditty because you're responding unconsciously to intense, intrusive Pavlovian conditioning thrust on you by the brain-raping industrial-advertising complex?"

"It's my fondest dream," Harry said.

"Why would you wanna be one of those things?"

"I wouldn't hafta go to work anymore. Whoever heard of a hot dog going to work?"

"That's true," she said. "They can't go anywhere, because they have no legs. Nor can they hear, because they have no ears. Need I remind you of their inability to see?"

"I know. But I'm willing to put up with that. I don't mind laying around all day in a package inside a nice, cool refrigeration unit somewhere in Beverly Hills."

"But you'd have to share the package with seven others," FG said. "Last time I checked, you were claustrophobic."

"I still am. But if I really was gonna be an Ozgur Mylar Wiener, I'd ask for individual packaging. With something fluffy inside so it'd be soft, and comfy. That way I'd sleep nice and sound."

"Sounds like a great idea. Sometimes I wish I could be one myself. However, I hope you understand what a low achiever you'd be for the rest of your life."

"I never was highly motivated. Runs in the family. I'm a victim of bad genes."

"Truer words were never spoken," she said. "Well, if this is what you really want, I'll change you into a separately packaged wiener right now. With fluffy polyester inside to ensure you'll always get a good night's sleep. And I'll make sure you end up in a refrigerated bin in Beverly Hills. Ready?"

"Yep."

She waved her wand over his head three times and cast the spell that changed people into hot dogs.

Harry's six-foot frame collapsed into a six-inch chunk of pink-orange meat. One side was nestled in spongy, blue polyester. Cute little pixies appeared and wrapped celluloid around the whole shebang. In seconds, the transformation was complete.

Examining the package, FG asked, "Are you comfortable in there?"

No answer.

Then she remembered Ozgur Mylar Wieners don't have mouths.

A sudden gust of wind blew the package from her hand, causing it to fall into the street. Unfortunately, it was rush hour. An eighteen-wheeler ran over the package.

"Gross!" FG said when she heard a loud squoosh. "Aw, hell! Now I gotta find a new godson. Oh well, that's how the cookie crumbles. Or maybe I should say how the wiener flattens."

Moments later, she heard a kid whistling the Ozgur Mylar Wiener song.

"Hey kid," she called. "Is that a real wish you have? Or are you whistling that inane ditty because you're responding unconsciously to intense, intrusive Pavlovian conditioning thrust on you by the brain-raping industrial-advertising complex?"

"None of those. I'm just weird. My shrink says it's because I don't have a fairy godmother."

"This is your lucky day. I'm a fairy godmother, and I just happen to be looking for a new godson. Want me to adopt you?"

"Oh, that'd be great! I can hardly wait until Christmas so you can bring me lots of fancy presents. And when my birthday comes, you'll grant me three wishes. Now that I'm a teen and my hormones are raging, I got some real neat wishes about leggy cheerleaders and Trixie the lap dancer."

"Sorry, kid. I don't do the gift thing. On the other hand, if you need to get to a Prince's Ball in a hurry, and your dad's car ain't running, and there's a public transportation strike, I'm good for a pumpkin with wheels. With custom interior. Drawn by white mice. Designer gown included."

"But since I'm a guy, I'd prefer a polka-dot tuxedo."

"Look, it's a package deal. It's either the gown, or nothing."

"Okay. When I get invited to the Prince's Ball, I'll give you a holler," he said.

"It's a deal," she said, shaking his hand. "Meanwhile, I gotta go to the courthouse and file adoption papers. Soon as they're approved, I'll call you."

"Instead of calling, could you come to my house? Like around midnight? And bring a Dallas Cowboy Cheerleader? As a welcome-to-the family gift?"

"Sure."

"What should I do in the meantime?" he asked.

"You could climb a few beanstalks and check to see if there's a giant hanging around. If you find him, remind him he owes me big time for losing a bet he made on the fights. Ever break somebody's legs?"

"Nope."

"Too bad. If he doesn't pay up, I was hoping you could let him know I mean business. Meanwhile, how about a nice hug for your soon-to-be fairy godmother."

When he reached for her embrace, he slipped and knocked FG into the street. An eighteen-wheeler ran over her. Like all fairy godmothers who get squashed by trucks, she vaporized and was never seen again.

When she didn't show up at her office in Ozgur Mylar Corporate Headquarters anymore, the owners were delighted. No work, no pay.

The kid she'd promised to adopt got invited to the Prince's Ball. He created a sensation when he arrived on a skateboard drawn by snowy white, giant praying mantises.

In time, the corporation declared Fairy Godmother a victim of alien abduction. Through underhanded manipulations, board members appropriated her vast holdings, sold them, and distributed the proceeds among themselves. They all lived happily ever after.

As to the kid FG almost adopted, he stayed weird his whole life because of acute fairy godmother deficit syndrome. However, FG's ghost cast a love spell so powerful, he ended up marrying a Dallas Cowboy Cheerleader, as well as Trixie the lap dancer.

They too lived happily ever after in the highly profitable nudist camp they established for bigamists.

LESSONS FROM GRANDMA

"Grandma, what's in this blue bottle?" asked Skip.

"Be very careful and hand it to me very slowly. And don't touch it again. I told you never to go into that closet, Skip. Not without my permission. Understand?"

"Yes, grandma. What is it?"

"One of my potions."

"Will I ever get to touch it?"

"Someday. When the time comes."

"You mean when I'm seven?"

Grandma chuckled. "No, when you're initiated."

"When's that?"

"The full moon after your first nocturnal emission.

"What's a noctal elishun?"

"Something very, very special. You'll have a beautiful dream that you are in a golden bed. In the dream, our magnificent Goddess Goona will come to you in all her glory, lie on top of you, and make you feel good all over."

"Oh," the five year old said, scratching his head and wondering why the Goddess would want to lay on top of him and not next to him. "Will she be heavy?"

Grandma chuckled. "She's going to make you feel so good, you won't care if she weighs as much as a bulldozer."

Skip laughed at the picture that painted in his mind.

"Hey, Grandma, the blue bottle has the same thing on it that looks just like the thing on the chain you gave me. I forget what it's called."

"Don't call it a thing. It's very sacred. It's a pentagram. Have you been kissing the pentagram on your chain when you wake up every morning, and before you go to sleep at night?"

"Yep. Just like I promised you, Grandma."

"Good. And do you say the special words to Goddess Goona I taught you, every full moon?"

"Uh-huh. They're funny words. But I say them."

"Have you kept the words secret?"

"Yeah."

"Good. Remember what will happen to somebody if you forget yourself and tell them those words?"

"Their arms and legs will wither and fall off."

"Right. Make sure you remember that."

"I promise I will. I wouldn't want that to happen to any of my friends."

"Me either. It would be terribly painful. Well, it's time for your next lesson. Today I'm going to teach you how to see things most other people can't. Things that will happen in the future. Take this blessed knife and cut the chicken open. From top to bottom. While you're making the cut, and the blood runs out, say these very special words…"

THE BREAK UP

The impact of the .44 magnum bullet decapitated the Barbie doll's head. Though the head flew across the room and landed hard on the kitchen floor, its bloody mouth continued to taunt Fred by repeating for the millionth time, "You're a jerk, you're a jerk, you're a jerk…"

Fred grabbed the severed head, threw it against the wall with all his might, then stomped it thirty-six times. Still, it continued to hurl invective. "You're a jerk, you're a jerk, you're a jerk…"

"Forget Barbie," said his new girlfriend, a Kewpie Doll he'd won in an Ebay collectibles auction. "I'm far more valuable and collectable than her, anyway. There's millions of her, but only a handful of me."

"Yes, and you're far more exotic," Fred said, raising the Kewpie to his lips and giving it a French kiss.

The severed Barbie head used the distraction to roll itself around the kitchen floor. Finding a wooden match, it managed to grab it between its bloodied teeth. Then it rolled back to where Fred was standing. Using all the energy it could muster, it scraped the match head across the floor. When the match lit, the head hurled itself upward to Fred's pants cuff. The cuff caught fire, instantly.

None of Fred's clothes were fireproof, contrary to the guarantees made by the Chinese manufacturer in Shanghai. Consequently everything he wore burst into flames.

Though the Kewpie Doll tried her best to douse the fire with a fire extinguisher, she wasn't successful. Since she was also made in China—at a factory right next door to the factory where all of Fred's clothes were made—she was just as flammable.

Soon the lovers were a pile of charred remains.

Savoring the revenge it had taken, the doll head rolled around until it spotted a tube of Super Glue. With the gyrations of an Olympic acrobat and herculean effort, the head managed to glue itself back onto its body.

The restored Barbie doll showered, then called the local newspaper, and placed an ad in the Personals column. Before long, a lonely, rejected man going through the middle age crazies, responded.

"Do you own a Kewpie Doll?" she asked before answering his question about her moving into his apartment.

"No," he said.

"Do you own a pistol?"

"No."

"Are all your clothes made in China?"

"Of course. I can't find any made in America."

"Good. I'm yours. Let's go to your place and fool around."

On the way, she suddenly realized how much fun she had when she torched Fred. As she replayed scenes in her head of him covered with flames, and how loud he screamed from the excruciating pain, she felt a powerful urge to do it again.

"Would you do me one big favor, even if it sounds weird?" she asked her new beau.

"Sure. Just name it, Honey."

"I'd like you to put a few wooden matches on the kitchen floor. There's a little trick I learned with matches that I'd like to show you."

CHERRY LOLLIPOPS

"Help me, Charley!" a woman screeched over the phone. "I'm surrounded by vampires!"

"Who is this?" asked Ed.

"I'm Selma. Hurry! They're getting closer!"

"My name's not Charley. It's Ed, and I don't know anybody named Selma. You have the wrong number."

"Please don't hang up!" the woman said. "Call 911 for me. Tell them I'm in Transylvania."

"Why don't you call 911 yourself?" Ed asked.

"I tried. It's busy."

"Look, lady, I'm in America. Transylvania's gonna be an expensive long distance call."

"Ouch!" she hollered. "One of the vampires just bit my neck."

Her phone toppled to the ground making a noise that hurt Ed's ear. "Hey lady, you okay?"

Ed thought he heard slurping sounds. While deciding if he should hang up, a man's voice said, "Hello. Who's there?"

"Ed Hart. Who's this?"

"Dr. Carl Zanker. I'm Selma's psychiatrist. She must've snitched my cell phone during our session. Poor woman's having delusions again. She has the worst case of multiple personalities and derangement I've even seen."

"So Selma's a goofball?"

"We have less crude names for the unfortunately insane," Zanker said. "Selma's a very nice old woman. Unfortunately, her illness gives her terrible delusions. Last night, werewolves were after her. The night before, it was the Loch Ness Monster. I figured things would get worse with Mother's Day approaching. Same thing happened last year."

"I'm sorry I called her a goofball. She said she was in Transylvania. Exactly where are you, Doctor?"

"Northwood, Iowa. We're a small, private hospital."

"Geez. I'm in Northwood, too. Is your place that Victorian a mile outside of town?"

"Yes."

"I know this is gonna sound strange," Ed said. "But could I visit Selma tomorrow? With it being Mother's Day and all? I lost my mom last year."

"That's a good idea. I don't recall her ever having visitors. I'll allow you thirty minutes. Perhaps you can come in the evening. Would seven o'clock work for you?"

"Sure," Ed said. "Would it be okay if I brought her something?"

"She likes cherry lollipops. She's eating one right now."

"So that's the slurping I heard in the background when she dropped the phone."

"Yes," said the doctor. Lollipops seem to calm her. That and a hefty dose of tranquilizer when she gets this bad."

* * * *

When Ed arrived with a box of lollipops, a nurse escorted him to Selma's room.

"I hope you don't mind," the nurse said, "but I must lock the door when I leave."

"I don't mind. Does she try to run away?"

"Oh no. She can't get out of bed. She's too old. If we don't lock the door, she starts to scream. She thinks she'll be attacked by monsters."

"Dr. Zanker didn't tell me she was that old," Ed said.

"You must be mistaken. You couldn't have spoken with Dr. Zanker."

"Well, he's the one who said it was okay to visit Selma."

"You must have him mixed up with somebody else." Lowering her voice, she said, "Dr. Zanker is a patient in the Holmes Institute for the Criminally Insane. It's a shame. He was such a brilliant psychiatrist."

Ed wondered what the hell was going on, as the nurse unlocked the door to Selma's room.

"Looks like Selma's sleeping," the nurse said. "I'll wake her and tell her you brought cherry lollipops. In her mind, anybody who gives her a cherry lollipop can't possibly be a monster."

The nurse spoke close to the old woman's ear. "Wake up, Selma. Somebody's here to see you. He brought lollipops."

Selma opened her eyes and coughed. The nurse hurried out and locked the door.

Ed had never seen such an ancient, shriveled face. It reminded him of an unwrapped mummy.

"Who are you?" Selma asked.

"My name's Ed. We talked on the phone last night." Extending the box, he added, "I brought cherry lollipops."

"Let's see," Selma said, reaching with a horribly shriveled arm.

Ed shuddered when the old woman touched his hand with blotchy, yellowish-gray fingers.

Raising a lollipop to beady eyes, Selma said, "It's so small. Why did you bring me such tiny lollipops? Dr. Zanker promised I'd get a king-sized one for Mother's Day."

"When did you see Dr. Zanker?" Ed asked.

"Five minutes ago. He came in to use my bathroom. I told him a million times he should use somebody else's. But he never listens."

Ed felt unnerved by the look in Selma's eye. "Well, I gotta be going," he said.

"Before you leave, could you help me sit up? My back's so sore." Selma raised her arms so Ed could reach around her.

As Ed tugged, Selma hit him on the head with a hammer. He fell onto the bed, unconscious. Dr. Zanker slid out from under Selma's bed and gave her a bed pan and scalpel.

Thirty minutes later, the nurse unlocked the door. "Where's your visitor?" she asked.

"Hiding under the bed," Selma said.

"Why?"

"We're playing hide and seek. Me, him, and Dr. Zanker."

When the nurse looked under the bed and saw Ed's headless corpse in a pool of blood, her screams turned to gurgles when Zanker's scalpel slit her throat.

"Yummy," Selma said, wrapping mottled lips around the oversized lollipop that looked exactly like Ed's head on a stick. Suddenly she spat. "It ain't cherry-flavored. Let me try yours."

"Sure," said Dr. Zanker, as he passed the nurse's head he'd just jammed on a stick and tasted.

A PLEASANT SURPRISE

Dr. Zangara was surprised when the corpse he tried to animate turned to a mass of yellow goo.

"How could I have failed so miserably," he cried. "What do you suppose happened, Eye-gore?"

"Don't know, Doctor."

"Did you press the Kazoo switch when the green lights over the corpse's head started to blink?"

"No, Master. The procedural manual said I should press the Kadidle switch."

"No wonder the corpse turned to gunk!" the doctor screamed. "Kadidle is used to compress molecules into mush! How could such a disastrous error occur?"

"You outsourced the job of typing your hand-written notes," Igor said, as he approached the yellow goo. "And they must've goofed."

"I'm gonna sue the bastards! Well, go ahead and examine what's left. See if we can salvage anything. Perhaps we can find some uses for that pile of goo. Maybe it can be used to grease the wheels on the wagons we use to haul corpses from the cemetery."

Eye-gore noticed the yellow stuff emitted a peculiar, pungent odor. He jammed two fingers into the mass, removed them, and stuck them between his gums.

"Mmmm. Tastes good. Reminds me of... mustard... and yet it's sweet. He tried another mouthful. "Master, you should try this."

Zangara thrust a spoon into the goo. Sniffing the spoon's contents, he said "Delightful! It doesn't have the horrid stink melted corpses always give off."

The doctor shoved the spoon into his mouth. "Mmm. You're right. This is unlike anything I've ever tasted."

"Now that I think of it," Eye-gore said, "It reminds me of honey. And yet it has the flavor of mustard. Imagine. Mustard and honey combined. Perhaps we should call it mustardized honey."

"Sound's catchy. On the other hand, perhaps we should put the words in alphabetical order and call it honey mustardized. Or better yet, honey mustard. Yeah, that sounds good. Who'd believe two such disparate things could be combined without causing a terrible explosion, and taste so good? I'm glad my experiment failed. Meanwhile, what do you suppose this stuff would be good for?"

"We could coat it on road kill to hide the gamy flavor. Remember how you tried to sell road kill carcasses to the village butcher, and he refused to buy them?"

"Yes. Unfortunately, that scheme failed to provide the funds I needed to finance my monster-creating experiments."

"Perhaps he'll change his mind if we spread our new honey mustard on the critters your carriage squashes along the cemetery road."

"Good thinking, Eye-gore. Tell you what: if my business plan works, I'll promote you from Switch Presser 6th Class to Culinary Specialist 6th class. As a bonus, I'll throw in all the road kill you can eat, as well as free honey mustard for life."

"That's very generous of you, Doctor." Eye-gore licked his lips.

"Meanwhile, check the castle for empty bottles. Fill them with this wonderful goo. I'll design some eye-catching labels. I think I'll call it Mother Zangara's Down Home Honey Mustard. Meanwhile, I'll tell the gravediggers to exhume more bodies. This way, we can make more honey mustard when this batch runs out. Just remember, when the green light blinks over the corpses' heads on the operating table, always press the Kazoo switch."

Zangara's business gamble worked. In fact, during the years of plague when cemeteries overflowed with bodies, he generously offered to dispose of the excess at no charge to the bereaved. The money the bereaved saved on funerals enabled them to buy lots of honey mustard that showed up on the village grocer's shelves. For Zangara, it was a win-win situation.

When the great flu epidemic hit Europe, Zangara was overwhelmed with so much surplus, he began to export.

For one hundred years, Mother Zangara's Down Home Honey Mustard has been the favorite of millions. Especially those who like to enhance the flavor of road kill.

TEENIE-BEANIE

"**B**lock the door!" yelled the security guard. "Don't let that damn Martian escape!"

Three heavily armed guards jumped in front of the mall exit door.

The naked Martian teen lowered his head and hit them like a battering ram.

The impact was so tremendous, the guards died instantly. The steel exit door behind them flew into the parking lot.

A SWAT team fired automatic weapons.

Unfazed, the teen kept moving toward them. Grabbing the nearest cop, the teenager hurled him a hundred feet.

When a burst of machine gun fire blew the teen's neck to smithereens, his head fell off and hit the ground. The rest of his body went forward a few feet, then toppled over.

"Look at all the freakin' damage," said a sergeant. "He knocked that steel door off its hinges like it was cardboard. I'll bet he was hopped up on Teenie-Beanie."

"Hey, what's that purple bubbly stuff coming from his neck?"

"Looks like foam. Collect it in some test tubes, Charlie. Have the lab check to see if it has anything to do with Teenie-Beanie."

Some mall shoppers came through the doorway to gawk.

"Get those people back in the mall. I don't want any rubberneckers. Seal the place. Get them to announce nobody leaves the mall."

"What's in that bag he was carrying?"

Somebody sliced the bag with a bayonet. A pile of multi-colored objects fell out.

"Looks like jelly beans."

"Hey, something's inside his mouth," yelled a cop.

"What is it?"

"Looks like a wad of jelly beans. Maybe he got all sugared-up and went nuts."

"Unless they really ain't jelly beans," said the captain. "Could be a way to conceal Teenie-Beanie. Sergeant, have somebody check the candy store. See if this bastard stole a bunch of jelly beans. Don't any of you let the press know it was a Martian teen. You know how the press hollers police brutality every time we arrest one of them. Tell them an old, nude American guy went berserk after nipping too much kick-a-poo juice. If this ever gets to the attention of *CNN*, who the hell knows what'll happen after they broadcast? Nutsoids will firebomb shopping malls all over the country just to get even with Martian teens. Everybody hates the bastards to begin with. And maybe some freaked-out American teen idiots will decide to play copycat. They'll chomp on jelly beans, disrobe, and run through malls yelling, 'I'm a crazed Martian teenager.'"

"Hey, Harris and Smith," the captain said. "Check out all the Martian teens in the mall. See if any of them have been chewing jelly beans."

"You gotta be kidding, Captain," Smith said. "Those freaks have such stinky breath."

"Borrow some ladies cologne and spray it under your nose. And double up on the rubber gloves. Never know how filthy their freakin' mouths really are. You don't wanna catch Martian Bird Flu, or something worse."

"What should I do if any of them has a mouth full of jelly beans?"

"Arrest the jerk. Put the jelly beans into evidence bags. Don't forget to read his Interplanetary Teenage Rights. I don't want some World Court Lawyer in The Hague getting a Martian released over a stupid technicality."

All of the seventy-nine Martian teens hanging around the mall were munching jellybeans. Some had wads consisting of several flavors. Others had only a single flavor.

Nobody knew what to make of it. To the best of their knowledge, nobody in the Space Administration had ever studied the flavor choices of Martian teenagers when it came to jelly beans. Nor were they sure if the stuff really was jelly beans, or a counterfeit version camouflaging Teenie-Beanie.

Lab results showed all seventy-nine Martians were bombed out of their skulls on Teenie-Beanie, and none were legal residents.

The local outrage was so overwhelming, every Martian teen who'd snuck across the Atmospheric Border was arrested and deported. But the same day, 482 Martian teens successfully crossed illegally and headed to shopping malls. The pockets of most were loaded with phony jelly beans.

Things got so bad, jelly beans were banned all over America. Lots of children wept bitterly when they found their Easter baskets completely devoid of them.

Meanwhile, Congress reminded America's children they had to make sacrifices so America could accommodate undocumented Martian teens to ensure diversity.

The nation's children banded together and formed Minute-Man Kid groups. They accomplished what the government couldn't, or was unwilling to do. They tracked down all illegal Martian teens, and assassinated them. They even built their own rocket ships and sent squads to Mars to guard all exit points.

The entire Solar System learned a hard lesson: don't ever mess with the contents of American children's Easter baskets.

A WORLD RECORD

"You're a no talent nothing!" Harry's wife screamed when she filed for divorce.

"You're wrong," he hollered. I can slap a 1,000-piece jigsaw puzzle together faster than anybody I know. Or anybody you know. And from the inside out, too!"

"She'll be sorry she divorced me when she sees my name listed in the *Guinness Book of World Records*," Harry mumbled. "And extra sorry when *People Magazine* pays big bucks to write my story. Then too when one of those reality shows does a TV special on me. Not to mention what I'll rake in when Hollywood offers a contract to do a bio-pic."

Harry pictured her begging him to take her back while he lollygagged on his million-dollar yacht on the Riviera: "I was wrong," she'd sob. "You're the most talented man in the universe. Please... take me back."

He figured things would start going his way after he mailed a notarized letter describing his jigsaw puzzle marathon to the *Guinness* editors. His letter told how he'd assembled a hundred of the most complicated puzzles in 39 hours, 16 minutes, and 52 seconds.

Three months passed without a word. Harry sent a telegram to the editors: "Where's your letter telling me I busted the world record for jigsaw puzzle assembly?"

Two weeks later he received a reply. "Dear Sir. We're sorry to inform you that the current record holder in your category accomplished the same feat eight seconds faster. In addition, his letter arrived a day earlier than yours."

Harry planned another record-breaking event. He bought three dozen jelly donuts for a practice run. Gobbled fifteen in one minute, seven. Then heaved his guts out.

Harry refused to give up.

That's when the idea of hot air balloons popped into his head. Checking *Wickedpedia*, he discovered the altitude record was 69,852 feet. The farthest one had ever traveled was from Japan to Northern Canada. The fastest speed ever achieved was 245 miles per hour.

Those seemed like formidable challenges until he this thought occurred: *These records are for height, distance, and speed from point A to point B. But there ain't any mention of how fast a balloon can descend to Earth. That's it! I'll set a record for how fast a balloon can fall to earth. Yahoo!*

Harry spent a year studying and riding in hot air balloons. He even convinced the guy in India who held the record for altitude to take him aloft to 69,852 feet. Afterward, he bought his own balloon.

On his first solo test flight, Harry almost achieved the world's record of 245 miles per hour during his descent. That alone was a record, because the current record was for horizontal movement, not vertical. But that wasn't good enough. He wanted to break the sound barrier by descending 700 miles per hour.

Then came the day he was to break the record. Rising to 69, 852 feet, he manipulated controls and raised the balloon two inches more. He broke the altitude record! He photographed his altimeter for proof.

Something inside urged him to land immediately and claim the new height record. But Harry overruled the impulse. *Why not break two records? One for height, and a whole new category for vertical speed of descent. By tonight, CNN and Fox News will plaster my face all over the world. I'll be drowning in wine, women, song, book and talk show offers. The President will invite me to dinner at the White House. And my wife will be on her knees begging me to take her back.*

He reached for the crossbow he'd brought, aimed at the balloon's mass, and fired.

The balloon exploded as planned. The reaction was so violent, his seat belt snapped, tossing him over the side—something not planned.

Harry reached a speed of 988 miles per hour as his body plunged; thus, establishing a record he wasn't even trying to achieve.

To date, nobody else has come anywhere near that rate of descent.

Unfortunately, Harry didn't survive to register his fantastic achievement with the *Guinness Book of World Records*.

DIGITAL MEMORIES

"Good morning." Joe said, throwing off the bed covers.

The woman with a hangover lying next to him, shrieked. Instead of the usual male equipment, a door appeared on Joe's lower abdomen. What shocked her even more, it had a handle.

"Did you enjoy the trip?" he asked.

"I don't know what you mean."

"Yeah, I suppose not. You were stinkin' drunk when you got here. But you paid your ten bucks, opened the door, made a wish, and went inside."

"What a kidder. What was I supposed to see in there?"

"Whatever you wanted to. Too bad you don't remember. Well, you can always go again."

"Sounds fascinating," she said dressing quickly, hoping to get out of there before the deranged nut attacked her. "How could a grown woman like me get through such a little door?"

"By magic. How else? When you paid and made your wish, my fairy godmother reduced your size. Hey, I have to pay her a royalty of five bucks per customer. But she does a good job. Nobody ever banged their heads going through my door."

"I see," she said, moving toward the apartment door. "Well, it was nice meeting you. See you again, sometime. Wait a minute. Before I go, do you mind if I take a picture of your door? I have a digital camera in my purse."

"And what will you do with the picture? Sell it to the *National Inquirer?*"

"Oh no. I'll go to one of those one-hour photo processing places and have a print made. As a keepsake."

"Too bad you didn't take your camera with you went you went inside last night," Joe said.

"Oh? What did I see?"

"It's a shame you don't remember. Well, you wished you were Cinderella and heading for the Prince's Ball. I'll bet when you got there, you found it fabulous. Well, if you ever decide to go again, take your camera. And make darn sure you have extra memory cards to store lotsa pictures. Now those would really be worth printing."

She snapped a picture of his door, then opened the apartment door to leave. Suddenly, she heard a loud knock coming from the door on Joe's abdomen.

"You better answer my door," Joe said. "It's obviously somebody for you. Nobody ever knocks for me, because I can't go inside myself."

"You really think it's for me?" she said, remembering the story of Cinderella and the pursuing prince.

"Hey, it was a slow night. You were the only person who went in there last night."

Wrapping her hand around the door handle on his abdomen, she pulled it open. Out came a teensy prince on a tiny white horse.

"Oh, Cinderella!" the prince exclaimed. "I'm so glad I found you. I've fallen in love with you. I want to marry you."

She was so startled, she froze.

"I'm a very rich prince. Come join me in my beautiful palace. I'll throw a ball every night in your honor. You'll have a wonderful life as my bride."

She thought about the unemployment checks that were about to end and four-buck-a-gallon gas. And about the nasty things happening in Iran and North Korea, which were causing so much tension.

"Okay," she said. "I'll come with you. But how can I get small enough to enter?"

"Just pay me ten bucks like you did last night," Joe said.

Checking her purse, she found only thirty-nine cents.

"I'm broke. But I have an unemployment check coming today. I'll run home, cash it, and return."

"Wait a minute," said the Prince. "You have no dowry?"

"No. I've had some bad luck. Downsizing, outsourcing, and things like that."

"But you came to my Ball in such a richly appointed carriage. I thought you were a princess from a faraway land."

"I'm Betsy Boomer. From Cucamonga, California."

"I obviously made a terrible mistake." The Prince turned his horse around and disappeared inside. The door slammed loudly behind him.

"Don't worry," Joe said. "Go cash your check and come back. You can go back in there tonight. By then he'll be so lovesick, he'll be only too glad to see you."

"You mean you'll let me go inside for ten dollars?"

"Not exactly. After all, you're gonna be rich and live happily ever after, while I'll be stuck out here worrying about the Russians and another

Cold War, not to mention what terrorists are up to. Plus nasty gasoline prices, and utterly terrible cost of home heating oil. Not to mention the latest strain of bird flu. The new entry fee is $100,000. Payable in advance."

"Impossible. My credit cards are maxed out. My credit rating is twenty points below the minimum. Can you give me a break?"

After pondering the situation, Joe said, "Tell you what. Buy some memory cards and extra batteries for your digital camera. I'll have my fairy godmother reduce the camera's size as well as you. Then take lotsa pictures of your pumpkin carriage from all angles, plus whatever you see on the trip to the Ball. Once you're there, take lotsa pics of the guests, and the palace. Don't forget the buffet table. And all the crystal chandeliers. Same with your wedding. Then bring the memory cards to the door and knock three times so I'll know it's you. I'll open it a bit so you can slide everything out to me."

"What are you gonna do with them? Print them at Wal-mart?"

"Hell no. I'm gonna sell them for a million bucks to the *National Inquirer.*"

EVIL VACATIONS, INC.

"**W**elcome to Evil Vacations. Our clients spend their vacations acting out monster fantasies. You have your choice of zombie, vampire, ghoul, werewolf, or Loch Ness monster. What's your preference?"

"Werewolf," said Bert.

"Wise choice. For $6,000, you'll enjoy three weeks on Planet Lycanthropia, which has three moons. Each remains full for seven days. Dense forests and populated villages are provided. Imagine the possibilities."

"I'll be able to rip villagers apart! Sounds relaxing."

"Many swear by it."

Bert had fabulous fun howling at the full moon, racing naked through the forest, and slaughtering villagers. Unfortunately, after two weeks, an asteroid destroyed the third moon.

Back on Earth, he hollered, "I want $2,000 refund. I lost a whole week. And I've become a REAL werewolf."

"As the small print of your vacation contract warned," said the travel agent. "But, I'll be fair. I'm low on cash at the moment. Will you accept payment in silver?"

"Sure."

Bert's body was found in a dumpster riddled with silver bullets.

A TERRIBLE SITUATION

"**B**ack off!" Larry yelled, clutching a yellow package to his chest. "If you shoot me, you'll set off a nuclear explosion. You, me, and this entire city will be vaporized."

The sheriff holstered his revolver. "Okay. You win. What do you want?"

"A Big Mac and a helicopter."

"We don't have a McDonalds here."

"What? A city of this size and you don't have a McDonalds?"

"Nope. Had to shut 'em all down for using the wrong kind of cooking oils."

"Then, I'll have a large bowl of Wendy's chili. With onions."

"Wendy's closed a month ago. They couldn't afford to install non-gas emitting cooling systems."

"No Wendy's. Hmm. Okay…I'll take Wal-mart's brand of chocolate chip cookies. Two boxes."

"We don't have a Wal-mart anymore. Too many people went there. Their combined body heat was accelerating global warming."

Larry went through a list of wants. But every place and brand he mentioned was no longer available in the city.

"What the hell happened while I was in prison?" he asked.

"The world became a better place," said the sheriff.

"What's left? I have the junk food crazies. If I don't get some soon, my nerves are gonna get real bad. And when that happens, I'll set this thing off. Okay… let's see. I still want the helicopter…. and… let's see…. a pack of Marlboro."

"They stopped making cigarettes."

"No smokes? Oh geez. Then get me a latte from Starbucks."

"You'd have to go to Brazil for that. It's the only country left that hasn't banned all caffeine products."

"Then I can't get a Hershey bar?"

"Nope."

"Just what the hell is it I can get along with the helicopter?"

"We got lots of nice treats made from soy: burgers, wings, pizza, ribs, hot dogs, cookies, soft drinks. Nothing refreshes like a good soy-Coke."

"Soy tastes rotten," Larry said.

"Not if you pour lots of soy-honey mustard on it."

"Mustard in Coke?"

"Yep. Hey, don't knock it if you haven't tried it," said the sheriff.

"All right. I'll have a soy-Coke. And some soy-pizza and soy-wings."

The sheriff made a call on his cell phone.

"Don't forget the helicopter," Larry said.

"That's not fair. We don't have enough funds to pay carbon offsets for a helicopter flight."

"Don't screw around…I'll set this thing off."

"Come to think of it," the sheriff said, "I wish you would. "

SANCTUARY

"Hey, Sheriff Spitz. I just captured an alien from outer space," said Jimmy Joe, as he dragged a greenish, jelly-like blob with a rope.

"Whew!" said the Sheriff of Santa Buffoona County. "That's one ugly looking sonovabitch. What're you gonna do with it?"

"Feed it to the hogs. I just wanted to show you want one of them looks like before I do."

"I don't think that's wise. What if his buddies are around and they have nasty ray guns?"

"Screw them and their ray guns," Jimmy Joe said. "They don't scare me. If they had any, I figure they woulda used them already. All these freaks do is sneak around at night and screw up everybody's crops by making those damn crop circles. That's where I caught this bastard—flattening my corn stalks."

"Regardless of what they do in our fields, I want you to let him go. You're violating his civil rights," the sheriff said. "He may be on Earth illegally, but even illegal aliens from outer space have certain unalienable rights in this state. And don't forget that Santa Buffoona County was declared as an official sanctuary for illegals."

"As far as I'm concerned, aliens ain't got no rights," said Jimmy Joe. "This one was trespassing on my property. And to me, that makes him a law breaker."

"True, but nothing in the law says you have the right to take matters into your own hands. It's my job to enforce the law. Turn him over to me. I'll lock him up and make sure he gets a fair trial. If you don't, his friends may get wind of this and start an interplanetary war."

"You been reading too many science fiction books, Sheriff. If I feed him to the hogs, there won't be anything left of him. His Martian pals will never figure out what happened to him."

Suddenly, a huge disk-shaped object swooped toward them. A voice roared from the disk, "You have three seconds to release our crewmember."

"Oh yeah?" Jimmy Joe yelled, waving his fist.

A blue beam from the disk struck Jimmy Joe in the head. In a split-second he was reduced to a pile of blue dust.

"Don't shoot me!" Spitz hollered. "I'm your friend. I like illegal aliens. We all like them around here. Your crewman is free to go. Look, I'm untying the rope."

The moment the rope was removed from the alien, a red beam flashed from the disk. The alien stepped into it and disappeared. So did the disk.

The sheriff tried to explain the incident to the emergency operator on the Homeland Defense panic line. The operator didn't believe a word.

Spitz swept Jimmy Joe's blue dust into a glass jar, then shipped it along with an explanatory letter to Homeland Defense Headquarters. He asked them for a DNA test of the dust. He figured that would prove that aliens had indeed invaded and killed the citizen whose remains were in the jar.

Two weeks later, the dust-filled glass jar came back with a note stating the jar contained saw dust that was dyed blue. And if Spitz knew what was good for him, he better not ever again try to joke around with the federal government. Otherwise, he'd find himself facing charges for frivolous waste of government time, effort, and money. He was also warned against messing with illegal aliens, no matter what planet they came from. Especially since he was an elected official of a county that had declared itself a sanctuary for illegals, regardless of their origin.

Spitz figured he better get rid of the blue dust. He didn't want his political enemies to use his run-in with Homeland Defense against him during the next election. Taking the jar to Jimmy Joe's pig farm, he poured the blue dust into the pig trough. Every pig that ate Jimmy Joe's dust turned blue and died from an unknown malady.

Somehow their carcasses ended up in the local hog processing plant.

Everyone who ate meat from those pigs died within days. Anybody who had come anywhere near the victims also died. Before long, the entire population of Santa Buffoona County died from an unknown, highly infectious disease.

Homeland Defense quarantined the County of Santa Buffoona, telling major press outlets that it had become the victim of an unusual strain of swine flu. Nobody outside of the county knew that all 1,537,264 citizens of the county had died.

Meanwhile, Homeland Defense continued its manic quest to encourage all counties in the Amalgamated States to declare themselves sanctuaries for illegal aliens. They succeeded admirably. In fact, they threw the biggest party to congratulate themselves that Washington had ever seen—at taxpayer expense.

When news of this reached the leaders of Mars, Mercury, Saturn, Uranus, Neptune, Venus, Jupiter, Pluto, and the Milky Way, they laughed their asses off. They joined forces to take advantage of their new sanctuary status by invading the Amalgamated States of America.

Every time somebody complained of the presence of an invading illegal alien from outer space, the alien hollered, "I have sanctuary." Homeland Defense used the mighty resources at their disposal to smash dissenters.

By Christmas of 2035, not a single American was alive, including members of Homeland Defense. However, members of that agency went to their graves feeling proud that they'd made the Amalgamated States a secure haven for illegal aliens.

Soon afterward, the entire land mass of the Amalgamated States of America was one gigantic, intricately carved, crop circle.

TOYS

"What can I do for you?" asked Father Myles Mahoney.

"Well, first off, I want you to know I'm an atheist. So's my wife. She'd go bonkers if she knew I was here. The thing is, something's happened that boggles my mind. Something right out of the Twilight Zone. Since I consider all religions to be nothing more than Twilight Zone fantasies, I figure you might have some answers."

"So what exactly is boggling your mind?"

"Remember last month when two planes collided in midair just outside of town?" I asked.

"Oh, yes. I was called to the crash site to give last rites. It was a terrible sight."

"Do you remember the head-on car crash on the road to the mall that wiped out two families?"

"Yes. They were members of this parish. It was a terrible thing."

"Do you also remember when an ambulance lost control on Summit Road and flew over the cliff?"

"I remember all these things," said Mahoney. "So what about them?"

"I think my six-year old son had something to do with all three accidents."

"Oh? How could a six-year old possibly be involved?"

"Well, my wife and I were in the kitchen when Jimmy came in with two toy airplanes. One in each hand. He made airplane motor noises, making believe the planes were flying. Suddenly, he slammed them into each other, and let them fall to the floor. The very next day, the midair collision happened when two planes crashed outside of town."

"Are you implying a cause and effect between what your son did with toy airplanes and what happened with two real planes?"

"It's the only conclusion I can come to after all the other things that happened. For example, two days later, Jimmy held a red toy car in one hand, and a blue one in the other. He made motor sounds, and rolled them along the floor. He talked about them crashing into each other. He imitated all the sounds of screeching tires, and people yelling, and slammed the cars into each other. The next day, two cars had a head-on on the way to the mall."

"Hmm. Were the cars in the accident red and blue?"

"Yes," I said. "I checked with the newspaper. They put me in touch with the reporter who covered the story. He verified their colors."

"I suppose you're going to tell me your son was playing with a toy ambulance the day before a real one flew over the cliff."

"Unfortunately, yes. He was running a toy ambulance along the arm of the sofa, when he called out, 'Look, Dad, the ambulance is out of control. It's going over the cliff.' He let it fall to the floor. It landed upside down. Next day, the same thing happened to County Hospital's ambulance. The picture in the paper showed that it landed upside down."

"It does sound quite strange," said Mahoney. "But the world's full of coincidences. However, our fantasies can sometimes get out of control. Perhaps you should discuss this with a psychiatrist. As to your son, I wouldn't be overly concerned. Sounds like he's normal, imaginative, and is just displaying normal, boyhood aggression. My brother was like that. He was always crashing toys together, not to mention dozens of kids he shot with his cap gun. He grew up to become the CEO of Amalgamated Airlines."

Checking his watch, the priest added, "I'm sorry to interrupt, but I have an appointment in five minutes with our Choir Master. Do come again any time you wish to talk."

"I don't mean to press the point, but is there anything you could do?" I asked.

"Sure. If I suspected something evil afoot, I could do a minor exorcism by blessing your house, your son, and even his toys with holy water. We never know what malignant forces can sometimes attach themselves to inanimate objects and create mischief. But you're an atheist, so I doubt you and your wife would tolerate my presence and my performing religious rituals in your home."

"You're right about that. I don't want my son exposed to anything religious. But it's kind of you to offer. Thanks for your time. Would you accept a donation?"

"Thanks, that's not necessary. But if you wish, you can put a donation in the poor box. It's inside the church vestibule. We'll use it to feed the poor."

I shook his hand and left. As much as I dreaded going into a church, I went into the vestibule where I found the locked poor box.

That afternoon Jimmy was playing with his Tonka truck—the one with a crane in back.

"What are you doing?" I asked, when I saw that he'd put rubber bands around a wooden block, had run the crane's hook under the bands, and was turning a crank to raise the block from the floor.

"This block's a giant piano. Somebody up high in a big building downtown wants it brought in through a window, because it won't fit in the elevator."

When he raised the block a foot off the floor, the rubber bands broke. The block fell onto a little plastic toy soldier.

"Looks like your soldier was in the wrong place at the wrong time, I said. A piano just fell on his head."

"It's not a soldier," Jimmy said. "I'm making believe it's a priest."

"Why a priest?"

"I don't know."

Next day, a weird accident was reported on TV. A piano that was being delivered through an outside window at the downtown high rise apartments, suddenly broke loose. It fell six stories and crushed a priest named Myles Mahoney. He was about to enter the building to visit a shut-in.

My hands shook, as I dialed the number of the Bishop's office to plead for an exorcist.

SNEAK ATTACK

"Relax and have another drink," said the mistress of the President of the Reorganized States of America. "Then we can get comfortable."

"How can I relax when a bunch of zombies are still running loose? The bastards won't turn themselves in. And the Army can't find them. With Election Day only two weeks away, if something doesn't happen soon, that bitch, Martha Goodman, could win. Do you want to see her become President? Between her and her damn Love and Compassion Party, this nation will be turned into a Fourth World toilet in no time."

"I don't understand why all the zombies aren't dead," she said. "You told me the Army was equipped with the latest portable flamethrowers and chain saws."

"Problem is, this bunch ain't the same as the kind that invaded us during the last zombie war. Back then, they were easy to defeat, because they walked slowly, were completely disorganized, and had no clear plan or objectives except to eat human brains."

"Oh? What's so different now?"

"They're a different breed. They're uniformed, organized, and have weapons. My guess is that a rogue nation refined the zombification process, and created a new class of zombies. They have some ability to think, although their brains were implanted, and are the size of a sugar cube. Those damn cubes contain computer chips. The CIA is still analyzing DNA samples to find out where they came from. We *will* find out. And I *will* severely punish the nation that perpetrated an unprovoked sneak attack against us on Christmas Eve!"

"Ohhh," she said. "I just love it when you get so stirred up. C'mon, let's get comfortable. Let me help you get rid of all that nasty old tension,"

As they disrobed, the President's red phone rang. He spoke quietly, so she couldn't make out what he was saying.

When he hung up, he said, "The CIA found out who created the zombies."

"North Korea?" she asked.

"Nope."

"Cuba?"

"Nah. They wouldn't dare."

"Let's see. It must have been Iran."

"Guess again."

"I give up," she said, nibbling his ear.

"Switzerland did it," he said. "I just ordered a massive nuclear attack. In a few hours, that beautiful, mountainous country will be transformed into a bleak, flat-as-a-pancake desert. Not to mention it'll be several hundred feet below sea level."

She kissed his neck and said, "What a shame. We had a wonderful time when we were there. Hey! Isn't that where all your gold and money are stashed?"

"Oy!" Grabbing his phone, the President called the Chairman of the Joint Chiefs of Staff. "Call off the bombers. I've been the victim of false intelligence. Reroute the bombers to—" He held his hand over the mouthpiece and asked her, "Which country was it where you had the worst vacation of your life?"

"Tahiti," she said. "A typhoon blew in and ruined everything."

Speaking into the phone, the President said, "Nuke Tahiti. They're the bastards responsible for the zombie sneak attack."

The President's decision provided a wonderful bonus. Turned out Martha Goodman had gone to Tahiti incognito to relax before facing the rigors of Election Day.

The President attended Goodman's funeral service. In fact, he had an empty coffin placed in the Capitol Rotunda to honor her. He even gave the most touching eulogy the nation had ever heard.

His ratings jumped fifty points and he was reelected.

After seeing what happened to Tahiti, Switzerland never again sent a zombie invading force to the Reorganized States of America.

GOO

"Welcome to the Buzz Beemer show where we discuss the wild, wonderful, and wacky. Let's get to our first caller."

"Hi, I'm Joe from Cleveland. I was just abducted by Martians. They grabbed me in the Wal-mart parking lot, and tied me to a table."

"Did they jam red hot needles into the most sensitive parts of your body?" asked Buzz.

"No. One of them said, 'All we want you to do is taste something.'"

"What kind of thing?"

"Well, they untied my hands, and gave me a box. When I opened it, I saw something that looked like a chocolate chip cookie."

"Did they force you to eat it?"

"Yeah. I thought it was poison, or something to knock me out. But it wasn't. The cookie was delicious. Best I ever tasted."

"Hmm. Then what happened?"

"When I said Yummy," they clapped their hands and jumped up and down. Like they were real happy that I enjoyed their cookie."

"Is this when they started to jam hot needles into the most tender and private parts of your body?"

"No. They took me back to Wal-mart and let me go. In fact, I'm on my way home now. Just had to call to tell you about my weird experience."

"So, you're okay? They didn't remove your lung or something?"

"I'm fine. I can't get over it. Sure wish I had more of those delicious chocolate chip cookies."

Buzz cut the caller off and said, "Ladies and gentlemen of the listening audience, from time to time we get somebody who shovels crap so thick it's up to our elbows. Aliens. Chocolate chip cookies. Sheesh! Did you ever hear anything so dumb? Does he really expect us to believe they didn't remove a vital organ or two, and ram dozens of needles into his privates? Hey, Joe from Cleveland, I think you better take your meds. You're hallucinating again. Whatta jerk. Okay, let's move on to the next caller."

"Hi Buzz. I'm Bill from Miami. Listen, I just heard what that guy just said. The same thing happened to me less than thirty minutes ago. Only they grabbed me when I was in the men's room of a hotel."

"You mean they gave you a box with a chocolate chip cookie inside, told you to eat it, then released you?"

"Right."

"Sorry, folks. I'm afraid we're gonna have one of those weirdo nights when all the nuts call. Is the moon full tonight or what?"

The next caller said the same thing happened to her. Meanwhile, Buzz received emails from people in the US, Canada, and Mexico who claimed they'd also experienced the same thing within the last hour.

"This is giving me a migraine," Buzz said. "Hey, hasn't anybody run into Bigfoot tonight or seen some black helicopters? If so, let us know. I'm tired of hearing a bunch of jerks trying to convince of us of the nuttiest thing I ever heard. Listen folks, if aliens grab you, it ain't gonna be so you can sample their stupid cookies. No way. They'll slice and dice you, rip your eyes out, and jam nasty things into every opening in your body."

Suddenly, a screeching sound came through everyone's radio. A canned announcement replaced the sound within seconds. "Due to technical difficulties, we will now play the Best of The Buzz Beemer Show."

Thirty minutes later, an announcer said, "We will now return to tonight's live broadcast of the Buzz Beemer Show."

"Ladies and gentlemen," said Buzz. "I'm sorry about the interruption. But the most incredible thing happened. I was abducted by Martians as I sat right here in my broadcasting studio in Los Angeles. To my amazement, they didn't mistreat me in any way. Instead, they gave me this thing to eat that looked like a chocolate chip cookie. Just like the ones the callers mentioned. I want to apologize to those callers. Like they said, the darn thing was incredibly delicious. Not only that, the aliens now want everybody on Earth to enjoy their fabulous cookies, at no charge. They said within the next twenty-four hours they'll deliver enough cookies to every Wal-mart, Kmart, Target, supermarket, and food outlet in the world so that each person on Earth can have a whole dozen. Don't worry if you're in a third world country that has no stores. The aliens said they'll drop your cookies by parachute."

The next day, every store on Earth received its quota of alien-produced chocolate chip cookies. They distributed the treats for free to everyone. Soon, every human on Earth, including those incarcerated, hospitalized, and in insane asylums, had received a dozen of the fabulously delicious cookies.

A week later, the entire population of Earth had melted into small pools of orange goo.

10-million Martian transports descended on all of Earth's continents. Each held 100 passengers carrying goo sucking machines. All the orange goo was collected and taken to Mars.

A month later, beings on Venus called radio talk shows. They all said they'd been abducted by Martians and forced to taste orange-flavored cookies, then let go. All said the cookies were incredibly delicious.

Mars was besieged with orders for their cookies from every store on Venus. This time the Martians charged the equivalent of $100 per cookie.

Anybody who looks at Mars through gigantic telescopes will be amazed to find it covered with millions of newly built mansions. In front of each are three luxury cars. Behind every dwelling is an Olympic-sized swimming pool.

Just goes to show what can happen when new businesses aren't restricted by repressive environmental regulations, crippling governmental interference, and endless red tape. Apparently Martians don't hate capitalism, don't punish entrepreneurs, and know how to get the most from free raw materials.

GOOD EATS

The table was immaculately set for twelve guests. Hand painted china, Waterford crystal glasses, heavy sterling silver utensils. However, not a morsel of food was in the house.

"Why does Mom do this three times a day?" Jane asked her emaciated dad.

"I suppose it reminds her of when we had plenty," he replied. "Before World War Five."

"I wish she'd quit. It only makes me hungrier. Ask her to stop, Dad."

"I did this morning when she set the table for our nonexistent breakfast. But she acted as if she didn't hear me. And if she did, maybe her brain turned my words into something else."

Just then, a fly flew by. Jane's mother shot out her hand and caught it. "Dinner's ready," she said, placing the squashed fly on an exquisite, china, turkey platter. "C'mon everybody and sit down before dinner gets cold."

Passing a carving knife to her husband, she said, "I'd like one of those lovely drumsticks. Jane, would you mind saying grace? Your father sounded a bit hoarse when he said it during lunch. He must be catching a cold."

"Sure, Mom."

During Jane's prayer, large patches of hair fell from her head onto her plate.

When Jane said, "Amen," her dad pretended to slice a drumstick from an imaginary fowl. Using magnificent sterling silver serving utensils, he managed to collect the fly and transfer it from the platter to his wife's plate.

As mom chewed the fly, she said, "Mmm. How supremely tender and delicious this is."

"That damn fly's probably carrying millions of germs," Jane told her dad. "And we're just sitting here letting her eat the stupid thing."

"What does it matter?" he replied. "She might not live long enough for an infection to take hold. Think of it this way: isn't it worth going through all this nonsense to see that wonderful look on her face just one more time? If I didn't know better, I'd say she looks as if she just ate the most delicious piece of turkey in all creation. Let's let well enough alone."

Suddenly Jane regurgitated from radiation sickness.

Tom had to restrain his wife from rushing to lap up what she perceived as fresh mushroom gravy.

Jane and Tom died from uranium poisoning the next day.

Mom survived two more days. For each meal during those days, she set an elegant table.

She didn't even notice Jane and Tom were dead. She spoke to them as if they were sitting at the table and enjoying hearty meals.

"Would you say grace, Tom?" she asked, as she carved the largest turkey drumstick she'd ever seen.

Before biting into it, she carefully removed the skin, which to an outsider would have looked like the pant leg from a pair of men's blue jeans.

AIN'T LOVE GRAND

When the Governor visited the orphanage, all the children were lined up for his inspection. As he passed each child, he asked, "What do you want to be someday?"

"A nurse," said a girl.

"Very commendable. We never have enough of them."

The next kid said, "Policeman."

"Wonderful. Crime is increasing every year. We'll always need brave police officers to protect us."

The Governor approached Billy. "And what do you want to be when you grow up?"

"A pizza."

"Why a pizza?"

"Nobody loves me. But everybody loves pizza."

"He's a lunatic! There's no sense squandering taxpayer money on the likes of him. Abandon him in the forest."

The director of the orphanage tore off Billy's T-shirt that said, "ORPHAN." He gave Billy a new one with much larger letters that read, "LUNATIC."

They put Billy on a helicopter and dropped him in a dense forest.

As he walked through the thickets, a chipmunk approached, pointed to his t-shirt, and asked "What's a lunatic?"

"Somebody who wastes taxpayers' money."

"What else are you, besides a lunatic?"

"A boy. But I wanna be a pizza."

"Why?"

"I wanna be loved."

"What kinda pizza do you wanna be?"

"Pepperoni."

"Well, you came to the right place," the chipmunk said. "Stand over there under that magic tree."

The moment Billy was under the tree, the chipmunk chanted strange words and waved a magic wand. Within seconds, Billy transformed into a freshly-baked pepperoni pizza.

"Are you happy now?" asked the chipmunk.

"Oh yes!" Billy replied, as he glanced at the golden crust, yellow cheese, red sauce, pepperoni slices, and bits of oregano that he'd become.

This is fantastic. Now everybody will love me. I don't know how to thank you!"

"Thanks is nice, but I have lots of mouths to feed. You owe me three million dollars for casting the spell. How do you intend to pay? I take cash, checks, and credit cards."

"Oh my. I'm an orphan. Orphans don't have money. Especially those who are lunatics."

"You shoulda told me before I performed my services."

"You didn't ask."

"True. But I assumed you knew that every professional expects to get paid for his services. After all, it cost me a fortune to get through eight years of Chipmunk Magic School. I'm still paying off the loans. What about friends? Do you think you can borrow money from them?"

"I don't have any friends."

"Oh dear. I'm afraid I'm going to have to sell you to raise the money to pay my fee."

The chipmunk whistled. Hundreds of chipmunks emerged from the bushes and gathered around Billy.

"My dear friends," said chipmunk magician (CM). "I did something good for this pizza, and now he tells me he can't pay. I'd like you all to help me to carry him to the city where I can sell him. Today is market day, and this luscious-looking pizza should fetch a good price. Okay, everybody, put your hands under the pizza. On the count of three, we'll lift it. Let's take it to the Interstate. I'll flag down a trucker and see if he'll give us a ride to the town market."

When CM said, 'Three," they lifted Billy.

Billy heard the pitter patter of countless chipmunk paws striking the ground, as they carried him through the woods. As the trees whizzed by, he was surprised at how fast chipmunks ran. He found himself wondering if he'd made a mistake by becoming a pizza. If he'd asked to become a chipmunk, he could run just as fast. Maybe he could've run so fast that he'd win a gold medal in the Olympic Games 100 yard dash. Then for sure people would love him.

"Hey," he called to CM. "I changed my mind. I wanna be a chipmunk like you guys."

However, CM didn't hear, because he was thinking about how much he'd make selling the pizza for $3.50 a slice.

Before long, Billy heard the sounds of passing cars and trucks.

The chipmunks laid Billy on the road. CM flagged down a huge truck loaded with logs. Unfortunately, the driver saw them too late, and ran over all the chipmunks and pizza. He stopped his truck, and examined the mess. A lover of road kill, he scraped the mashed chipmunks and pizza mess from his tires and the road, and put them into a container.

That evening, the driver said to his wife and beautiful daughter, "I have a wonderful surprise for you. Mashed chipmunk pizza."

"I love chipmunk pizza!" the daughter said. "Especially when it's mashed."

As the gorgeous girl sank her sharp teeth into the pizza, Billy sighed deeply and said, "I'm finally loved."

BIZZARE BEHAVIOR

Only a handful of people knew that Santa Claus was born in Tahiti and lived there for hundreds of years. Even fewer knew that he always wore grass skirts, was beardless, employed only human union workers in his toy factories, used horses to pull his gift-filled carriage, and that he delivered presents to children by entering their homes through the front door.

During one of his Christmas Eve toy deliveries in Haiti, he was ambushed by marauding, famished zombies who had no respect for anybody. Those nasty creatures bit his skull open, used razor sharp ice cream scoops to tear out his brains, and ate every scrap.

This happened just as Santa left the final house of the 82,756,281,429 houses on his route. If the zombies had jumped him sooner, lots of kids wouldn't have received presents that year, and would've been very sad. To the credit of those rotten zombies, at least they jumped him at the end of his route. No doubt that would have been brought up in their defense, if they had ever been found, arrested, and appeared in court.

Fortunately, Santa's brainless body was quickly discovered. Even more fortunately, Haiti was the home of Dr. Frankenfutz, head of the Frankenfutz Institute For Brain Swaps. He just happened to have a wonderful selection of fresh brains on hand. All came from villagers killed during a terrible earthquake.

The moment Santa's grass-skirt-clad body was delivered to the Institute, the good doctor began emergency transplant surgery to give him a new brain. After eighteen grueling hours, Frankenfutz declared the operation a success. The world rejoiced.

When Santa recovered, everyone was surprised when he didn't jump on a boat heading for his native Tahiti. Instead, he hitchhiked to the North Pole. As soon as he arrived, Santa traded his grass skirt for a fire-engine red suit. Even worse, he grew a long beard, hired only non-union elves for his new toy factories, used reindeer to pull a gift-filled sleigh, and delivered presents to children by entering their homes through chimneys.

The world was shocked by his bizarre behavior. Especially since lots of homes don't have chimneys.

The greatest behavioral scientists on the planet were consulted. None was able to explain Santa's goofy behavior.

The Congress of the United States held hearings. Hundreds of witnesses were subpoenaed to testify. However, they came to no conclusion.

After years of intense research in the Frankenfutz archives, the mystery of Santa's radical behavioral changes was solved. Turned out that Santa's new brain came from a village idiot.

Millions volunteered their brains for a new transplant. A lottery was held to decide who the lucky donor would be. The entire world held its breath, as the General Secretary of the United Nations reached into a gigantic barrel and picked a slip of paper containing the winner's name. To protect the winner's privacy, his or her name was never publicized.

The operation was a success. As soon as he recovered, Santa hurried back to Tahiti.

Once again, he wore grass skirts, was beardless, employed only human union workers in his toy factories, used horses to pull his gift-filled carriage, and delivered presents to children by entering their homes through the front door.

The entire world rejoiced when *CNN, BBC,* and *Fox News* reported that Santa had returned to his good old, normal self.

252 Michael A. Kechula

SNEERS

During his first visit to a psychiatrist, fifteen year old Jimmy asked, "Do you believe in vampires?"

"The question is, do you believe in them?" replied Dr. Stone.

"If I didn't, I wouldn't be sitting here. My parents think I'm totally obsessed with those blood suckers."

"When did you become interested in vampires?"

"When I read about those people from town that were missing. Turns out they weren't missing at all, according to a blog site. They were quietly buried by the cops so nobody'd find out they had large holes in their toes, and all their blood was gone."

"I thought vampires bit necks."

"I think this is a different breed. Hey, you're supposed to keep secrets, right?"

"Yes," Stone said. "Nobody will ever find out what you say here."

"Then I'll show you my secret invention." Jimmy pulled a small box from his pocket. "This is a vampire detector. See the red bulb on top? It'll flash when I point at anything that has blood inside. There's a tiny dowsing rod in the box that was hexed by a witch. Whenever it recognizes the presence of blood, the light flashes. I'm gonna point it at you. See how the bulb's flashing?"

"What'll happen if you point it at my desk?"

When Jimmy did, the bulb stopped flashing.

"What are you going to do with your vampire detector?" asked the doctor, while jotting in a notebook.

"Go to the mall, find vampires, and kill the bastards."

"What happens if you succeed?"

"No doubt I'll be on Oprah's show. Meanwhile, I'll file for a patent. Once I have it, I'll get rich, considering the world's overrun with vampires. I figure I'll sell my detectors for a million each."

They discussed Jimmy's belief that vampires abounded in their city. He figured the reason why the cops couldn't find them was because they slept inside hollow mannequins at Macy's, instead of coffins. In fact, after his session was over Jimmy was heading to Macy's to test his detector.

"What'll you do if it blinks when you point it at a mannequin?"

"Stomp on the freaking thing's guts. Since it'll still be daylight, the vampire inside will be powerless and won't be able to do a damn thing.

Then I'll drag it to a dressing room and torch it. Fire destroys them like sunlight does."

Stone wrote on his pad, "Mildly delusional. Harmless. Won't act out. Apply reality therapy."

After the session, Jimmy headed for Macy's.

Five days later, the local newspaper claimed Jimmy was missing.

A few weeks passed. Something about Jimmy and what he'd said kept nagging Dr. Stone. He called the Missing Person's Bureau to find out if they had any news. When they said they had no leads, Stone decided to visit Macy's.

Meandering among the mannequins in the men's department, he checked the floor. He figured if James had gone there and come to violence during his vampire search, perhaps the match box might still be around. When he found nothing, he chided himself for getting caught up in Jimmy's silly delusion.

As he was about to leave Macy's, something inside nudged him toward the women's department. Entering, he noticed far more mannequins than he'd seen on the floor below.

Well, if that isn't the damndest thing, he thought. *Every one of these mannequins has a sneer on its face. But the ones downstairs had neutral expressions. I wonder what that's all about?*

He asked a sales clerk if she'd noticed the sneers on the mannequins. She gave him a strange look, and hurried off without answering.

Stone checked the area around each mannequin, but found nothing. When patting the bra of a mannequin in the undies department, he felt something odd. Ensuring nobody was looking, he reached inside. His hair bristled when he removed a little match box with a bulb on top. He jumped when the light flashed like crazy.

"Jimmy said if it doesn't have blood inside, the light will go off," he mumbled to himself, pointing the box at the floor. The light shut off immediately. He raced to the men's room to avoid wetting his pants.

Trembling, he decided to leave the mall for the world outside. The real, tangible, world of crime, stench, hatred, and disasters. The mall was not the real world. How could it be with phony music? With clerks having artificial smiles glued to their faces? With the nicely scented atmosphere that elevated the mood? With beautifully decorated store windows? With super-cleanliness everywhere? With mannequins inhabited by vampires?

Savoring the fresh air and sense of reality outside, he jumped into his car. He headed to his favorite lounge to talk to the regulars about sports, to check the weather on the bar's TV, to feel the stark reality of whiskey burning his mouth.

After drinks and pleasant chatter, something nagged him. Before long, he found himself back at Macy's standing in front of the mannequin where he'd found the matchbox.

"I'm on to you, blood sucker," he whispered in the dummy's ear.

Remembering what Jimmy would have done, he pushed the thing to the floor, and stomped its gut with all his might.

Blood flew from its mouth, staining his expensive suit.

Angered, he dragged the thing to a women's dressing room, impaled the mannequin by slamming it against a clothes hook, grabbed his cigarette lighter, and put the flame against the thing's foot.

Within seconds, the foot was ablaze. Immediately, the fire got out of control.

Several days later, newspapers reported that a psychiatrist named Stone was missing. Nobody connected his disappearance with all the others.

A fireman found the little bulb-topped box in the scorched dressing room. He didn't notice how wildly it blinked, as he walked past smirking mannequins.

The vampires within the mannequins sighed in relief when he tossed the box in a trash can.

TILT

"Hey, Robo-Dad. I got bad news. I'm calling from jail."

"Sounds like good news to me. So, what'd you do now, Robo-17?"

"I was playing with my pea shooter and shot the wrong robot."

"You and that damn pea shooter."

"You shouldn't have bought it for me," said Robo-17.

"I did it so you could have fun, not end up in jail," said Robo-Dad. "Didn't I tell you to shoot peas only at girl robots? But, no, you wouldn't listen. Damn teenage pain in the rear circuitry!"

"Don't get mad. I did just like you said. Honest. But this old model came down the street. I let her have it, but good. You shoulda seen her try to get away. Only problem was one of the peas hit her in the fourth eye. She fell over and broke."

"Whadda you mean, broke?"

"She didn't get up," Robo-17 said.

"Didn't you try to help her?"

"Yeah. But she kept falling down again."

"Did you check the screen on the top of her head?"

"Yeah. It said, TILT."

"That's bad news," Robo-Dad said.

"Don't I know it. The cops said she's inoperable forever. They're charging me with robotocide."

"Holy smoke! What hue was she?"

"Purple."

"Oh, you freakin jerk! Purple robots are a protected class. If you harass or hurt them, the fines and jail time are triple. I told you that."

"She was short and looked kinda bluish to me. From a distance she looked like a little blue girl robot. Turns out she was an old lady robot who needed a paint job."

"Well, they'll say you should've known she was really purple, even though it was hard to tell."

"They already said it. They're gonna charge me with a hate crime on top of everything else. I told them I don't hate anybody. That some of our best friends are purple robots. You gotta help me. You're the one who told me to shoot peas at girl robots."

"Well, I meant little, blue-hued girl robots," Robo-Dad said. "See how you listen?"

"Don't get mad at me, Robo-Dad."

"Don't get mad? Do you realize the press will turn this into an interplanetary incident? Your screw-up could set us cream-hued robots back a hundred years. Protected class robots like the one you hurt have more rights. More of everything. Didn't they teach you that in school?"

"Maybe I was absent that day."

"Well, I bet they'll melt you. They'll march you to a room tie you down, and turn up the heat. You won't be able to breathe. It'll hurt real bad. Then they'll reduce you to a bunch of base metals and turn you into a dozen towel racks, or toilet flush handles."

"Stop it. You're scaring me."

"Scaring you? I'd tilt your ass if I could get my hands around your scrawny circuit cards. And I'd get away with it too. Because you ain't a protected class. You're nothing but a cream-trash robot. A freaking hunk of junk. I shoulda never adopted you."

"Don't hang up mad. The sacred Blue Words on our Holy Ancient Blueprints say you shouldn't let the sun set on your anger."

"That's what your Holy Ancient Blueprints say, not mine," Robo-Dad said. "Besides, I don't believe in any stinking Blue Words. It's all a stupid myth."

"You're a heretic," Robo-17 said."

"Maybe so. But I ain't the one in jail, Jerk-o. You're just like your factory. Like factory, like robot. That's what my blueprint says. Come to think of it, I do believe in some Blue Words."

Robo-Dad slammed the phone so hard, it came off the wall. "Why did I ever adopt that pitiful robot?" he mumbled. "He used to be a good kid. Now that he's a teen, he's been one aching circuit after another. Don't let the sun set on your anger, he says. Stupid jerk doesn't even know our sun burned out eons ago."

NEXT

"**Y**ou're next, Charlie," said the Angel of Death to the chubby guy at the head of the line.

When AOD lowered the rope barrier, Charlie raced toward the railing of the Golden Gate Bridge. Climbing over, he yelled "Geronimo!" and jumped.

Applause broke out in the line.

"It's your turn, Marcia." AOD tapped her shoulder.

Marcia skated toward the railing, and managed to leap right over it on her first try. "Life stinks!" she yelled on the way down.

The folks in line applauded even louder.

"Hey, Boss," said AOD's assistant. "Look up there. Somebody's standing on top of the bridge."

AOD peered through binoculars. "By golly, you're right. Never fails. Some idiot always manages to screw things up."

"Hey you, on top of the bridge," AOD yelled through a bullhorn. "What the hell do you think you're doing?"

"Jumping," the guy yelled back.

"Hold on a minute. What's your name?"

"Frank Higenlooper."

AOD checked his daily planner. "You can't jump today. You're on tomorrow's list."

"Does it matter?" Frank hollered.

"Yep. Affects the entire cosmos. Climb down. Come back tomorrow. Bring beer. I'll bring pepperoni pizza. We'll party first."

"But I can't stand another day of my wife's constant bitching."

"Then don't go home. Check into a hotel. Go out and have a great dinner at Fisherman's Wharf. Find yourself a nice streetwalker. What the hell, it's your last full day on this planet. Might as well live it up big time."

"I don't know if I can get down by myself. I feel dizzy." Frank said.

"Hold on. I'll call the rescue squad." AOD grabbed his cell phone.

While waiting for them to arrive, AOD let three more people in line rush to the bridge's railing and leap over. When he heard them hit the water, he put a checkmark next to their names in his daily planner."

"How you doing up there?" asked AOD.

"I been thinking things over," Frank replied. "Even if I go to a hotel, she'll find me. You have no idea to what lengths she'll go to nag me. And if I have an expensive meal, she'll carry on like a lunatic. It'll be a thousand times worse if I bed down with a streetwalker. I think I'm just gonna jump and be done with it."

"Don't do it! You'll botch up the cosmos!"

Frank jumped anyway.

The entire cosmos collapsed into nothingness.

BooksForABuck.com Books by Michael A. Kechula

Michael A. Kechula's flash and micro-fiction tales have been published by 149 magazines and 50 anthologies in Australia, Canada, England, Finland, Ireland, India, Scotland, and US. He's won first prize in twelve flash fiction writing contests and second prize in eight others. He owns and moderates Muse Speculative Fiction Flash, a Yahoo writing site that specializes in the creation of flash and micro fiction for potential publication.

The Area 51 Option
A Full Deck of Zombies
I Never Kissed Judy Garland
Writing Genre Flash Fiction the Minimalist Way